Return to Rebecca Farms

A Novel

Heather Fahy Serrano

The Cover: Designed by Getcovers.

I dedicate this book to all the Indie authors I've had the pleasure of getting to know, and those I have yet to meet.

We keep the dream alive by
creating and publishing our work.

Special thanks to Joe Garland. He is always there to lend his helpful (formatting) hands and eyes.

Kay Springsteen
Your thoughtful editing made my words shine brighter.

The Rebecca Farms Family

Proprietors

Robin Robinson
Farah Robinson (The Wife)
Rebecca Robinson (Robin's younger sister)
(Richard, Rachel, and Ricky; Robin's deceased parents and brother)

The Aunt and Uncle

Diana and Philip
Emily Robinson (Daughter)
Josh Marshall (Fiancé)
(Adam; deceased son)

The Right Hand Man and Wife

Joe and Maria Gonzalez
Joe Jr. (Son)
Marisol (Daughter)
Cristina (Daughter)
Diego (Son)

She's Back for a Reason...

Barbara Fletcher
Ben (Son)
Brandi (Daughter)
Carole (Mother)

And He's Back for a Reason...

Carl the Ex

Prologue
April

The white wicker rocking chair softly creaked as Robin Robinson sat on his front porch, moving it back and forth, his whiskey resting on his knee between sips. The longer days had finally given into the star-filled sky. In the still air, he welcomed the chatter of crickets, a few of his boarders not settled for the night, and barking dogs in the distance.

The two fingers of amber liquid swirling in his glass usually signaled the end of a long, hard, and satisfying day. But tonight, he was thinking about Farah, looking at the empty rocker next to him. He looked at his phone. They'd just spoken ten minutes ago, and then she was taking a bath, but still he looked to see if she'd sent a text like an anxious teenager, though he was now a man of forty-two.

Around town he had been considered "tall, dark, and handsome," or so his mother always claimed. *"Those eyes aren't staring at this truck because of me,"* she used to say when they drove the truck down main street, leaving Robin with the urge to slouch down in embarrassment. He did so even now out of habit, remembering.

In simple detail he was six-two and sinewy, with dark curly hair and deep green eyes to complement. And that smile! He drove the girls crazy with his smile. When he wanted to, that was. But he was also aloof, and he, like everyone else, thought his farm would remain his one true love, and his life.

Until seven fateful years ago when he'd met Farah.

His thoughts were interrupted by sudden, loud popping sounds. *Firecrackers? In April?* He sat forward and spotted headlights in the distance slowly coming into view.

Ross and Charlotte Meeker's farm sat across the road from his, and farther to the left, Cal Davidson's place. Pete and Susan Baker's farm was a quarter mile to the right. Like his, these properties had been family owned for years, and he knew all their vehicles. From where he sat, the approaching car wasn't one he recognized. This was truck country. Robin couldn't make out the model of the small car with the sputtering engine, but he felt it didn't belong.

"Someone took a wrong turn," he said and chuckled as he stood to go inside and pour a second whiskey. But he paused as the car seemed to slow right in front of his farm. *My imagination.* Then a small light shone from the inside. *From a phone?* This was not his imagination. He couldn't see who was driving, though he could make out long hair in the small light.

He was about to walk down the steps to get a better look when the car sped up, gears grinding with more firecrackers exploding from the engine as it drove away.

Shrugging, he turned and entered the house. As he locked the front doors and made his way to the kitchen for that second drink, his thoughts settled back on his wife. He knew the second whiskey would help him get to sleep, and tomorrow his farm would keep his attention and the hours moving quickly along. And by the time he was through working for the day, she'd be home.

This gave him great comfort as he climbed the stairs to his bedroom.

Chapter 1
Happy Birthday Farah
(And it's a Big One!)

Maria was cracking fresh eggs into a glass bowl in the kitchen when her phone rang. She smiled when she saw it was Farah Face Timing her. "You're up early, Birthday Girl," she said, putting the phone on speaker then leaning it against the toaster.

"I'm waiting for a lousy cup of coffee from a lousy little coffee maker. There's no aroma! I miss my French roast and my kitchen."

"It's your rare opportunity to stay in bed!"

"I know, I know. I had this crazy dream, and I couldn't get back to sleep after I woke up. You were in it."

"Hold on a sec. So far, your replacements are no shows." Maria walked over to the stairs. "Becca and Marisol, I could use a hand. *Ahora!*"

"You're busy. It can wait," Farah said, smiling at her dearest friend. Though Maria was short in stature, she was mighty in demeanor and Farah marveled at this strong, proud woman and mother of four.

"Yeah, and of course, Em...oh wait, here she comes. There you are!" Farah heard the sliding glass door open. "You're supposed to be helping me this morning, Emily," Maria said.

"I can't eat breakfast. The wedding dresses have arrived! Where's Rebecca?"

"Hey, Emily," Farah said.

"Hi, Farah! Happy birthday! It's a big one!" Emily looked at the phone and waved.

"Thank you, I am well aware of the number."

Maria came back into view. "You don't have to eat it, just help make it. Go to the fridge and get the biscuits and start putting them on baking trays. Now, Farah, what about the dream?" Maria asked, back in front of the phone. Her warm brown eyes filled the screen.

"Well, it was Easter, and you and I were on the porch drinking mimosas."

Maria laughed. "We *did* just celebrate Easter last week and we *did* drink mimosas on the porch."

"I know, but it gets better. Emily was..."

"Reporting for duty!" Rebecca said, saluting Maria, spotting Farah, and rushing to pick up the phone.

"Hey, girls!"

"Happy Birthday, Farah! It's a big one, right?"

"Thank you, Becca. It's just a number," Farah smiled, shaking her head.

"The dresses are in, Becca," Emily said, flinching as the can of biscuits she was holding popped open.

"Have you seen them?" Farah asked.

"Marisol, you need to go back to the house and finish getting ready for school. Make sure your brother is up and help Christina with her shoes. And Rebecca, please start setting the table outside," Maria said, bringing the conversation back to reality.

"They just arrived, Farah," Emily said, moving back into the phone frame. "Mama is coming with me to work so we can see them together. I can't' wait!" Her petite frame, youthful looks, personality, and childlike voice made many people forget she was almost thirty.

"I don't want to go today. We have a lot to do before the party. I'm sure the dress is fine," Rebecca answered.

Emily put the can of biscuit dough down and walked over to her cousin, gently placing her hands on her shoulders. "Remember, we talked about this. We must try the dress on to see...where we are at...and what we want to accomplish. We only have five months."

Rebecca, still holding the phone, looked down at Marisol. "She's saying I'm fat."

In unison, Farah and Maria said. "You are not fat!"

Emily sighed exasperatedly but looked at her cousin and smiled. "You're my maid of honor. You're going to be front and center, right next to me. I just think...we could...you know...tone up a little."

"I'm a full-figured woman, and I'm proud of it!" Rebecca answered, handing Maria the phone before grabbing placemats and heading toward the door.

"Me too! Full figured and proud of it!" Maria announced. "Marisol, get going. *Prisa!* The bus will be here in a half hour." As her daughter hurried out behind Rebecca, Maria turned to Emily. "I know your heart is in the right place, but that child is not going to be able to 'tone up a little' as you put it. She is who she is."

"This is true, Emily," Farah said. "Listen, I'm going to let you go. I'm seeing my sister first this morning."

Maria turned toward the window, "I hate that you have to do this on your birthday of all days."

"It's all right. This time rolls around every year, like it or not. By the time I get home to all of you later today, this morning will be a distant memory. See you later, Emily," Farah said before hanging up.

"Bye," Emily said absently, staring at the oven, watching the biscuits slowly rise and brown as the buttery aroma began escaping the oven. Her mouth might have been watering, but Emily wouldn't be having any biscuits this morning.

Marisol, Christina, and Joe Jr. rushed back in with Rebecca. Maria already had toast and scrambled eggs ready for her three school aged children and they sat at the big farm table and began to eat.

"So, you don't want to see your dress today, Becca?" Emily asked, taking the first trays out of the oven.

"Not on Farah's birthday! I want to help Maria. The dresses will be there tomorrow and the next day and the next," Rebecca said matter-of-factly.

True. The dresses were to *The Yardstick*, the fabric store where Emily and Rebecca worked. Back in high school, when Emily should have been studying math, history, and English, she had been studying her mother as she'd worked her magic with a sewing machine. These days many women sought out her advice and alteration services.

Maria kissed her daughters and son, handed them their lunches, and escorted them to the door. "Hurry on up the road. The bus will be here any minute. And hustle out after school. Mr. Clark doesn't have all day. *Te amo*."

"Me and Mama can get them after we see the dresses," Emily said, putting one more tray in the oven.

"Are you sure?" Maria asked.

"Positive!"

Maria walked out and called to her son, "Joe, honey, look for Emily and Aunt Diana instead after school. And don't forget your sisters!"

Joe Jr. waved back and Maria watched her children run up the long driveway that led to the road, waving to Mr. Clark, and waiting until they were on the bus and on their way. Then she glanced over to the house on the right where Philip and Diana were sitting on their porch drinking coffee.

"I have the bacon cooked and ready to go," Diana called out.

"I can tell. It smells delicious. We'll need it in about fifteen," Maria called back.

Bursting out of the house, carrying two pitchers of orange juice with Emily and a basket full of hot biscuits right behind her, Rebeca asked, "What kind of cake are we making, Maria?"

"Well, we better make Farah's favorite since it is her birthday."

"Your cakes are everybody's favorite," Rebecca said.

"Ugh, more fattening calories," Emily moaned. "I better skip lunch."

Chapter 2
The Dream

Farah smiled as she waited for the single serve coffee maker to fill a white plastic cup, imagining what happy chaos was ensuing in her absence as Maria coordinated breakfast this morning. She was also thinking about her dream, which, surprisingly, had stayed with her in its detail. It was taking the sting off the big day.

We were on the back porch...

Raising my raising my glass as the effervescent bubbles tickle my nose. It is odd we only drink mimosas on holidays. They're so delicious and I'm feeling decadent. Silly because it's just orange juice and cheap champagne. At least on this farm.

Maria is on my right, smiling, sipping her own mimosa, and my niece Emily is on my left, also holding a flute filled with a virgin version this year as she awaits the birth of her second child in early July. It's a girl! And in July! I can't believe we will have another little girl to celebrate in July.

But this morning, the focus is on the impending Easter egg hunt. Robin is not doing a very effective job of explaining the rules to the anxious group of hunters who are squirming, ignoring him, looking around, hoping to spot a few easily hidden colorful eggs.

Joe Jr. and my boy, looking more like his dad every day, are acting like they were too old for this, but they've been assured there are special eggs hidden for each child and they will not be disappointed.

"Ready, set, hunt!" Philip calls.

We root the kids on as they scramble. Grandpa Philip and Grandma Diana help two-year-old Sam, Emily, and Josh's first child, while Sam's dad films the little boy on his phone.

"We will never see that video," Emily says, and Maria and I laugh knowing how technically un-savvy Josh is.

Joe is leading Christina and Diego over to the chicken house, while Rebecca, Marisol, and Brandi have teamed up. I wonder how my girl is going to find any eggs with her crazy curls bouncing in her face. She was so excited this morning she wouldn't let me do anything with her hair.

It is quite a sight, and when Robin looks up at me, I could pinch myself. It sometimes feels like I'm living in a dream. I had all but given up hope of a husband and children. And not only did I get that, but I also got all of this! This deserves another mimosa.

The front door slams, and Maria and I give each other a knowing look.

"DID YOU START WITHOUT ME?"

Farah stirred in powdered creamer, and watched it coagulate and swirl at the top. I mean it was just Easter this past Sunday. We did have an egg hunt. But Emily is NOT pregnant. She's not the blushing bride yet.

She looked at herself in the mirror as she took her first sip of coffee. "Happy Birthday to me!" she said, lifting her coffee cup to toast her reflection. It *was* a big one. One of those numbers that hits hard. Though she doesn't look her age...or so she'd been told...whatever that meant anymore.

Later, she will visit her old hairdresser and get her shoulder length, naturally wavy light brown hair highlighted, trimmed, and straightened. Then she might visit one of her favorite boutiques and splurge on a birthday treat. And speaking of treats...she will have to stop by her old business and indulge in a treat of the mouthwatering sugary variety and a good cup of coffee.

With that thought, she poured the flavorless coffee down the sink before showering and gathering her things. Her sister

MaryAnn wouldn't care that she hadn't bothered with any makeup, or that it was her birthday. She won't care that *her* own birthday was two days ago, or that Farah made this effort once a year because their parents would have wanted it that way. MaryAnn wouldn't care about her life now, even though she was partially responsible for it.

My life now... Farah pushed the elevator button and began the ride down. Her life was as perfect as her dream. She had Robin and the farm and her wonderful extended family. She had all of this...but unlike her dream, she didn't have any children.

Chapter 8
It's Party Time!

Robin stood at the doors of the stable and looked at his home and the welcoming signs coming from the big kitchen windows as Maria and Rebecca moved around. Outside, the large white gazebo with climbing vines covered two long picnic tables in the center of the property. Tonight, they were adorned with red-and-white checkered tablecloths, white plates, wine glasses and two big vases of fresh cut flowers, ready for Farah's party. Though the sun was shining bright in the sky, Robin knew by the time it set, the charming outside dining room would glow with lights strung throughout the gazebo. He started to walk, hoping for a shower before his wife arrived home, but in an instant, he realized he was too late.

Farah had just walked out the back door behind Maria, who was hurrying her children down the stairs. Was it because he hadn't seen her all day, or because her hair shone brighter and styled in a way he rarely saw, or she was wearing a blouse he had never seen before? Whatever it was...she looked even more beautiful than normal.

A moment later Rebecca ran out of the house and down the stairs toward her big brother. "She's home, Robin. Farah is home!"

He took her in his arms and spun her around. "I see that, sis. By the looks of things, I can tell you've been busy around here."

"We have been. Maria even let me help frost the cake!" She beamed.

"I can't wait to eat it," he said, kissing her forehead. Robin always had a special fondness for his sister, and it had grown through the years as he became her father figure.

"I can't wait to eat it either. Shall we skip dinner?" Farah asked as she approached and wrapped her arms around them.

"No way! Maria would be so upset," Rebecca said.

"I'm just kidding! The kitchen smells fabulous. We're not skipping dinner!"

"Good. Now I'm going to change for the party," Rebecca said and turned to leave but stopped. "And since it *is* a very special occasion...I put a wine glass in front of my plate, just in case."

Robin laughed. "A little one. And just one!" Then he pulled his wife into his arms for a proper hug. "I missed you today. How is my birthday girl? It's a special one."

"Not you too!" she groaned, gently punching his side. "It was like any other day, I just wasn't at breakfast," Farah said, resting her head in his neck, breathing him in. The combination of hay and sweat was as appealing as any expensive aftershave she might have once preferred.

"It's always different when you're off the farm. Plus, you always come back looking like the city slicker I first met. How was your sister?"

She looked up at him. "Same as she was last year. I had plenty of time for a little birthday pampering and catching up with my old hairdresser."

"Good. I'm going to jump in the shower before the festivities start," he said as they walked toward the house arm in arm.

"And while you do that, I think I'm going to pour *myself* a little glass of wine," she said and smiled.

Robin turned her towards him and gently kissed her on the mouth, "That's a great idea, Birthday Girl. I'll clean up and join you."

Sitting on her porch with a crisp glass of Chianti in her hand, Farah savored the familiar sounds. She could hear the stable workers singing to the horses in Spanish and smiled at the thought of the mares and stallions knowing the language better than her. She could hear Maria and Joe talking and laughing with each other while gently urging their children to wash up. Uncle

Philip and Josh came out of the second stable. Sweet Joshua, with his arm over his soon-to-be father-in-law's shoulder, guiding him along while they talked. And just as they reached the porch steps, Emily burst through the doors and into her fiancé's arms. This place was the stuff fairy tales were made of. Truly, it was. *Only one regret...*

She tried to shake these thoughts. They had reared their ugly heads today. It's this darned birthday. A big one. I'm now in a different decade than Robin.

Standing quickly, Farah turned towards the door and the solace of another glass of wine.

By 6:30, the birthday party was in full swing with everyone feasting on Maria's hearty lasagna, green salad, and Diana's crusty garlic bread and Farah's antipasto platter. *Antipasto?* They had never heard of it before the first time she'd made it. Now it was a family favorite. The red wine was passed around and Rebecca was excitedly nursing her glass and eagerly toasting to anything she could think of. When the last of the sun fell and the gazebo lit up with hundreds of lights, everyone sat a little closer to one another.

"Farah, we saw the dresses. They're just the way I imagined them," Emily said.

"They really are lovely," Diana agreed. "Right out of a Jane Austen movie."

"I want the whole place decorated like the English countryside," Emily said wistfully.

"Let's take a ride to town tomorrow to see them," Farah said.

"I'm busy," Rebecca said, making everyone laugh.

"Oh, and I almost forgot. You'll never guess who I saw today!" Diana exclaimed.

"Mom, you were mistaken," Emily said.

"No, I'm sure of it. I saw Barbara Fletcher!"

"Barbie?" Maria and Rebecca asked in unison.

"Well, I heard her first. I was outside the store, and this old car was coming up the street. It was making loud popping noises, like firecrackers. And when it passed me there was no mistaking who was in the driver's seat."

Robin tensed, suddenly paying attention. *The same car he saw last night.*

"Are you positive?" Maria asked.

"I've only seen three women in my life with that color hair and they're all Fletchers. It was her. Anyway, I'm seeing Carole in the morning. I'll get the scoop." Diana shook her head. "I smell trouble."

"Who's Barbara Fletcher?" Farah asked.

"She was a friend of my brother's," Robin said with a definite edge in his voice, still thinking about the drive-by the night before. *It was no coincidence.* "She's been gone...for years."

"She was bad news. We always thought so, right Maria?" Diana asked.

"She was...unusual, I'll say that."

"Well, she's back, and I just know this is trouble. I can feel it," Diana said.

"Diana, stop," Philip admonished. "You don't know why the poor girl's back. Maybe to help her mother. Carole's not very well. You said so yourself."

"Exactly," Emily said. "Now, I think it's time for birthday cake! This might be the last cake we have for a while. Right, Becca?"

"Speak for yourself! I've seen all your Jane Austen movies and they all eat a lot of cake!"

"Do you want to talk about MaryAnn?" Robin asked, from inside their bathroom at the end of the night.

Farah sighed, full stomach, lying in bed, scrolling through her phone. "There really isn't much to say. The nurses are always pleasant. We spent the morning sharing family pictures. What about this Barbara person's return? The mention of her name brought tension to the table. I felt it in you too."

There was a pause. "It's...nothing. My aunt's always thought she had something to do with the accident."

"Why?"

"Because she disappeared right after it."

"That is an odd coincidence," she said, absently, coming upon a text she had yet to read. "Well, whatever the reason she's back, she sure has caused a stir."

Robin slid in beside her. "Having you home with me has caused a stir," he said and they both laughed. I hope you've had a good birthday. I just realized...I didn't get you a gift."

Farah chuckled. " You've given me the best gift of all. This farm and this family. It's been a lovely day."

When Robin had drifted off to sleep. She looked at the unread text. It was from Carl. He did surface each year to wish her a happy birthday. She can't say she remembers his...but April will be forever ingrained in their memories.

* * *

In high school, she worked at a popular bakery called "Buttercream." Wide-eyed and enthusiastic, soaking up everything taught to her, by the time she graduated high school she was the weekend manager, known by most of the clientele and in high demand for her cake decorating.

She had no interest in applying to colleges or leaving home. But with her parents' gentle persistence, she signed up for classes at the community college and suffered through mandatory classes during the day, while measuring, mixing, icing, and piping to her heart's content by night.

Two years into college, the owner of the bakery told her he was looking to sell. Farah said yes before she knew what owning a business involved. The owner was a better teacher than any she had ever met in a classroom and five months later, after working out the financial details, taking out a loan from her parents, and revamping the menu and the bakery, Farah had a small grand re-opening.

On a beautiful Saturday afternoon in April, right after her thirtieth birthday, she was putting the final touches on a wedding cake when a dapper group of groomsmen boisterously entered the bakery in classic black tuxedos.

One of them nervously approached the glass cases. "Um, hello. We need...um...pastries." He looked at the selection, shaking his head. "We have a little while before..." He stopped talking and stared at her, seeming taken aback by her simple beauty in blue jeans, white tee shirt, white apron and her long curly hair pulled back off her face. He leaned in and whispered. "You're the prettiest woman I've ever seen."

Though she guessed they had already been celebrating, she was flattered. Maybe because of her age or the fact she was preparing to send another wedding cake on its way to a reception, by the time she had filled a box with chocolate croissants and banana nut muffins, she had invited Carl Crabtree back for coffee.

A week later, he had traded in the black tuxedo for an ill-fitting brown suit. He was pale and looked like a guy who didn't spend too much time outside, but he was warm and kind. They talked about their professions. He, a lawyer following in his father's footsteps.

They dated for six months before she ended it. He professed his love early and often. She professed her love once, and immediately regretted it. Farah wanted to feel what he felt...but it wasn't there.

Soon after she broke it off, he started dating her sister, MaryAnn, and within six weeks they were engaged. And to top it off, she picked Farah's birthday for her wedding, just a few months away. Her parents were always uncomfortable with it, wondering what their unhappy and unstable daughter's motives were.

Farah knew what they were. Her sister wanted his money, family status and to make Farah regret her decision.

Years later, Carl would tell Farah he felt responsible for what happened. He wasn't in love with MaryAnn, just like Farah hadn't been in love with him.

"If I'd only found her diary sooner," He'd lamented...

If only, were Farah's last thoughts before drifting off to sleep, thankful April was nearing its close.

Chapter 4

Much Ado about Many Things

Robin watched the first of the twenty-three family-friendly horses in his care escorted out for exercise. His focus should be on planning the day, just like his father had taught him. *Was the farrier scheduled? How many trainers were coming to give lessons? Were any horses heading out with their owners?* He normally had all this information in his head. But this morning all he could think about was the odd little girl that used to hang out with his brother. He hadn't thought about her in years. Or her mother. And *their* secret...

Robin shook his head, trying to get his thoughts back on his farm, purchased by his father Richard and his Uncle Philip when they were both in their twenties. Though he had been only five, he remembered the first time he came to the farm vividly. There was the big main house, and the two smaller homes that needed repair. There was only one stable and one arena, but his dad and uncle had plans and vision and, in the years to come, they would grow, prosper, and become among the most beautiful farms in the area. And now it was all his. Three beautiful houses, two modern stables, was a busy arena, and the lush acres where he stood.

Robin thought about his mother, Rachel. While he was growing up, she was in and out of the stables all day making sure his father was okay, even though she had more than enough to do with two other children who were ten years plus younger than him. *"We thought we had all the time in the world,"* his mother had told him once when Robin asked why they'd waited so long after him. *"And then we lost two before your brother. And then our miracle four years after that."*

His mother would have loved Farah, and the bond between her and Rebecca, now twenty-seven born with Down syndrome.

Rachel would have loved to see the wonderful, smart, and happy person his sister had become. He hoped she knew.

He turned around and saw Joe. They had been out since 6:00 overseeing the morning feeding and stable cleaners. Josh Marshall was also here this morning, checking on their expectant mare. But he was at the farm every day because of Emily. It had been love at first sight when Josh started coming to the ranch two years ago, taking over the duties of his father.

Soon, Robin breathed in the welcoming aroma of bacon and started to walk through the stable. But more welcoming than the aroma was the sight of his wife.

On her way back from getting the bounty from the generous hens, Farah waved to Philip on his front porch drinking coffee as she walked. "Diana sent the bacon over before she left with Emily," he said, waving back.

Inside the kitchen, Maria was busy icing warm, fragrant cinnamon rolls, the house smelling like a holiday morning. "Wow, you're going to spoil everyone, Maria." Farah laughed, placing her basket of eggs on the center island.

"Just like you taught me," Maria beamed.

"You have far surpassed me," Farah said, leaning in close to the pan and breathing in warm cinnamon.

"Never, never," Maria turned away, pink blooming across her cheeks.

A moment later, Rebecca bounded down the stairs and caught off guard by the heady aroma, she asked, "Is it Christmas?" Then she laughed and looked around. "Is she here? Where is Emily? She won't want me to have any today," she moaned.

Farah laughed. "She headed to town earlier with Aunt Diana. Go for it."

Inside *The Yardstick*, Emily was a ball of energy as she fussed over her three bridesmaids, Cassie, Anna, and Sasha, looking lovely, waltzing around the shop in their long lavender chiffon dresses with square necklines, simple capped sleeves and a thin velvet belt cinched right under the breast line. Emily was elated, and her friends seemed equally pleased with her choice.

When she saw her family come in, she squealed, "Oh, my God! Look at these! Aren't they perfect?"

"They are! They're beautiful!" Farah and Maria agreed.

"Where is your mom?" Farah asked, looking around.

"Still at Carole's getting her hair done. Where is Rebecca? I want her to put her dress on too."

Where was Rebecca? Farah found her hiding behind large bolts of fabric. She winked and took her by the arm. "Let's go."

"Can't I take it home and try it on?"

"Rebecca, c'mon, I'll help you," Emily said, and they disappeared behind a big curtain in the back of the store where customers tried on their clothes for fittings.

Maria started looking through books to get ideas for Marisol and Christina's flower girl dresses she would be helping Diana make. "Fingers crossed," she said quietly to Farah.

"I know. There doesn't seem to be much room for alterations with this style," Farah said.

As Rebecca emerged from behind the big curtain and stood on the small stage before the large mirror, everyone let out happy and relieved sighs. The dress fit perfectly. And Rebecca, usually preferring denim to dresses, was transformed. Her smile beamed as she turned around, feeling the soft, delicate fabric between her fingers.

"I knew it would be perfect on you," Emily said, her eyes filling with tears.

Farah and Maria were also having a tough time holding back tears of relief and joy, as all the bridesmaids gathered in front of the mirror, seeing Emily's vision come to fruition.

"Why are you all crying?" Rebecca laughed. "It fits! The dress fits!"

"They are lovely on all of you," Maria said, wiping her eyes.

"They are," Farah agreed with a sigh. "Now, Emily, it's your turn. Put yours on for us!"

"Okay. I will," she said before disappearing behind the curtain with Cassie and Sasha, where they whispered and giggled for several minutes.

When Emily appeared, you could have heard a pin drop. The Ivory gown complemented her golden blond hair and fair skin. The style was like that of her bridesmaids, except the fabric was organza, and the sleeves were long and made of lace and delicate beading. Christina and Marisol were silent, watching their beautiful aunt with big smiles on their faces...perhaps envisioning their own weddings one day.

All at once everyone was talking, hugging each other, discussing flowers, veils, and shoes. The happy chatter was so loud, no one heard the bells on the front door as it opened, signaling a customer coming in. And it took a few more moments to realize that the person who came in was Diana. But instead of smiling at the sight of her beautiful daughter...she looked stricken.

"What is it, Mama?" Emily asked. "You look like you have just seen a ghost."

"It wasn't a ghost. Barbara is back. I saw her with my own two eyes. She came into the salon."

"Why after all this time? What did Carole say?" Maria asked.

"I bet *I* know why she's back," Rebecca said absently, still staring at herself in the mirror.

"You know, in all the years I've been here, I've never met Carole. I've just seen her in passing." Farah shrugged. "I do remember the red hair. It's quite a color."

"Well, her daughter is back and guess what?" Diana started.

"Mama!"

Diana glanced at Emily and froze. "Oh, my goodness. Look at you!" She walked over and took Emily in her arms, clearly forgetting what she'd been about to say.

Loading up the van outside the shop, preparing for the ride home, Farah glanced up the street. Just a few storefronts up and on the left was the salon. The rundown little car was parked in front. It was out of place on the quaint Main Street. When she was strapped in, she looked over at Diana who sat next to her. Her eyes were also on the salon. "Are you okay, Diana?"

She glanced over with a puzzled expression on her face. "Hmm? Yes. Fine. Just...can't believe my baby girl is finally getting married."

"She really did pick out a beautiful gown, didn't she?"

"It's lovely," Diana agreed, but her mind was elsewhere. "I know everyone thinks I'm crazy, but I know Barbara was involved in...she was the reason Ricky wanted to come home."

"Well, All I know is Robin has insisted that wasn't it."

"He knows something more. I've always had the feeling he knows something more."

Of course Diana knew a few things of her own that she'd never had the courage to share. And as the years had passed, she had thought they were tucked away in a safe place.

* * *

Growing up on the farm just a year apart, to say Ricky and Adam were close would be an understatement, And early on, Diana had a suspicion Adam had feelings for Ricky that went far beyond cousins, or even best friends. Feelings he should have for a girl.

After high school, Ricky was encouraged to follow in Robin's footsteps and help run the stables. Within six months in, it became clear he had no passion for horses, and he asked his parents if he could go to college. It wasn't that he wanted the college experience.

With his parents' reluctant blessings, Ricky packed up and enrolled in a community college, three hours away in Sacramento. He found a room to rent and got a job at a restaurant.

The night before he left, after a family going-away party, Diana saw the two cousins head out to the stable with a six pack of beer. She had no idea what was going on as she sat in the dark at her bedroom window, watching the stable doors for an hour. Ricky hurried out first, followed by Adam, perfectly timed, five minutes later.

After he left, Adam counted the days until he would be home for Thanksgiving. But Ricky didn't come, so Adam counted the days until Christmas. But he still stayed away, claiming he needed money and it was the best time for tips. He made more excuses until school was out for the summer and his parents pleaded with him to come home.

Upon his arrival, the changes were obvious. He had traded in his flannel shirts and Levi's for black tee shirts, and jeans so tight they all wondered how he got into them. The cowboy boots were replaced with something called "Doc Martens," Rachel had filled them in with a heavy shrug.

On his first night home, Diana walked by Adam's room. He was pacing, visibly upset. "What is it, Adam? What happened?"

"Ricky went into town."

Diana laughed, "Well what the devil is wrong with that?"

"There is only one reason he'd go into this town. Barbie."

"Oh, well, they did...were friends before he left. My goodness, you can ask if she has a friend and you can double date," she said, knowing how ridiculous those words sounded.

Adam took a deep breath and blurted out, "I don't want to date girls, Mom. I want to date Ricky."

The right thing to do would have been to throw her arms around her boy and tell him it was okay. Instead, she'd laughed and said, "Oh my heavens, you two have spent too much time together. You don't know what you want."

Adam yelled, "I do know what I want! You just don't want to hear it!"

Diana stood wringing her hands in her apron. She was about to say something when Philip appeared behind her.

"What's all the shouting about?" he asked, placing his hands on his wife's shoulders.

"It's nothing. Adam just had a rough day at work, that's all," she said meekly. "He was just venting to his mama."

"That's not it at all, and you know it!" Adam shouted back.

Diana held her breath, fearing what would happen if her son said anymore. She silently pleaded with him with her eyes, and finally he clamped his lips and stormed past them into the bathroom, the door.

After Ricky went back to school, he invited Adam for a weekend. Her elated son left on Friday morning and returned the following Monday, and Diana. He was happier than she had ever seen him and constantly on his phone. Looking, waiting, texting, smiling. If Diana had to put a finger on it...she'd say her son was in love. But it was short lived, and Ricky never asked Adam to visit again.

Several times she heard him leaving messages. They were always the same. "Hey, what's going on? I've been calling and texting and you've gone silent. I want to see you...I miss you...call me."

Whatever happened after that, Diana didn't know. The days and weeks turned into months, and Adam was more depressed than ever, spending his time alone in his room when not working. Philip was angry, and Diana tried to be the buffer.

"What's the matter with that boy?" Philip asked her. "It's high time he grew up and acted like a man! I had already met you by the time I was his age. I already had a plan."

"He's a late bloomer," Diana returned. "He's sheltered on this farm. Look at Robin. He is almost thirty and he hasn't met anyone."

"Well, that's true," Philip admitted. "But he's the only one we can trust to run this place. That's not right. He needs to learn the ropes around here."

Diana didn't argue. She didn't have the heart to tell her husband Adam didn't want anything to do with the farm. But she agreed it was wrong to let him hide in his room, hoping for the impossible with Ricky.

* * *

As they pulled into Rebecca Farms and Farah parked the van, Diana turned back to Maria and said, "I almost forgot. Barbara is the mother of two. A boy and a girl."

"Is she married?"

"No, never married. And the kids have different fathers."

"Are the father's part of their lives?" Maria asked, unstrapping her girls.

"I asked Carole and she gave me a funny look. She said we'll find out soon enough. Something is up. I can feel it."

Chapter 8
Dark Secrets

Farah came onto the front porch in a long black silk robe and Robin welcomed her onto his lap, offering her his whiskey.

"You usually sit out back," she said, taking a sip. Farah tilted her head back as the warmth of the liquid hit the back of her throat for the first time.

"I just wanted a little quieter space tonight," he said, wrapping his arms tighter around her silken body. *And waiting for unwelcome visitors again...*

"Well, it's quiet now. The day wore everyone out."

"Rebecca seemed happy. I've never seen her so excited over the thought of wearing a dress before," he said with a chuckle.

"She...they all looked lovely. And Emily is going to make a beautiful bride," Farah said, taking another sip. "And you know Diana got her hair done by Carole."

He laughed, "I *always* know when my aunt gets her hair done. That helmet could stop a bullet."

Farah playfully smacked his arm. "Well, she confirmed Barbara is back. *And* she's brought her two children with her. A boy and a girl."

Robin whistled and shifted uncomfortably. He did not like the way the past suddenly was cropping back up. "Is she married?"

"She's not. And the kids have different fathers."

Robin took the whiskey back and quickly gulped the last sip. "She dated Ricky for a while. I mean I guess you could call it that," he said, trying to take the edge off her return.

"Oh, really? So, she *was* involved with this family at one time."

"They hung out, like teenagers do. Diana has always assumed Barbie was the reason Ricky wanted to bail out of college. Which of course led to... Anyway, it wasn't." He put the glass down and held her tighter.

"Yes, she thinks you know more. Something you've been keeping from her."

"I don't," he added quickly.

"Do you know Carole, her mother?"

Robin cleared his throat. "Well, yeah. For many years her mother's place, "*Hair Biz*," was the only place in town to get a haircut. Carole took over from her mother. Why?"

"Because when Diana asked about the children's fathers, she said we'll learn more in the future."

"No idea what she's talking about," he murmured as he kissed her neck, hoping to get her mind elsewhere. Her on his lap was certainly taking his mind elsewhere.

Farah sighed and ran her fingers through his hair. "I bet she loved getting to run her fingers through your sexy head."

He pulled her closer and brought her mouth to his, while his hands moved up and down her back. His desire surged. His tongue searched for hers, and she welcomed him in as she held onto his cheeks. His hand moved inside of her robe where he found a naked breast and she shuddered with pleasure as his rough fingers massaged a nipple. He stood and lifted her into his arms. He didn't want to talk any more tonight.

Up in their room, they fell onto the bed and each other. Farah rid herself of her robe and Robin stepped out of his jeans then tossed his tee shirt at the side of the bed. He cherished her naked body as though it was the first time he'd seen it, his hands exploring tentatively. And her body responded, arching, opening, guiding him. He loved that she knew what she wanted. He loved that she took his mind off everything except pleasing her. Her gentle sighs, building to feverish moans, her fingers digging into his flesh while he caressed her with his hands and teased her with his tongue. Driving her crazy with pleasure was all that mattered.

* * *

He was fascinated with her long curly red hair, her glossy pink lips, her hip hugging jeans, and her bare midriff as she reached up to trim his hair. Her loose flowy tops never quite hid her braless breasts that swayed and bobbed as she circled around him in the chair. He was often thinking about those breasts under the sheets at night.

One afternoon she was drinking a beer when he came in and she offered him one. They made their usual small talk; with her doing all the talking while he did all the fantasizing. Sitting in her chair, he was craving the body he craved at night. After she finished, she walked over and locked the door and closed the window blinds.

Then, without saying a word she came over and put a hand on him. On him, on him! And then she whispered into his ear, "Ready, baby?"

He was. "I...am," he managed to say, though not sure for what.

She undid his pants and freed him. He had never seen himself at this angle, jutting straight up, long, and thick. He had never felt a hand on himself other than his own, and having her stroke him up and down almost made him pass out. And when she took him in her mouth and he watched her shiny pink lips go up and down, he knew he was going to pass out...until he came.

To say it was all he could think about was an understatement and counted the weeks before it was time for another haircut. This time, she locked the doors and shut the blinds before she started. This time, she wore a tight yellow sweater with a front metal zipper, and Robin could see her hard nipples through the fabric. And this time, with a pile of hair at her feet, she stood in front of him and unzipped her sweater, letting him see her ample breasts.

"Go ahead, touch them if you want," she encouraged.

Robin didn't need to be asked twice. He tentatively took one in each hand and squeezed. She sighed and he thought that was a good thing. He was right. Next, she took him by the hand and led him to a small room with a curtain. There was a bed, more like an examining table and Robin looked confused.

"It's for waxing," she said.

"Huh?"

"Never mind, baby," she cooed, unbuttoning his jeans.

After laying him on the table, she took a small, shiny square out of her skirt pocket. It could have been a piece of candy, but Robin knew it wasn't and blushed. She carefully tore it open and expertly slid it on him before hiking up her skirt and climbing on top.

"Wow," he said, trying to breathe, feeling marvelously confined inside of her as the blood pulsed through him. "I mean WOW!" he screamed blissfully.

She chuckled, and when he caught his breath, she climbed off, lowered her skirt, and excused herself.

After dressing, he joined her back in the salon. All she said was, "Fifteen for the hair, baby. See you in a few weeks."

And when those few weeks were up and Robin was back, she said, "We have to stop meeting like this."

After she finished cutting, she stood in front of him and ran her fingers through his thick head of hair. He could feel her sweet breath on his face. He could see her breasts under her sheer blouse. He could see a bead of sweat make its way down her neck to the middle of her breastbone. This time he knew what to do when she took her shirt off and dropped it on the floor. And he even had some idea of what to do when she brought his hand between her legs.

This time she was the one who said, "WOW" as she lifted her leg onto his lap while he rubbed his fingers back and forth. He felt so powerful, watching her breath quicken and her legs start to shake. And then she quickly undid his jeans and climbed on top of him. It felt different this time. She was different this time. It wasn't all about him and he concentrated until she got there...

* * *

Robin's eyes popped open. He had not thought about that time of his life in years. He knew it had ended abruptly but couldn't remember why. He'd called for an appointment and was told it would be better if he found another salon.

So, his hair grew, and after a year, it danced off his shoulders, up and down like a horse's mane when he rode, blowing in the wind. And Carole had become a distant memory. Until tonight.

Chapter 6
"Something About Her..."

Maria was in the kitchen peeling potatoes for dinner, watching Farah and Diego feed the chickens. It had been five days since the news about Barbara Fletcher's return, and like Diana, Maria had a strange feeling this was no coincidence. She hadn't thought about her in years. There was their life before the accident, which Barbie was an interesting part of, and their life after, where the girl fell out of sight...and mind.

Her family had found so much love on this farm since arriving ten years ago. She recalls the day vividly when Joe came in from work and told her to sit down, their lives were about to change.

He'd been asked to make a special delivery to a farm forty minutes away. "I met the owners last week when they came in for supplies. They board horses. They had two on a trailer with them. Beautiful animals. They called asked me to deliver their supplies personally today," he'd on his way out that morning. "I might be a little later."

When he arrived home, he was talking fast and non-stop and Maria had to ask him to slow down. The bottom line...they had offered him a job...and a new home!

* * *

Driving up to the big white house with hunter green window shutters, and wrap-around porch, Joe was in awe. And when he followed the road around to the right, he saw the second house, a smaller version of the main one, with the same white paint and green shutters. When he was all the way around to the back, he saw one stable, and next to it, another one under construction. And finally, there was a third house on the other side of the property.

Robin was there to greet him at the truck and Joe was given a tour of the stable, the new one about six months from being complete, the new arena in the back. Finally, he was invited to stay for lunch.

"We can start getting the little house ready for living in. You got a family?" Richard asked during lunch.

"I have one son and a daughter on the way," Joe answered nervously, staring at the fried chicken on his plate.

"Well, the house is a two/one right now. But there is plenty of room out the back to grow." Philip offered. "Think about it."

When Robin walked Joe to the truck, Joe said, "I can't believe this. I don't know what to say."

"Say yes! We need another person, We saw you with the two horses we had hitched last week. You're a natural. My dad can tell. Go home and talk to your wife. I promise, you'll be happy here."

* * *

Maria couldn't believe her ears when Joe had finished. "They saw you pet a horse and offered you a job and a house? *Ellos estan locos!*"

She chuckled, remembering that day, but it was true. Joe said the place had a special feel to it. In the brief time he was there...he said it felt like home. And he was right.

Maria was seven months pregnant with Marisol the day they arrived and Rachel insisted they stay in the main house while their house was under construction. She wasn't used to relaxing, but as the weeks dragged on and her belly and feet swelled, she was grateful for the comfortable surroundings, and the extra hands to help with Joe Jr.

She also enjoyed her ringside seat on the couch watching all the comings and goings of the hormonal teenagers. Ricky, Adam, Emily, and Rebecca were on constant highs and lows, laughing one minute and yelling at each other the next. And there was one visitor who added an extra layer of tension whenever she was around...

* * *

*"Wow, that's a big bun in the oven you got there, lady,"
Barbie pointed to Maria as she walked through the back door
one afternoon, sucking on a big cherry red lollipop, turning
her lips and tongue the same garish color.*

*Maria was on the couch with her feet up, and Rebecca was
on the floor building blocks with Joe Jr. Her first impression
was she looked sickly. Or maybe it was the bright red head of
hair against her pale skin. It was a color Maria had never seen
before, except on a famous rag doll. It hung wild and loose
and overwhelmed the rest of her skinny body.*

*"It's not a bun it's a baby," Rebecca said to her, in a matter-
of-fact tone.*

"I know what it is, you re..." Barbie caught herself.

Maria gasped. "Watch your mouth, little girl."

*"I'm not a little girl," Barbie sneered, her lollipop
protruding out one side of her cheek.*

*Ricky came over carrying two sodas. "C'mon, let's go
upstairs."*

*"You're not supposed to be up there alone with a girl.
Mom's rules," Rebecca said, smiling, pleased with herself.*

"Shut up!" Ricky yelled.

*"It's okay, it's okay," Barbie said, not paying any attention
to Ricky, as her eyes stared out the window.*

*And when Maria followed her gaze...she could see Robin
walking from one stable to the other. And when she looked
back at Barbie, she could see the same look on her face that
she saw on Adam's face when he looked at Ricky. Barbie was
also smitten.*

*Yes, since her arrival, she had figured out a couple of
things. Adam had an ill-fated crush on his cousin, and Barbie
was here to admire the long haired cowboy from a distance.
And Ricky seemed oblivious to both.*

By the time Marisol was born, Maria watched the odd couple, while rocking her baby girl, from her renovated front porch.

Ricky and Barbie hung out on the big picnic table under the gazebo. Whenever Robin came into view, Barbie would grab his hand, peck his cheek, touch her thigh to his.

The pecks on the cheeks turned into long awkward kisses. Now, along with Maria and Adam, the hormonal couple had the attention of Rachel and Diana, who'd sit in the kitchen turned into long, messy, teenage kisses drinking lemonade, watching the side show at the picnic table.

Rachel wasn't happy with the couple. "There's something about her. I can't put my finger on it. She seems a little...off," she said one afternoon holing Marisol, staring out the window while Maria chopped vegetables. "I know that doesn't sound nice."

"I'm sure it won't last. If she is anything like her mother, she'll get tired of him and look for another," Diana said, chuckling. "That wasn't very nice either."

"Well, the good news is, after graduation, Ricky will be putting his attention into the farm. There won't be any time for this. Richard won't put up with it," Rachel said.

Diana sighed. "At least Ricky has found someone. Adam has never even had a date."

"Never?" Rachel asked.

Diana hesitated. "Not yet. Hopefully, his luck will change at the grocery store," she said.

I don't think so, Maria thought but couldn't dare speak as she looked out and saw Robin coming from one of the stables.

He usually ignored his brother and Barbie, but that one time he said, "Get a room you two."

"Jealous?" Ricky said, loud enough for everyone to hear.

"He's not jealous of us. He likes his women older," Barbie said.

Robin stopped at the door but did not turn around before walking quickly past all the curious eyes in the kitchen.

* * *

As Farah came in with Diego, Emily and Rebecca came rushing through the front door.

"You're never going to guess who we saw walking in town," Emily said breathlessly.

"Okay, then just tell us," Farah laughed.

"We saw Barbie Fletcher with her little girl!"

Maria turned, wide eyed, the image of her still fresh in her mind from years ago. "How did she look?"

"Same. Sickly...like you always used to say," Rebecca said.

"Stop, young lady. I wasn't that bad."

"What is all the interest with this girl?" Farah asked. "Robin said she dated Ricky, sort of."

"She *dated* Ricky, but she *liked* Robin," Rebecca said nonchalantly, peeling a banana.

"That's silly, Becca," Farah said. "She was much younger than him. What makes you think that?"

"She told me. I told her she looked gross, always kissing Ricky. And then *she* said, 'shut up, dumb retard.' And then *I* said, 'I am not a retard,' and then *she* said, 'you are dumb because you don't get that I'm only kissing him to make Robin jealous,' and then *I* said, 'he would never like a skinny girl like you,'" Rebecca finished, taking a big bite out of her banana.

Maria couldn't believe her ears. "How could you possibly remember, *mija*?"

"I don't know. I just do. She was always calling me stupid, and I am not!"

"You two never did get along," Emily said. "She was probably just trying to make you mad or something." She waved her arm to dismiss this. "Anyway, her daughter is darling. She's a tiny thing with lots of curly strawberry blond hair."

"I feel sorry for her having Barbie for a mother," Rebecca said, and Emily and Maria both chuckled.

"Alright, that's enough. Hopefully, motherhood has...changed her," Farah said. "Now let's help Maria get this dinner going."

"Let me go see if Mama needs any help," Emily said and hurried out the back door.

"That means she's going to look for Josh," Rebecca said.

Farah laughed. Rebecca was anything but stupid, never missing a thing. "Just make a salad and I'll go set the table."

Farah was placing silverware at each plate when Robin emerged from the second stable. She loved watching his big, purposeful stride and she smiled broadly as he approached and gently kissed her lips, "Hey, there."

"Hi," he said, kissing her again. "How was your afternoon?"

"Good."

"Anything I need to know before I go in? Do we have flowers picked out yet for the big day?"

"You might be saved from flower talk. Emily and Rebecca came in with *other* news."

"What's that?"

"They saw Barbie Fletcher in town with her little girl." For a split second she thought he stiffened.

"Oh?"

"And what's more interesting, Rebecca thought Barbie hung around here so much was because she had a crush on *you* and not your brother."

Robin seemed to breathe a sigh of relief. "That's crazy. She was just a kid." He leaned in and kissed her cheek, "I got to get cleaned up."

Farah watched him walk away and into the house. It was an odd feeling thinking he was keeping something from her. Something that had to do with Barbie Fletcher. She was back for a reason. What did it have to do with this family?

Chapter 7
The Accident

Robin was awake long after Farah fell asleep, thinking about Barbie's ominous return. He had not seen or heard from her since the accident that killed his parents, brother, and cousin eight years ago. Though he would never forget, these past years had been so happy since his marriage, Joe and Maria having two more children, and most recently, Emily getting engaged. But now it was right back on the surface. That horrible January night Ricky called. It was pouring rain on the farm, and across the state. Robin and Adam were in the kitchen finishing off one of Rachel's apple pies when the phone rang.

* * *

Ricky screamed over the line. *"I want you to come and get me as soon as you can!"*

Rachel asked, *"What is going on?"*

"I can't...over the phone. When can you come?"

"What about classes?" His father asked.

"I...I don't have any tomorrow. And...could you just get me?" he pleaded.

Robin stood from his chair and took the phone from his mother. *"Hey, Ricky, you can't expect Mom and Dad to drop everything. Especially in this weather. Grow up, man. What could be that bad? Did you flunk a class? Anyway, you have a car. Get your own ass home!"*

"Shut up! You don't know anything. Dad? Mom? Please."

Richard took the phone back. *"Son, where is your car?"* Then there was a long pause. The only sound was the pouring rain, saturating the grounds outside. *"Ricky, your car?"*

"It hasn't been running for a couple of months," he blurted out. "I...um... had an oil leak. I didn't know."

Robin sighed in disgust. But after more pleading, his parents agreed to go in the morning. He was pacing back and forth, expressing his concern. "It's supposed to be lousy weather all week. Let me go."

"No, you're needed here even more than me. Besides, you and Ricky don't see eye to eye," his father replied, rubbing his forehead.

Adam, who had been sitting quietly, jumped up. "I'll go with you. I can help drive."

His parents looked at each other before his mom said, "Go and check with your parents. It would be nice to have you come along."

Adam hurried out as Robin was about to express more objection, but his mother put her hand up. "I'll need you to help with Rebecca. I'm going to tell Maria we're leaving."

And that was that...

The rain was still coming down in the morning as the three of them loaded into the truck just before 7:00 AM with a big picnic basket of provisions.

Philip, Diana, and Emily were watching the departure from their porch, and Maria stood with Rebecca.

Robin was at the truck, leaning on the door of his mother's side...as if it could keep the truck from moving. But soon enough it gently pulled away...

They arrived at Ricky's apartment four hours later and Richard told Robin he would let him know when they were on the way back.

"But the weather! Spend the night, at least." Robin argued.

"We'll be fine. It seems better here," his father said. "We're going to gather up your brother, hopefully get some answers, fill our thermoses with fresh coffee and be on our way. We should be home by eight or nine."

"Dad, please stay on the freeways. Stay on the main roads," Robin said, knowing his father loved to find shortcuts, though they never were.

"Sure, sure. See you later tonight. Love you, son."

* * *

Robin quietly got out of bed and went into the bathroom to splash water on his face. When he looked at his reflection, he saw his red, watery eyes. He was hot and nauseated, not wanting to think about what came next for fear he would throw up. These memories brought this reaction even after all these years. Remembering the last time he heard his father's voice. The night Ricky called was horrible, but the next morning was worse.

* * *

The rain had stopped but a thick, low fog hung in the air, blanketing the farm. Diana and Emily stood at the edge of their porch, with a blanket wrapped around them. They stared at the road, hoping for a familiar truck to come into view.

Robin was on his porch, huddled in a chair with a blanket, watching his aunt and cousin, hoping for the same thing. He'd made his last call to his dad three hours before. His father's familiar voice was replaced with; "The number you have dialed is not in service."

Philip and Joe were in the stables. It was easier to keep moving, avoiding the inevitable. Whatever it was, it wasn't going to be good.

Maria had just come out and handed him a hot cup of coffee when they heard Diana whimper, and the sheriff's car came slowly around the corner and stopped. There were no sirens, but the lights were on, spinning round and round, red lights breaking through the thick fog.

As the Sherriff slowly exited the car, Robin knew what he was going to say just by his body language. It was a long walk up the steps for Sheriff Paulson...the longest, heaviest steps he

*had even taken. He waited until Diana and Emily joined them
before he spoke.*

*Seconds later, Philip heard guttural screams coming from
his wife, and he fell to his knees as Joe rushed over to him to
catch and keep him from falling further.*

* * *

When Robin's beathing had settled, he slowly made his way
back to bed where his wife still peacefully slept. He had managed
not to get sick, even though his aunt and uncle's agony still rang
in his ears. And worse, the life in their eyes was gone for years
after.

He had less than three hours before his day would begin on his
beautiful farm. The farm that had protected them from the worst,
and now was rewarding them with so much happiness.

Robin had kept a couple of secrets close to the vest after the
accident. Secrets he wanted to stay buried. It was all to protect
his family.

There was no way Barbie was back to unearth anything, was
she?

Chapter 8
A Mother of a Mother's Day!

Rinsing strawberries and blueberries for shortcakes in the kitchen, Farah was enjoying some rare quiet on a Sunday afternoon. The mothers of Rebecca Farms were in town for some well-deserved pampering and Robin was out in the stables. He had been quiet and distant in the past few days and had had a couple of restless nights but assured her everything was fine. He hadn't wished her a Happy Mother's Day, even though she's taken on the role in many ways. *Stop, Farah.*

This was always a tough day for her, bringing back memories of the last time she'd seen her mother. It was that fateful afternoon just before the final dress fitting for MaryAnn. She could still see her beautiful mother coming into her bakery like it was yesterday. How could she know they would never spend another Mother's Day together?

Farah had invited her mom to the bakery because she wanted to tell her about her recent diagnosis. *Endometriosis.* She had long been suffering with pain each month, and never really addressed it, but getting on in her thirties she had started to take better care with her health...still hoping one day to have a family.

"Those flowers look so lifelike!"

She can still hear her mother's voice sing out when she came into the bakery.

Farah was supposed to go to the fitting but a couple of late orders were keeping her at work. She was about to tell her about the diagnosis when MaryAnn called and said she was running late. *"I'll be glad when this wedding is over and she's off on her honeymoon,"* her mother had said.

After that call, seeing her mother's obvious stress, she decided this news could wait, and as they said goodbye, they looked forward to talking later. But Farah didn't hear from her mother that night...

* * *

She poured a glass of wine when she got home and looked at her calendar and the schedule for the following week. "And my birthday!" she said aloud. "Of course, you picked that day for the wedding, MaryAnn. Bitch."

She was about to call it a night when there was a knock on the door. She answered, and two police officers stood before her. There had been a car accident. They believed alcohol had played a factor in the other driver losing control of the vehicle. Her parents had been killed, and her sister was at the hospital. In the days that followed, the details fell into place, although more details would never change the outcome and Farah wished for less.

Because of MaryAnn, the final fitting started forty-five minutes late. And because of MaryAnn's constant complaints about the dress—a stitch here, a bead there—they were there longer than they should have been.

Perhaps if the appointment had started on time and MaryAnn wasn't a "bridezilla," they wouldn't have crossed paths with the young woman on her way home after having drinks with co-workers.

Unfortunately, there was no time to properly grieve in the days after the tragedy. Farah and Carl were at MaryAnn's bedside while making calls and canceling the wedding. Farah would remember later they both were in overdrive, and she couldn't remember Carl shedding one tear for her sister. Neither did she. She had forgotten all about her recent diagnosis, her birthday, or the talk she wanted to have with her mother.

After a week, there was no brain activity and no signs of life in MaryAnn's lifeless body. Farah would have pulled the plug immediately but kept her on life support so any friends could come and say goodbye. There were just a handful that trickled in over a week's time. And before she knew it... three weeks had passed.

Except for a few hours spent at her bakery, and a few more hours spent at home sleeping, Farah had been at MaryAnn's bedside with Carl. She wasn't so sure whether it was out of guilt or obligation. But now it was time to decide. And Farah didn't take long. She signed the papers to have her sister removed from life support.

Carl grabbed her hand as the nurses turned off the machines and the room became eerily quiet. Farah couldn't wait to turn her over to the funeral home. She hadn't even planned a service for her parents yet. She had her coat in hand and purse over her shoulder, waiting to make a quick exit, but there was no flat line. MaryAnn kept breathing. The nurses said this should be a temporary thing...

A week later, MaryAnn transferred to a long-term rehabilitation facility and Farah threw herself back into her work. She rarely thought about the condition she'd found out about right before the accident. She never thought about dating. She thought that part of her life was over. Her sister remained in a Persistent Vegetative State...and in a way, so did Farah, for five years. Until the day Robin walked into her life.

* * *

Walking toward the staircase, Farah saw the car approaching the house. She stood at the front door as the engine puttered before it died. It took another minute before the driver's door opened and a skinny leg appeared, dangling outside the car before the rest of the body slowly emerged, followed by a slight woman with flaming red hair whipping in the breeze, stood, hands on her hips, eyeing the home from top to bottom and side to side.

It was Barbara Fletcher.

Farah opened the front door and the two women stared at each other. Slowly, she walked out and down the front porch steps until she stood six feet in front of her.

Built like a lanky boy, wearing a faded sleeveless denim blue dress, cinched tightly around the waist by a worn brown leather belt, she whistled before saying, "Wow wee! This place has changed. I had to drive by a couple of times just to make sure I got the right farm, even though the sign out front's still the same. Who are you?"

"Farah," she answered, eyeing her warily.

Barbie chuckled, "Like the faucet?"

"Funny. Who are you?"

"Barbie."

"Like the doll?"

"Yeah, yeah, I get that a lot. So, who *are* you?" she asked again.

"I'm Robin's wife. I'm Farah Robinson."

Barbie suddenly felt small and insignificant looking up at Farah. All the bravado she had worked up on the drive over was slowly melting away in the hot sun, but she tried not to show it. She knew Robin was married. It wasn't like she wasn't *expecting* someone beautiful. Of course, he'd marry someone beautiful.

Farah's soft curly hair shone brightly in the warm sun. Her capri jeans and yellow tee fit her slim figure perfectly. *She even smelled great*, Barbie thought as the breeze carried her floral fragrance over to where she stood. There was one thing that took her by surprise though. *She's got a few years on him.* "Yeah, I heard he got himself a wife. Huh. Looks like you've done wonders with the place."

"Thanks. What brings you here, Barbie?"

"Funny you should ask. I...um...thought it was time Robin, well, and now you, and the rest of the family I guess," She took a deep breath, "I thought it was time to introduce you to my kids."

"Why?" Farah asked.

Barbie turned to the car and leaned in. "C'mon, get out, it's okay," she said as two little bodies slowly climbed out of the back seat.

Farah looked like she was going to pass out and leaned on the porch rail. *She can't take her eyes off my boy, and I know why,* Barbie thought, feeling very pleased with herself having dropped this bombshell, her bravado building again.

"What...what are their names?" was all Farah could manage to ask.

"Ben and Brandi. I wanted to do that same initial thing with my kids, like the Robinson tradition and all. But the birth certificates say Fletcher. Poor things."

"I see," Farah said meekly.

Barbie had just rocked this woman's entire world. Her perfect world. She had never had a perfect day in her life...but this moment was close to it. She laughed again and walked closer to Farah so that her kids couldn't see her face. "Listen, the look on your face has made my Mother's Day, but I shouldn't completely ruin yours. Ben is not Robin's son. He's Ricky's."

"Oh, Robin. Let me get..." Farah turned, ready to go when he came through the front door.

"Barbara?" he asked, coming down to Farah's side.

"It's Barbie."

"What's going on?" Robin asked but hurried down the steps and right over to the little boy.

"I thought it was time you meet your nephew."

He turned back to her, "What...my nephew?"

"Ben, meet your Uncle Robin. And I guess this would be your Aunt Farah." Robin stared at the child in disbelief. "He looks just like you when you were a boy, right? I remember all those school pictures on the walls heading up the stairs."

"Listen, Barbie, this is huge. This is beyond huge." Farah moved closer to her, keeping her voice quiet. "This was not the best way to do this. Not for us, and certainly not for your kids. You should leave, and Robin and I will, um, come to you tomorrow."

"I'm glad you think you can call the shots," Barbie answered, not bothering to be quiet.

Robin turned to her, "Please, Barbie, don't turn this into a circus. Think of the rest of our family."

She shrugged and kicked the ground like a scolded child. "Fine. Get in the car, kids."

"Wait," Robin said as he took Farah's hand and they walked over to the children. He kneeled. "Hi, Ben, and..."

"This is Brandi," Farah said, also kneeling.

"Ben and Brandi. Well, I'm your Uncle Robin and this is your Aunt Farah." He held out his hand and the boy took it. The little girl slid behind her brother.

Both children looked hot and confused. "Hi," Ben said, softly.

"We are very happy to meet you," Farah said.

"We're going to come and visit you tomorrow, okay?" Robin said.

"Okay," Ben answered back.

Robin rose and turned to Barbie, "What time works?"

"Golly, you name the time. I got nothing to do and nowhere to go."

"Fine, we'll come around eleven o'clock."

"Great. Should be fun," she said and opened her car door, but before getting in, she turned back to Robin and said, "I guess I don't need to tell you where to come. You remember the place."

Farah and Robin sat on the front porch long after Barbie drove away with her kids, leaving a cloud of dust and more questions than answers. At first, they were a loss for words.

"This explains why she's back." Robin said finally.

"I can't get over how much Ben looks like you."

"Farah, he's not mine. You know that, right?"

"Yes, I know. It's remarkable, though. If she'd never left town, what a scandal this would have been. It would have been hard to convince people he was Ricky's." She chuckled and nudged his side. "This could be the reason she left. And *this* is why your brother *really* wanted to come home."

He sighed deeply, knowing the real reason. It had nothing to do with Barbie, or the fact that he was going to be a father. At least he didn't say. "I'm ashamed to admit, I never really knew my brother."

"There was a ten year age difference."

"I know that, but that's not the only reason. He was different. I thought he was soft. He didn't want anything to do with this place. I resented him for that instead of trying to appreciate his interests."

Farah turned to him. "Do you know what they were?"

"I...uh...don't really know that either. I tried to get some information out of the roommate when I went to get his stuff, but he didn't know him either. That was the day I met you," he said grabbing her hand. "It was still all so painful. Just a month after the accident."

"I know," Farah replied, squeezing his hand just as a familiar car turned into the farm. "Well, looks like the family's back."

They stood together. "We have to keep this quiet until we know more," Robin said, waving as the car pulled up to the front of the house.

Emily stopped and opened her window. She had a big smile on her face and she asked, "Did we miss anything?"

Chapter 9
A Brother's Secrets

Much later Farah and Robin were by side in the bed, staring at the ceiling. They had managed to get through the rest of the day without the life changing news getting out.

"You prepared a lovely meal," Robin said.

Farah laughed softly. "Really? You hardly touched the salmon."

"It's great once a year. I know Maria and Diana loved it."

"They did? I can hardly remember getting it on the table. I hope I didn't forget a key ingredient."

"They wouldn't have known."

They both laughed at this before Farah said, "We would get some sleep. Tomorrow is going to be a big day."

Robin responded with a warm embrace and kiss on her forehead. All he's been able to think about is his brother since Barbie's return to the farm today. He was ashamed he never really knew him. And what he found out later...well that secret had to be kept from the family.

Like Farah's mixed feeling for her sister, he'd had them for his brother. Sad for the loss...but anger too. None of this should have happened.

* * *

"Nathan, right?" Robin said, holding out his hand to the skinny young man who looked like he'd just crawled out of bed when the apartment door opened.

"Yeah. Man...I'm sorry about what happened."

"Thanks. I'll get out of your way as soon as I can."

"No problem. Take your time."

Robin walked into the living area with a small kitchen and round table straight ahead. He looked to the right and saw two bedrooms. One room looked neat and the other looked *like a pig pen. He knew which one was his brother's. He had brought garbage bags and started sifting through the paper covering the bed. "Look at this shit. How did he get anything done?"*

"Yeah, probably why he got into trouble," Nathan said absently from the other room.

Robin had forgotten about Nathan. He walked out to find him sitting at the kitchen table. "What trouble? What are you talking about?"

Nathan moved uncomfortably in the chair. "Oh, um, I guess I thought you knew. Isn't that why he wanted to go home?"

"He didn't say over the phone. What do you know?"

Nathan scratched his head. "Well...he was on academic probation." He swallowed hard. "He was caught cheating. He had to go before the Dean with a plan for getting back on track."

Robin scoffed. "That idiot!" He went back and started throwing things into a bag, cursing under his breath. But then he came to something that stopped him in his tracks. It was a picture of Ricky and Adam. Not just one picture. There were four on a strip; the kind folks got from sitting in a photo booth at the fair. In the last frame...they were kissing...on the mouth. "Oh. Oh No. No. No!" He turned to see Nathan who was now standing at the door.

He looked like he'd rather be anywhere but in this apartment. "Man, I'm sorry. That was his buddy, Adam."

Robin bitterly laughed, "No... actually..." he stopped.

"I only met him one time. I mean he could have been here more, but I usually split on the weekends to my girlfriend's," he said, but Robin was absorbed in the picture. "Listen, I'm going for a coffee. Can I get you one?"

Robin sighed. "That would be great. Thanks."

While Nathan was gone, Robin sat on the bed. He knew his brother and cousin were close, but he'd never sensed they had a romantic connection. He thought about his aunt and uncle.

They could never know about this. They had been devastated enough.

He stood and began stuffing bags again when Nathan came back in with a welcoming cup of coffee. "That was fast."

"Yeah, there's a place right around the corner. The owner's cool. At the end of the day, she'll give us free stuff. She's kind of motherly. I brought cream and sugar if you want," he said.

"No, black is fine." He sat and sipped the steaming hot coffee. It was good and he looked at the label on the cup. "Buttercream."

"Hey, I'm sorry to be invading your privacy like this."

"Hey, no worries, man. I'm leaving for class anyway. Take your time."

"Can I ask you something? I...ahh...feel like a barely knew my brother."

"Sure," Nathan said, but he looked anything but sure.

Robin shook his head. "I don't even think I knew his major."

"Business."

"What did he do for fun? Did he have other friends? Was he involved in, I don't know, clubs?"

"Not that I knew. But, you know, we were just roommates. We didn't hang out. There was this girl, though. She came a few times."

"A girl? Like, a girl he was dating?"

Nathan was gathering his books and putting them in his backpack. "I don't know. Her name was Barbie."

Robin was confused. "Barbie Fletcher?"

"I just got Barbie."

Well, there could only be one, Robin thought. "Did she have red hair?"

'Flaming."

That's the one. "Yeah, thanks, man."

"So, I have to get to class," Nathan said, easing toward the door.

"Can I ask you one more thing?"

"Sure," Nathan said, releasing a sigh.

"I didn't see his car. He said it wasn't running. Do you know where it is?"

Nathan looked at the floor shaking his head. "He gave the car away. He gave it to someone in exchange for an essay. That was the cheating."

Robin was so disgusted in his brother, he didn't bother to look through any of his belongings. He stuffed everything in bags and hauled them to the dumpsters. He threw away his clothes too. And the pictures of Ricky and Adam, he tore to shreds and flushed them down the toilet.

Chapter 10
Confessions over Cherry Pie

"**I** knew you had something going on yesterday, Farah. I could tell something was off," Maria said, shaking her head after she and Joe found out about the new situation they found themselves in.

"Was the dinner that bad?"

"No, that was delicious, right, Joe?"

"It wasn't bad for fish," Joe chuckled, winking at Farah.

"Rebecca's right when she said Barbie only came around here to see you," Maria said, looking at Robin. "I saw the way she stared at you. I never thought she ever had *those* kinds of feelings for Ricky. When did this happen?"

Robin shook his head. "I guess when he was at college. I know she visited. His old roommate told me. Not many red heads named Barbie. We hope to get more answers out of her today. I mean...if she is just going to disappear again, what good will it do to tell the rest of the family."

"You have a nephew! So does Rebecca! Don't you want to get to know the children?" Farah asked.

Robin rubbed his tired eyes. "Of course I do. But not at the sake of upsetting Diana and Philip again. If she *is* part the reason Ricky wanted to come home, and my aunt's suspicions were right, Barbie us going to wish she never returned."

When they pulled up to the front of the salon, they sat, holding hands, bracing themselves for what lay ahead. Robin was sick to his stomach. He had not walked through these doors since the last time he had been with Carole. His brain was telling him to move...but his body wasn't cooperating.

"Robin?" Farah asked. "Should we go in?"

But before he could answer, Barbie was there, knocking on Farah's window. "I was thinking we should have coffee without the kids first. I know I shocked the shit out of you yesterday."

"You shocked the shit out of your children too, I imagine," Farah answered.

"Ha!" Barbie said. "So that's how this is going to go."

"Let's just get coffee," Robin said, getting out of the truck. "We can walk to Sam's."

"Yeah, sounds good. I like their pie," Barbie said, wearing the same ill-fitting dress as the day before.

They sat in a booth, Robin, and Farah on one side, Barbie across from them twirling a lock of hair between her fingers. When the server approached, Farah imagined a waitress from the 1950s in her tight yellow dress and overly teased hair wrapped in a chignon and a name tag that read Bev.

"Just coffee for us. We've already eaten," Farah said.

"I'll take a piece of cherry pie and throw some ice cream on it too, would ya, Bev?"

"Yeah, you're looking thin, Barb. I'll make it an extra big slice," Bev said, snapping her chewing gum.

"Yeah, well, you know Mom don't have much of an appetite these days and hates me eating around her. So I'm taking advantage."

Bev delivered the coffee and pie and after two big bites Barbie looked up. "You two don't look so happy."

"Let's talk about your son," Robin started.

"I have a daughter too. They come as a package."

"What does that mean?" Robin asked.

"In a minute!" She took another bite, staring at Farah. "How did you two hook up? You look...um...How long you been together?"

"Why?" Farah asked.

"If I'm going to be letting you...spend time with my kids. I should know. Duh!"

"We met shortly after I lost my parents...and...Ricky and Adam," Robin said quietly.

"Yeah, that was the pits," Barbie said and paused. "That was right after I found out I had a bun in the oven."

"Right. I knew you visited him at school. Is that when...it happened? Did he know?"

"Nope," she said, finishing off her pie, scraping the plate with her spoon hoping for every crumb. "I'd just found out."

"Jesus," Robin said, shaking his head. "What were you going to do?"

"We never talked about playing house or anything, but I'm sure he would have let me stay with your family. I mean it wouldn't have been good for the baby living above the salon with all those chemicals and smoke in the air."

"Did you trap him? Did you try to get pregnant?" Robin asked.

"Hey, it takes two to tango. It's not like he ever bothered with condoms. He was trying to prove something to himself."

"And what was that?"

"Nothing. And anyway, right when I found out about the baby, he got the boot from school. We were a fine pair."

Robin sighed. "You knew about that?"

"Yeah, I knew. I thought I shouldn't spring fatherhood on him in the middle of all that. He was a disaster. He told me he wanted to come home and I thought that would be good. He could settle down and then I would tell him. And then," Barbie took in a big breath and let it out. "Well, shit. Then he died."

They were all silent for a few seconds before she continued. "I was real sorry about that. I thought I should just get rid of the kid. I never even told Mama. She had, still has, a friend in Carson City, so I asked to go and stay with her to figure things out. Then I got a job in a casino and never got around to it. Getting rid of the kid, I mean." She could see the disgust in Farah's narrowed eyes. "Hey, it's not like I had a mother I could turn to. Don't judge me!" She shook her head, "I'm guessing you had a great mom, right? Well, mine would have driven me to the nearest clinic."

"Well...thank God you didn't...do that," Farah said.

"Oh, one of those, are you?"

Farah glared. "If you mean I'm a person who doesn't think dumb little girls should be getting pregnant and then using abortion for birth control, then yeah, I'm one of those."

"Alright, alright," Robin jumped in. "Let's talk about Ben. Why *did* you come back? Why do this to him, and all of us now?"

"And where have you been?" Farah asked, frustrated by the whole conversation. "Has your mom been involved in your children's lives?"

"I've been in Nevada. My mom hasn't been around much. She didn't even meet Ben until Brandi came along," she quickly held up her hands. "Don't ask about her daddy. Not related in any way and not...around. After Ben was born and I saw he was going to be the spitting image of a Robinson, I decided to keep my distance. I thought it all might be too much for you...after...you know. And when my mom met him, she agreed. Like her good name could be tarnished," she grunted.

"So why now," Robin asked again.

She sighed, looking down at her empty plate, like she was searching for the right words. "I thought they needed more family. It's just me and my mom and she has less maternal bones in her than I do. And we, well, she's not so well. I want them to get to know you, Robin. And I want them in a better...environment."

"I want that too. I do." He looked at Farah. "We do. But we must prepare the family first."

"Yeah, whatever. I'm not going anywhere. You know where to find me." Barbie shrugged and went back twirling her hair.

"Can we take the kids out for an ice cream? You can come with us of course," Robin offered.

"Yeah, fine. They like ice cream."

"You should come," Farah said. "They might be afraid to be without you."

"Nah, they're tough little guys. I taught them not to be clingy. Can't stand it."

Why am I not surprised? Farah thought as they scooted out of the booth.

Twenty minutes later, Robin and Farah were sitting in another booth at Swenson's Ice Cream, waiting for hot fudge sundaes and looking across at Ben and Brandi. They had asked to be seated in a corner booth away from watchful eyes, though their young server knew who they were...and knew they didn't have children. She couldn't help but notice the young boy who looked just like Robin. Her eyes darted back and forth several times while writing down the order.

"I'm sure this is confusing. Finding out about us, I mean," Robin said when they were alone.

Ben looked thoughtfully at Robin. "We look alike."

Robin nodded. "We do."

"I don't look like my mom or my sister or my gran. I like that I look like someone."

Farah had to hold back tears. "You're lucky to be so handsome like your uncle." Then she looked at Brandi. "And you're lucky to have those wonderful strawberry blond curls and big blue eyes." Though Farah was wondering when the last time those curls had a good wash or comb through. *Like mother like daughter.*

"But I don't look like anybody," she said softly.

"You look just like you. One of a kind." Farah winked, reassuring.

"Can we come and see your farm?" Ben asked.

"Sure. We take care of horses," Robin said.

"I love horses!" Ben said, wide eyed.

"And we have chickens, and a couple of dogs named Fred and Barney, a cat named Ruby, and a vegetable garden," Farah added.

"And...we have a big family. Your family," Robin said, looking at both children.

"We have more family?" Ben asked.

"Yes, a wonderful family," Farah said.

"When can we come?"

"Very soon, we promise," Robin said.

Robin and Farah walked, hand and hand, with the children right down Main Street. They were all talking and laughing and in their own little world, forgetting all about The Yardstick...until they passed the front door and out rushed Emily and Rebecca.

They all froze. Emily and Rebecca kept looking back and forth between Robin and the boy.

Too late, Farah recalled that Barbie had suggested they return by a different street and enter in the back to avoid the curious eyes of the town. *"You know the talk that'll start if the town sees Robin walking with a kid that looks just like him."*

Finally, Farah asked, "Girls, what are you doing here? The shop's closed on Mondays."

"We came to work on my dress. The better question is what are *you* two doing here?" Emily asked.

"That *is* the better question," Rebecca said, staring wide-eyed at the children.

"Girls," Farah cautioned.

"He looks just like you, Robin," Emily said, and then gasped, "Is he...?"

"My nephew. He's...Ricky's son. He's your second cousin, I guess." Robin wasn't sure of his answer.

"So, he is my nephew too?" Rebecca asked.

"Yes," Robin nodded.

"That is so cool!"

"Yeah, but..." Emily started.

"Emily, take Becca home and we'll explain all of this later," Farah said quickly.

"And don't say anything to your folks. I want to do it. Got it, Emily?" Robin stated firmly, though thinking the odds of this remaining quiet before they got home were slim.

"Got it!" she said. "C'mon, Becca," she said, taking her hand as they walked to the car, still staring at the children.

When the car had driven out of sight, they hurried the children across the street, where Barbie was already out waiting for them. "I told you to go around the back."

Robin and Farah both knelt to talk to Ben and Brandi. "See what we mean about a big family? You're really going to like it on the farm," Robin said.

"When can we come? I want to see the horses!" Ben asked, excitedly.

"I want to see the cat!" Brandi said, giggling.

"Very soon," Farah said and took her hand.

They stood. Robin asked quietly, "Can I call you tomorrow? We'll set up a day. You're welcome as well. I know we have a lot more to talk about."

Barbie chuckled, "You got that right. I hope you're ready!" Then she looked directly at Farah. "I hope *you* are ready..."

Eerily quiet when Farah and Robin walked into the house, Maria, sitting at the kitchen table drinking iced tea, and she got up when she saw them. "Well, I guess the cat's out of the bag," she said, wringing her hands.

Robin rolled his eyes. "Where are they?"

"I sent them over to my house while Diego naps."

Robin put an arm around her. "Thank you."

Cheeks blushing pink, Maria pulled away and went to the refrigerator. "I'm going to make enchiladas tonight."

"It's my turn for the main course," Farah protested.

"Forget it. You have enough on your plate."

"Well, I'm going to work while you two hash this out," Robin said then kissed Farah on the cheek. "We'll get through this."

When Robin was gone, Farah said, "Oh, my God, Ben is the picture of Robin! Seeing them side by side is remarkable. And Brandi is adorable. Her father must have been good looking. These children don't resemble Barbie at all, except for Brandi's curly hair."

"Let's hope they have none of her disposition either," Maria said and chuckled. "Where is the little girl's father?"

"He's not in the picture, but Barbie wouldn't elaborate. So odd," Farah said, shaking her head.

"I'm concerned about her showing up after all this time. Did she say?"

"Um...she said she wants them in a better environment."

"I guess it could be as simple as that," Maria grabbed a big pan from under the stove and turned on a burner.

"Remember that dream I started to tell you about a few days ago?"

"The one about Easter?"

"Yes, but it was much more than that. I had a dream about those kids. There was a boy who looked just like Robin and a curly haired little girl. They were...my kids."

Maria subjected her to a strange look. "Honey, I know you wanted children, but..." Before she finished her thought, Joe Jr., Marisol, and Cristina came in from school. "Hey guys! Sit and I'll make you a snack and you can tell me about your day." She touched Farah's arm. "Go and get some rest. It's going to be a long night."

Chapter 11
Love at First Sip

Maria's look had said it all. Farah knew she sounded crazy. She was supposed to be the level headed one. On her bed, she gazed out her window, watching Emily and Rebecca coming out of the house with Diego. Philip and Diana were on their porch with their afternoon iced tea. Joe Jr. came into view, racing over to his house to change into his stable friendly clothes as Robin and Joe talked outside the stables. Looking at him now, so confident and sure of himself, always with his emotions in check. He knew his role as the strong leader of this family.

After they met, he would tell her she was the reason he chose to get back to living. That fateful day the unfamiliar man with long dark hair, pulled back in a ponytail, and emerald, green eyes walked into her bakery. He'd captivated her. His plaid shirt, faded jeans, and well-worn boots told her he wasn't from her neighborhood. It had been a long time since she'd thought about a man...

* * *

As she moved closer to him, she realized something else. Something tragic had recently happened in his life. Bloodshot whites surrounded those green irises. His furrowed brow told the story of a heavy burden. She knew this look of hopelessness.

"Can I get you something?" she asked. He stared at her holding an empty coffee cup from her bakery. "I have coffee and..." she glanced over at her glass cases, "...several pastries still to choose from."

"Um, coffee," he said, lifting the cup. "I had some earlier. It was good."

"Sure," Farah moved around the cases. "Are you certain you aren't hungry? There's banana bread or coffee cake," she said, feeling she was rambling. "I tend to give it away at the end of the day."

"No, just coffee."

"Cream and sugar?"

"Black."

She directed him over to a small table and put the coffee down. "You look like you need to sit."

He did, staring at the steaming cup of coffee. Then he glanced up. "Thanks."

Farah sat down across from him. "Are you okay?"

He shook his head. "I...ahh...just came from an apartment around the corner. I had to pick up my brother's stuff."

"Is he a student?" she asked. "We have a lot of students living around here."

"He...was," Robin said, shakingly lifting the cup to his mouth and taking a sip. Then he looked at her. "He's gone. He's gone and he took my parents and cousin with him."

She grabbed his hand from across the table, suddenly recognizing the kind of pain he was in. He had no idea she knew just what he was going through after he told her his story, but there would be time for that later. If there was a later. All she wanted to do now was take care of him. "You're going to come to the back with me. I have a few things to do for tomorrow. There is a couch and a bathroom, and I can warm soup. I always keep soup here."

"I should get going. I have—"

"No, you need to stay here with me for a while. My name is Farah." She squeezed his hand a little harder.

"My name is Robin."

After locking the bakery's door, she led him to the back. "Can I heat you up some soup? I make a mean lentil?"

"I...don't think I've ever had...lentil."

"Well, then you can't say no." Farah went to the refrigerator and pulled out a plastic container and put it in the microwave, never taking her eyes off him.

He was looking at the two large stainless-steel worktables. On one of the tables were cupcakes, half decorated, half not. "I hate to keep you from your work," he said.

She brought a hot mug of soup over to him. "Those will take no time. I can frost cupcakes in my sleep. They're for a one-year-old. Crazy."

He took a sip of the soup. It was delicious, and he was suddenly famished. "This is great."

"Well, I have more." She stood in front of him for another moment before moving back to the cupcakes. "Where do you live?" she asked.

"I live in a town called Honeysuckle. It's a little over three hours from here, up north. We have a farm."

Farah stopped piping, her heart sinking at the thought of him three hours away. "Is there more family?" she asked, skirting around the question she did not want the answer to.

"My aunt and uncle are there. My cousin was their boy. They have a daughter. Then I have Joe and Maria and their two kids. They are not blood, but they might as well be. And then there's my younger sister, Rebecca. The farm is called Rebecca Farms."

"After her? How sweet."

"She likes to think so. My folks bought the place with the name and never changed it. My mom vowed if she ever had a daughter..." He trailed off.

Farah packed up the cupcakes and put them in one of the large refrigerators. Then she pulled another cake out and set it on a worktable.

"You seem so busy. I should go and let you work."

"No!" she quickly said and went over to him. "I mean unless you want to go. I just have one more cake to finish. And if you can stay... I can offer you something else to drink. Something a little stronger than coffee?"

"Sure," he said softly. *"If it's no trouble."*

"No trouble," she said back.

After bringing him a small glass of bourbon, Farah went back to work. She knew the hopelessness Robin was feeling. She knew he felt like there would never be any happiness again. And honestly, she couldn't vouch for the happiness part, but time had certainly numbed the heart wrenching grief.

When she turned around after the first layer of frosting was on, Robin was asleep. His head was resting on the back of the couch, his drink, almost gone, still in his hand. She gently removed it, and he didn't budge. She took the last sip herself and sat next to him. Farah wanted to touch him, rest her head on his shoulder, stare at him all night. She grabbed a blanket she kept in a cabinet and draped it over them. She just wanted to look at him. If she never saw him again, she didn't want to forget. She knew she was older, and she thought he would never, so she just wanted to sit and stare for a while.

When he awoke in the morning, they talked over fresh coffee and blueberry scones. He told her about Rebecca, and it was clear from the moment Farah met her that she was an adored and capable force to be reckoned with. In the weeks to come, and their daily phone calls, he talked about all his farm and family and she felt she knew them before the first time she came to the farm.

* * *

Now watching Maria head over to Joe with Marisol and Christina, knowing they were just as much family as if they had been born Robinsons. They had welcomed her in just as Robin and his parents had welcomed them.

Finally Farah glanced over at Philip and Diana on the porch as Emily walked up and kissed both of their cheeks, heartened to see they were finding contentment again such losses.

She was content too, as she looked down at her beautiful family, but there was room for more.

"This dinner can't happen fast enough. Emily and Rebecca are busting at the seams down there," Robin said coming into the bedroom.

"Are you nervous about telling Philip and Diana? This brings back such a painful time."

"It's going to be fine. They wouldn't have any grudges against these two kids," he said reassuringly, sitting on her side of the bed.

"When Diana hears about Ricky getting Barbie pregnant right around the time of his wanting to come home...it will be upsetting."

"It will, but I will reassure her Ricky didn't know. And it's good news, right? There's another Robinson boy. A real Robinson."

"It's wonderful," Farah said, moving closer to him. "It's better than wonderful. It's just what we've been missing."

He tilted his head and gave her a questioning stare. "What do you mean 'missing'?"

"That was a poor choice of words. I meant to say..." She scrunched up her face thoughtfully. "I meant to say it will be nice to have more children around. That's all. Now I better get down and help. I've been up here too long. Poor Maria."

Robin stayed on the bed after she left. He hadn't thought they were missing anything. He had thought they were complete, even without children of their own. He had her, his family, and his farm. It was all he needed. But he'd heard it in his wife's voice. Her words. In her mind something was missing. And the answer was these children.

Chapter 12
A Night to Celebrate

Downstairs, Maria was setting the dining room table. The table, nestled in the spacious room off the kitchen, surrounded by big bay windows, and, when lit up in the evening, could be admired by the road below.

"I invited Josh," Emily said, bringing in plates. "I hope you made enough to eat."

Maria leaned towards her on the table, "Don't you think you should have asked first? This isn't an ordinary night. It should be just family."

"He's *almost* family. I mean he *is* family. The wedding is just a formality," Emily said.

"A pretty pricey formality, *su Alteza*," Maria said.

"What does that mean?" Emily asked.

"You probably don't want to know," Farah laughed, coming in carrying small votive candles.

But there was always more than enough food at any meal on Rebecca Farms, and soon the entire family was at the table, except for Christina and Diego, who were happily missing the meal for a chance at one of their favorite movies.

Chicken enchiladas, pinto beans, rice, salad, chips, and guacamole lined the table. White sangria was passed around to all who wanted it.

"This looks great, Maria," Philip said, heaping two enchiladas on his plate then sipping his beer. "What's all the fuss about tonight? Did I forget a birthday?" He chuckled.

"No, it's not that. But we do want to talk to you about something," Robin said, clearing his throat, clearly not knowing how to begin. He looked at Farah for help.

"Well, we found out some big news yesterday," she started, but now she too was at a loss for words. "We found out..."

"Do you need help?" Emily asked.

"No!" Farah said quickly back. "You know Barbie Fletcher is back?"

"Yes, I told you that," Diana said.

"And she brought two kids with her," Farah added.

"Yes, I told you that, too," Diana said.

"Well...her son...her son..." Farah started.

"Her son is my nephew!" Rebecca blurted.

Joe choked on his beer and Maria slapped his arm.

"What are you talking about?" Philip asked.

"We just found out. Barbie was pregnant with Ricky's child when he died. He, um, looks just like my father when he was a boy, and a lot like me. There is no mistaking it," Robin said.

"There *is* no mistaking it. The little boy looks just like Robin!" Emily added.

Diana and Philip had put down their forks and were staring at Emily. "You knew about this?" Philip asked.

"Becca and me were downtown today. We saw the kids. He could be Robin's son!"

"But he's not," Robin added quickly. "There's a daughter too. She's four. Barbie would like them to get to know all of us."

"Well, this is something," Diana said. "I can't believe Carole never mentioned this to me. In all the years I've known her, she's never mentioned these children."

"She didn't know Ben was Ricky's until she met him and by then he was already a toddler," Farah said. "Barbie left before Carole even knew she was pregnant. She hasn't been a part of their lives."

"What brought her back now?" Diana asked.

"We don't have the answers yet. But we have met the children, and they're sweet."

"Well, in that case, when can we meet them?" Philip asked and scooped salad onto his plate.

"I don't want to meet them," Diana said. "And I don't want anything to do with her. Just look at the timing! I know she was involved in—"

"Could it be true," Robin?" Philip asked quickly, putting a gentle hand on top of Diana's. "Did Ricky know about this?"

Robin stared at his plate. After all this time, the only thing they knew was that Ricky had flunked out of school. He had never told them about the cheating, and he'd never told them about the picture with Adam. "She wasn't involved, Aunt Diana. She told us today Ricky didn't know, and we believed her. We shouldn't hold anything against her kids. They're innocent, and Ben is family."

The rest of the meal was calm, while everyone processed the news and asked questions there were still no answers to. The family stayed around the table longer than usual, nibbling on chips and spoonful's of beans and rice and slowly sipping the sweet wine, any excuse to keep from getting up. It might not have been a holiday, but it was a day and night to remember.

What they were all unaware of was the loud, rundown little car they had all become familiar with was slowly driving by the house again. Barbie stopped in front of the "Rebecca Farms" sign and looked up at the house. It looked like the cover of a Christmas card. Hell, it looked like the stuff dreams were made of. Big windows, a brightly lit chandelier, and a big happy family. She wondered if she could ever fit in at a table like this.

"They'd probably photoshop me out," she said and chuckled, putting the car in gear and driving away.

She had grown up with no family traditions. There were never any men sitting at the head of the table during a holiday dinner telling old stories. She never knew her grandfather or her father and had always been intimidated watching the men of Rebecca Farms move about, always looking dignified and purposeful. Robin didn't look at her twice back then, but she knew her return would finally get his attention.

Then again...she might not need him. Someone else knew how important she would become to this family. Someone knew there were two missing pieces of a puzzle, and she had them.

"Farah, Farah, Farah," she hummed as she circled around and passed by the farm again. "This is going to be fun."

A hand touched Robin's shoulder and a kiss graced his head as he drank his bourbon on the back porch. "What a dinner!" Farah said sitting next to him. "Today's felt like a year."

He nodded but still did not speak.

"Is something wrong?" Farah asked.

"It was something you said earlier. You said these kids were the answer to something that's missing. What did you mean by that? I didn't think we were missing anything."

She let out a sigh. "It came out wrong, but...and you're going to think I'm crazy, but I had a dream about these kids, even before I knew they existed. I had a dream about a boy who looked just like you."

"Farah..."

"It's true. And now he's...they are here."

"They are not our children," he whispered forcefully. "We only met them today. Yeah, you are sounding a little crazy."

The last thing she wanted to do was cry, but she felt embarrassing tears welling up. "I get it," she said before rising and walking into the house and hurrying up the stairs. She wanted his body next to hers, telling her everything was going to be okay. Of course they would have had a boy that looked just like Ben and a curly haired daughter just like Brandi. Her dream wasn't crazy. These kids were real, and from the looks of things, they could benefit from some happy, healthy farm life.

Robin knew from the beginning Farah couldn't have children. But did he know how much she'd longed for them? How cruel to have two bodies so in tune to one another when they touched, and yet she could not give him a child. Farah would think this many times in the beginning whenever they made love. She could still feel his breath on her face as both their pulses quickened, their bodies were touching and squirming in anticipation as his mouth finally found hers for the first time, three weeks after they met, when Robin drove back to her.

* * *

Their mouths would stay together as they stumbled toward the bedroom. Their mouths would stay together as they hurriedly got out of their clothes. It was the passionate kiss of first-time lovers. It was the passionate kiss of lovers who couldn't get enough of each other after many years.

Their mouths would stay together until he sat her on the bed and his greedy lips moved down to her breasts. Farah sat back on her elbows and arched herself, letting him take in all of her. He stayed there until she laid back and opened her legs for him. He climbed on top of her and found her mouth again with his.

Just before he entered her, he asked, "Wait, should I? Do we?"

She looked into his beautiful eyes. He was the man of her dreams. "We don't have to do anything. Just make love to me."

Afterwards, wrapped in each other's arms, Farah was crying. "Either I was really good, or really bad," Robin said, kissing her forehead.

"There is something we should have talked about. Something I should have told you."

"What is it?"

"I can't have children. I have a condition. Not to mention my age," she said, burying her face in his chest.

Robin held her tighter. "I don't care about your age. And I don't care that you can't have a child."

"How can you say that? What about the farm? Who will take over?"

He sighed. "I've never thought in those terms. Before you, I expected to live out my days as a single man. There's Joe and his boys. There will be options. In fact, I'd sell it tomorrow if you wanted a partner in the bakery."

This made her laugh. "Alright, you can have your first icing lesson tomorrow."

"You mean I can stay?" he said, pulling her on top of him, not waiting for her answer as his greedy mouth found hers again.

* * *

Farah instinctively reached for Robin, but his side of the bed was still empty. She got up, threw on her robe and slippers, and headed out of the room.

He wasn't in either of the two empty bedrooms. He wasn't on the couch downstairs. That left only one place and she headed out the door and across the yard to the stables. There were times that he slept in one of them. Sometimes when a sick or pregnant horse needed overnight monitoring. But this was not one of those nights. Their pregnant mare was not due for another month, and Josh was staying in the first stable to keep an eye on two horses with bacterial infections.

She entered the second stable as quietly as she could, hoping not to disturb the resting occupants. Moving to the back, toward the small room, more like a cubicle in the back with a small single cot, table, and light, she found Robin, covered up with a thin green blanket like a soldier in an Army barracks.

She knelt and touched his shoulder. "Hey," she said.

"Hey," he said back, scooting over so she could sit.

"I'm sorry about earlier. Of course, I don't think there's anything missing. It's just that—"

"No, I'm sorry. I know how much you would have loved children. I see how you are with Maria's." He pulled her in. "I still don't need anyone but you."

Farah closed her eyes as his lips met hers. He sighed with pleasure when he felt her bare breasts under her robe. He sighed again as her hand caressed his hard penis through the jeans he was still wearing. Soon, they both forgot where they were, or who they might be disturbing.

Chapter 13

Let the Game Begin

On the first Saturday in June, Farah and Robin stood on the porch, hand in hand as the car approached. Farah squeezed tighter as Barbie pulled the seat forward so Ben and Brandi could climb out, followed closely by Brandi who clung to his shirt. They looked bewildered, disheveled, and tired, as did their old clothes. Like mother like daughter, Brandi's hair hung in her face, seeming to have a mind of its own.

Barbie looked at them, "Well, come on. They don't bite," she snapped, pushing them forward like a game piece on a board. "At least I don't think they do," she laughed.

Farah walked down the steps and over to the kids then took Brandi by the hand. "We're so glad you're here. Come on in," she said, gently urging them toward the house, then turning to their mother, "You too."

Once inside standing in the foyer, Barbie let out a big whistle. "Wow, would you look at this place. It's like it's twice the size as I remember!"

"Um, we took a couple walls down and opened up the space and added the bigger doors out the back." Farah said.

"La ti da. Right out of a magazine." Barbie chuckled, looking straight ahead at the big kitchen with white cabinets and countertops, farm table and great room with oversized white couches. There were splashes of bright color throughout with artwork and decorative pillows in reds and yellows. "Fancy, schmancy. I can tell who's the boss around here."

"It's...very comfortable," Farah said, wondering why she was justifying her home to this woman. She was hoping her husband would jump in and say something, but he was staring out the back. "Robin?"

He put his arm around his wife. "She's in charge in doors and I am in charge out there," he said, pointing toward the stables. "And speaking of that, kids, want to see the horses and the rest of the farm?" he asked, winking at Farah.

"Yes!" Ben said, releasing his sister's hand and taking Robin's as they walked through the house to the back sliding French doors. They stood for a moment staring as Joe and Joe Jr. came out of the first stable, dressed in flannel shirts, jeans, cowboy boots, and hats.

"Wow!" Ben said. "I've always wanted boots and a cowboy hat."

"Really?" Robin asked with a smile. "I think we can make that happen." He looked back at Farah who had come onto the porch and gave her a *thumbs up* before walking out.

Philip, who had been sitting on the porch, stood quickly, staring at the boy walking across towards the stables. Farah saw the mesmerized look on his face. Telling him about the family resemblance was one thing. Seeing it in person was different. Ben *did* look just like his brother when they were boys. He did look like Robin. Philip hurried down his steps and walked toward them.

Farah couldn't hear the conversation, but Philip rested his hands on Ben's shoulders, shaking his head and smiling, and soon they were in the stable and out of sight. She looked at Barbie. "Do you want coffee...or something?"

"No. I'm good. If you don't mind, I might slip out for a bit. I could really use a few hours to myself. Cooped up in the apartment with kids and my mom has been too much. You know what I mean?"

Farah looked down, still holding the little girl's hand, wondering what her reaction would be. But Brandi's eyes were on Maria and her two daughters, who were planting flowers around the chicken house while the happy hens roamed and squawked.

"Would you like to see the chickens, Brandi? Ruby the cat is usually there too. She loves her naps under the chicken house," Farah suggested.

"Yes, I'd like that."

"Okay, you head on over and after I walk your mom out, I'll join you."

"You don't have to walk me out. I know where the door is," Barbie said.

"No. I want to," Farah subjected her to a hard stare, conveying *stay put!*

Brandi gave her mother a shy little wave and turned away. "Have fun, peanut," Barbie called after her.

Farah called to Maria as Brandi went down the steps and hurried over. "This is Brandi. I'm just going to walk her mom out and I'll be right back."

"We'd love another set of hands," Maria said and smiled as the little girl approached.

Farah turned and walked with Barbie back in the house. "We need to talk."

"What about?" Barbie asked.

"You and your children. I know what you said...but there must be more."

Barbie laughed. "Jeez, can we get through the first visit? I don't know that all of this is your business."

"Oh, it's my business all right. Robin is my husband. This is my family, and I won't let you come here and tease those babies under *m*...our noses and then disappear."

"Yeah, I heard you couldn't have kids."

Farah felt her anger rising. "*That* is none of *your* business.

"Relax! I'll tell you everything you want to know." Barbie could tell she was getting under her skin and she loved the feeling. "Although, be careful what you ask for."

"What do you mean by that?"

"I'm just saying...I've known Robin longer than you. There might be a few things you don't want to know about him."

Farah stayed quiet, not daring to take the bait. She cleared her throat. "Well, the children are in good hands if you want to leave. You can all stay for dinner. We're barbequing hot dogs and hamburgers."

"Alright, that'll work. I'll be back by five o'clock," Barbie said, then she turned and left.

Later that afternoon, Farah was sitting on one of the couches, with Brandi at her side. She had taken the liberty of combing through her rosy, red curls and pulling them off her face with two braids. There was no mistaking the lingering odor of cigarette smoke in the children's clothes and Brandi's hair. It angered and saddened Farah.

They were looking at dresses on her laptop and the little girl sat in wide-eyed wonderment as if she had never seen a screen on a computer scroll up and down with dresses beyond her wildest imagination. They'd agreed on three when the back door flew open and Rebecca rushed in.

"Hey!" she said when she saw Brandi. "Welcome to our farm. You know it's named after me?"

Farah laughed and looked at Brandi. "It's actually the other way around. But, yes, this is Rebecca." She looked back at Rebecca, "Barbie is coming back for dinner."

Rebecca gave Farah a funny look. "This should be interesting."

"Rebecca..."

"Brandi, want to come up and see my room?" she asked before Farah could say anything else. She held her hand out and Brandi got up, and the girls disappeared up the stairs.

Farah smiled as she walked to the refrigerator and pulled out hamburger meat and a bottle of wine. Just as the cork came out, she saw Barbie at the back door, almost childlike in baggy denim jeans and a loose-fitting yellow tee shirt, her hair in pigtails.

"Come in!" Farah called. "I was just pouring a glass of chardonnay. Would you like to join me?" *I know I'm going to need it.*

"Don't know what that is, but I'll try a little." As Farah handed her a glass, she took a big sip and shrugged her shoulders. "Not bad."

"Well, we've had a lovely day. In fact, I've barely seen Ben. Just in for a quick sandwich and then back out to the stables. It was two sandwiches. He seemed very hungry. Did he eat breakfast?"

"Yeah, I feed my kids breakfast if that's what you want to know."

"I didn't mean to...offend."

"What do you cook for breakfast?"

"Well, this morning was a little different because we have a small bacterial infection breakout among the horses. The stable workers were here extra early to clean and move the sick horses together. We made a big breakfast for everyone. Pancakes, scrambled eggs, sausages, and fresh fruit."

"Well my kids had Cheerios." Barbie said.

Farah wondered if Ben had any formal schooling. How far behind is he? Have the children been to regular doctors or dentists and have they had their vaccinations? Calm down, Farah. Instead she asked, "When are their birthdays?"

"The boy's is October twentieth and the girl's is July twelfth."

"Oh, a birthday in July! That's coming up. Christina also has a July birthday. She'll be seven. I was wondering...if you wouldn't mind...would it be helpful if I got Brandi and Ben some new clothes," Farah said, feeling like she was walking on eggshells. "I mean if that would be okay with you."

"Why, the gals at the country club wouldn't approve?"

"Funny."

"No, go right ahead. I know they need new things. I've been a little short on funds lately."

"I'm sorry to hear that." How had she supported these kids all these years? She wanted to start from the beginning, but that wasn't going to happen tonight as she looked out the window and saw Robin and Ben crossing the yard. She smiled at Ben, now wearing jeans, boots, and a cowboy hat.

"Wow, look at you!" Barbie said when he walked in.

"They were Joe Junior's. He looks darn good, right?" Robin said and smiled warmly at Farah.

"He does!" Barbie said. "This place agrees with him."

"It's fun here, Mom. Can we come back?" Ben asked eagerly.

"Yeah, yeah. I'm sure you'll be invited back." Barbie winked at her son.

"You can come back whenever you'd like," Robin said, putting an arm around Ben. "Now, I need to go and wash up before dinner."

When they gathered outside at the picnic tables filled with hamburgers, hot dogs, corn on the cob, watermelon, and a colorful coleslaw, Barbie counted heads in amazement. *Two, four, six, eight...thirteen people.* She had never been at a table with thirteen people. Add her kids, that's fifteen. *What's a couple more...*

When the colorful slaw landed in front of her, she took a tentative spoonful. "It's a tri-colored peanut slaw," Farah said.

"What? Good ol' fashioned coleslaw doesn't work for you?"

"Farah's taken everything up a notch," Diana said.

Barbie then took a tentative bite, the tangy peanut sauce hitting the back of her throat. She *loved* it but hesitated to say so or take more. She could hear her mother in her head. *Don't eat much. Stick to the plan.*

Ben was between Robin and Joe Jr., who had taken a "big brother" liking to him, and Brandi sat between Rebecca and Emily, who were doting over her like she was a princess.

This is going to be so easy, Barbie thought, grabbing more salad when the bowl came around again.

After homemade brownies with ice cream, she stood and said, "Alright kids, let's not overstay our welcome on day one."

"We'd love to have them back whenever it works for you. Especially with summer right around the corner. All the kids will be out of school in another week," Robin said.

"In fact, next time you can spend the night. All of you," Farah said.

"Yeah, well, it's not like we're going to Disneyland or anything. I'll call you," Barbie said, walking out.

"And...when do you think that might be?" Farah asked, following behind her.

"I don't know. Maybe tomorrow. We got granny to think about, right kids?"

But neither answered.

As they watched Barbie drive away, Robin took Farah's hand, "It was a really good day, wasn't it?"

"It was. I'm sorry I wasn't much help with the horses today."

"We got a good handle on things today. We just need to keep a close eye on them for the rest of the week. And keep our mommy-to-be isolated. I'm going back right now and check on things. Josh is spending the night in the stables."

Farah smiled as she walked upstairs. If Josh was going to be in the stables...that meant Emily would be sneaking out at some point. *Oh what beautiful babies those two would make someday. Just like the ones in her dream...*

Chapter 14
The Sleepover

Three days later, Barbie, Ben and Brandi arrived, each carrying a paper bag. Ben, in the same jeans, boots, and Stetson he'd been wearing when he left, dropped his bag at his mother's feet and hurried past them through the house. And Brandi, in another sundress meant for a girl a couple inches shorter, dropped her bag next to Ben's and hurried into the kitchen where Maria and her daughters were baking cookies.

"So, why don't we go upstairs and I'll show you the rooms, Barbie," Farah suggested, pointing to the staircase. "Can I help carry anything?"

"Nope, we travel light," Barbie said, picking up the three bags. At the top of the stairs, Farah said, "So here is the first extra room." She opened a door on the right. "It has a single bed so I thought it would be good for Ben."

Ricky's old room. Plain and unassuming, Barbie thought.

"And the room next to it is bigger with a queen bed. This is for you and Brandi," Farah said, opening the door.

Barbie walked inside.

The room was spacious and light, with a big window looking down on the farm. The bed was plush with all white bedding. A vase of fresh flowers stood on the pale blue dresser.

"Is everything okay?" Farah asked.

"It's..." Barbie chuckled and shook her head. "I've never been in a room this nice. Not that I want your pity or anything."

"I do not pity you," Farah said.

"I see the way you look at me. How my kid's dress. You have it all, and I have nothing," Barbie said, staring out the window.

"I don't have everything, Barbie." Farah sighed deeply. "I don't have children."

"Yeah, well, I probably shouldn't have any either."

"Don't say that! They're wonderful children."

"They are. But it's really despite me."

Farah wasn't sure what to say. With the little she knew, she might have wanted to agree with her guest. "Well, you did something right. And we can talk about anything you want...whenever you want."

"Right now, I think I'd like a little rest. My mother zaps all my strength. Do you mind?"

"You go right ahead. I'll go and take care of Brandi." She looked hard at this strange little woman, and it dawned on her: *maybe she's sick!*

When she was alone, Barbie got up and walked toward the dresser. She didn't tell Farah that she *had* been in this room before, but it looked different back in the day. This had been Robin's room. It was true, she wasn't supposed to have been upstairs alone with Ricky, but there were times when she used the excuse of needing to use the bathroom, and she had discovered Robin's bedroom early on. Aside from his parents, Robin had the biggest room. *The favorite son,* Ricky had referred to his big brother.

He was a tough act to follow, and Barbie had snuck up to Robin's room whenever she could. Back then, the room had dark blue walls and bedding a similar color. It smelled like him. Farm life and spicy soap. She would come up and stand in the doorway and breathe in. She'd ventured in a couple of times and touched the items on his dresser, the one that was now a light blue. But most of the time she had just stood in the doorway. Even as a naïve teenager she had known Robin was out of her league.

As she lay on the bed and closed her eyes she thought about her mother. She wasn't in Robin's league either, but there they were all those years ago. *What was I, eight or nine?*

* * *

Barbie knew Robin was always the last appointment of the day, and she usually stayed downstairs when he came in. She felt a tingling in her stomach whenever she saw him. She renamed her Ken doll Robin. She doodled "Robin loves Barbie" in her school notebook and drew hearts around it.

The last few times he'd been scheduled, her mother sent her upstairs. But one time as she walked a client out, Barbie decided to hide behind the curtain of the waxing room.

When he came in, her mother locked the doors and closed the blinds. There was little talking. After the haircut, her mother wasted no time taking off her top and throwing it behind her. Then Robin grabbed her mother's bare breasts and started kissing them. When Robin stood and slid down his pants, Barbie could barely breathe.

In another moment, her mother was leaning against the chair and Robin was behind her, putting himself somewhere between her legs. Barbie had no idea how this wasn't hurting her mother and, in a couple more seconds, they were both making weird grunting sounds. Her mother didn't say stop. She didn't try to get away. She kept saying stuff like, "That feels great, baby." And then the grunting got louder and they were both shaking back and forth, her mother's breasts bobbing up and down. Barbie was so scared, she thought she'd wet herself.

It finally ended with gasps, laughter, and hard breathing. There were no words, just Robin quickly dressing and hurrying out, letting the door slam behind him.

Finally, Barbie let out her breath and coughed. Carole froze, turning and looking at the curtain before walking over and sliding it open to find Barbie's watery eyes staring up at her... Suddenly Barbie lurched forward and heaved all over her mother's bare feet. She expected a spanking, or at least at least a good tongue lashing, but she got neither.

After putting her daughter in a bubble bath, Carole spoke to her gently as she washed her back. "You know, Barbie, you can't tell anyone what you saw down there. We weren't doing *nothing wrong. We're both adults. This is what adults do...sometimes. It's just that the town folk might not see it that way. And the Robinsons have that big fancy farm, and I just have this little, tiny shop. We would have to leave. And I got nowhere to go. So, we must keep this just to ourselves. Okay, sweet pea?"*

Barbie hugged her knees to her chest and nodded her head. But she never forgot.

* * *

Downstairs, Farah, Maria, Emily, and Rebecca were in the kitchen in a lively conversation, looking at a box of cards.

"They're just what I wanted!" Emily said, looking up and seeing Barbie come down. "Come and look at my wedding invitations!"

Barbie walked over and took the square white card Emily handed her. She had never held or seen a wedding invitation before. The gold writing was so fancy, she had a tough time reading it. "They are pretty. I guess the day will be here before you know it."

"Yes, and about that, I was wondering if Brandi can be a flower girl with Marisol and Christina. We can whip her up a dress in no time."

"Really? I'm sure she'd get a kick out of it," she paused, looking at the invitation, her mother's voice ringing in her ears loud and clear. *Plant the seeds. Don't waste this opportunity...*"I mean it's really not necessary," Barbie said. "Y'all just met us. It's not like we expect to even be at the wedding. Or even in this town for that matter."

The room went quiet...

"She makes a good point," Rebecca said.

"Rebecca!" Farah and Emily said in unison.

Maria turned away, going to the refrigerator, pretending to be looking for something while laughing under her breath.

"Of course they're included. They...are...family," Farah blurted.

Another stretch of silence...

"You can think about it," Emily said. "We're working on Christina and Marisol's dresses, and I have plenty of fabric for Brandi."

"That's real nice. I'll think about it," Barbie said.

Farah opened her mouth to say something but then closed it. She was already envisioning the sweet little girl walking down the aisle holding a little basket of rose petals, wearing white patent leather shoes and white laced ankle socks, her curly hair tied up off her face with ribbon. She was already envisioning the little girl hopping on her lap during the ceremony when she got tired.

"Well, I better go and see if Mama needs any help," Emily said, bringing Farah out of her trance. "She's making her famous fried chicken tonight. Ugh, not that I'm eating." She rolled her eyes before heading out of the house.

Maria shook her head, packing up the box of invitations. "That girl will be as skinny as you, Barbie, if she keeps this up."

"Well, you know the old saying. Can't be too rich or too thin." She snorted.

"Don't you have to work to get rich?" Rebecca asked.

"Hey...," Barbie started.

"Alright, ladies!" Farah said. "Please, give it a rest."

"Fine. I'm going out to see my kids," Barbie said and headed out the door.

Rebecca shrugged her shoulders. "I don't get why everyone is being so nice to her. She's only back to steal Robin away from you."

"Becca, that is not happening," Farah said, exasperated.

"Good. Because there is no way I'm taking orders from her."

"And I'm not either," Maria said, winking at Farah.

Farah and Maria laughed. "I could use a glass of wine. Maria?"

"Absolutely!"

"I could use one too," Rebecca said.

"NO!" Both women exclaimed before she turned and headed up the stairs, laughing.

Chapter 18

One Shock too Many

Diana's fried chicken was a hit! Ben, Brandi, and Barbie all ate two pieces, along with a fresh corn and tomato salad and biscuits.

"I've never had corn like this," Barbie had remarked, scooping more corn onto her plate. "Mine usually comes straight from a can. This is how the rich eat it, I guess."

"Glad you like it," Farah said, squeezing Rebecca's leg, urging her to keep quiet.

Rebecca was too busy eating to comment anyway. Emily decided to skip the family dinner and go into town to have dinner with Josh and his parents. It was the perfect chance to show them the invitations, and the ideal excuse to get out of the greasy, tasty chicken. This allowed Rebecca to enjoy hers more without her cousin's watchful eye.

Now, as Robin Farah sat outside enjoying a nightcap while Barbie put her kids to bed, he looked around and whispered, "Those kids nothing like her; looks or personality."

Farah laughed, "I know. They're shy and polite and so appreciative. Emily even asked Barbie if Brandi can be a flower girl."

"What did she say?"

"I said I'd think about it!"

They quickly turned to find Barbie standing at the door.

"I do like me a little whiskey now and then. Mind if I join you?" she asked, taking a seat next to Farah.

"Sure, let me get you a drink."

"Bring the bottle," Robin said.

After refreshing her husband's drink, Farah asked, "Did the kids settle down all right? Are the beds comfortable?"

"At Mom's, Ben's using a sleeping bag, Brandi is on my old bed, and I'm on the couch. So yeah, you'll get no complaints from us," she said, taking a big gulp of her drink and wincing as it went down.

"Well, we're really enjoying getting to know them," Farah said.

"Yeah, they like you too. And this place! I remember seeing it for the first time myself." Barbie leaned over and poured herself more whiskey. "I was already a teenager, and I was in awe. I can only imagine it through their eyes."

Farah was feeling the effects of the alcohol, or she may have never asked, "We have heard you were only here because you...um...were interested in Robin." She heard a deep sigh coming from him and quickly added, "I mean it's common for a younger girl to have a crush on an older man. Is that why you were here?"

"Thought so at the time, I guess. But I knew Robin long before I started hanging out here. I first met Robin when I was about the age of my son, and he was a teenager. He used to come into my mama's shop to get his hair cut. Remember Robin?"

He sighed. "Yes, I remember." He leaned forward and searched her eyes.

Farah looked at him. Even in the near dark, she could tell his eyes were wide open and bright. They were pleading with her not to say something. "What's going on?"

"Well, you said you wanted to hear my story. This is kinda the beginning," Barbie said and chuckled. "Do you want to tell her or should I?"

"Tell me what?"

"I was with her mother!" Robin blurted out. "When I was eighteen, I...had sex with her mother." He put his glass down and cradled his face in his hands.

Farah's first instinct was to laugh, but she held her breath until it passed. "Well, this is news. But...I'm guessing it was all consensual."

"Yes, of course it was." Robin kept his head down, too embarrassed to look at this wife. "How the hell do you know about this?"

"I saw you!"

"Oh, my God!" Robin groaned.

"I saw him buck naked before you did, Farah!"

This time Farah couldn't hold in her laugh, and she erupted.

"I'm glad you're finding this whole thing funny," Robin muttered.

"It's pretty funny. And it was a long time ago." Farah turned to Barbie. "I don't need details, but after you saw them, what, you developed a crush?"

Barbie sat back. In the dim light, her eyes glittered and her cheeks were flushed. Whether from the memory or the alcohol, it was impossible to tell. She looked relaxed, though. "I had a crush on him even before that," she said with a chuckle. "I even named a doll after him. I used to read the appointment books so I knew when he was coming in. It was always the last appointment of the day. And this one time, when Mama thought I was upstairs, I was hiding."

"I think we get the picture," Robin said, pouring another shot of bourbon.

"I didn't even know what I was witnessing. But after the haircut was over, they both took their clothes off. None of Carole's other customers did that." She laughed.

"Enough!" Robin said.

"After you left, Mama found me hiding. I remember barfing all over the place and after she got me in the tub, she told me that I could never say a word to anyone about it or we'd have to leave." She lifted her shoulders and let them fall. "So I didn't."

"And I never went back," Robin said. "Carole called me and told me to find a new place to get my hair cut. I never knew why, but now I get it."

"But you never forgot Robin?" Farah asked.

"I never forgot him. I still would see him around town now and then. His hair grew and grew through the years. And then I met Ricky."

"Did you use Ricky to get to me?" Robin asked, suddenly sitting upright.

"I guess so, in the beginning. But we became good friends. And after coming here, well, who wouldn't to want to come back. And then I realized something else."

"What?" Farah asked.

"I loved coming here because it made Carole so nervous. She was so afraid her little secret was going to come out."

"Maybe she wanted to protect you," Farah offered.

Barbie snorted. "She wanted to protect herself. She couldn't care less about me. She knew it would ruin the business. She hated it when I came over here. She would question me over and over. It was pathetic." A twisted smile curled her lips. "It was great."

They were all quiet then. So much had just been said, and Farah knew this was just the beginning. "Well, maybe we should call it a night," she said. "We can talk more tomorrow."

"Yeah, I need to get to bed," Robin said, standing up, leaning on the porch railing for balance. "I'll...see you in the morning," he managed before walking unsteadily into the house.

"I hope I didn't upset you," Barbie said when he had left.

"Really? I think that's *exactly* what you were trying to do," Farah said, smiling and amused.

"After getting to know you a little, I knew you wouldn't be mad. I see the way you two look at each other. All mushy and stuff. It's what all little girls fantasized about with the Barbie and Ken dolls."

"Well, it took years for me. And I never thought it would happen."

"How did it? I mean you are older, right? It can't be that my mother ruined him for a woman his age."

Farah sighed, suddenly feeling very tired and very much her age. "That's for another night." She stood and Barbie stood with her. When they walked into the house, Farah had the urge to put an arm around her, but she didn't.

As they got to the top of the stairs, Farah asked in a whisper, "You aren't leaving again are you. You mentioned earlier you might not be around for the wedding?"

"Oh, *that* definitely is for another night too," Barbie said and walked into her room.

Farah, feeling uneasy with that last comment, found Robin lying on top of the bed with a washcloth on his forehead. She chuckled and enough for one night. "Did you take aspirin?"

"Maybe I'm so drunk I'll wake up tomorrow and forget tonight ever happened."

She sat down next to him. "It's no big deal. You were both consenting adults. I had a feeling I wasn't your first," she poked him in the side and laughed. "I should thank her for being a good teacher."

"Oh, God. I to need sleep. Or get sick. I'm not sure."

"Of course, honey. You sleep." She kissed his hand and got up and walked to the bathroom and closed the door behind her.

Robin's head was spinning, but he could hear the toilet flushing and the sink running. Then he thought he heard a phone ringing and Farah's muffled voice behind the door. Then a long silence.

When the door opened, Robin was blinded by the light, and he shielded his eyes as he sat up. "Was that a phone I heard? Were you talking to someone?"

Chapter 16

The Diary

Farah reached under her pillow and pulled out the diary. It had been hidden away in a shoe box since the accident. She never knew MaryAnn kept a diary. And after reading some of the entries, she wished she hadn't.

Carl had met her at the rehabilitation center on the day MaryAnn moved to live out the remainder of her days. Farah hadn't asked him to, but there he was, waiting for her at the door when she arrived. She was appreciative of his support, but wanted this whole thing behind her, and that included him. She agreed to one final cup of coffee, and that's when he presented her with it.

"She left it on my bed the last time I saw her...before the dress fitting. I had left before she did, and when I got home...it was open," he said, shaking his head. " I shouldn't have read a word of it. I should have never let it get as far as it did..."

Farah had listened to him lament, let her coffee grow cold and bid him farewell. She read the final entry when she got home that day...and again last night after Robin fell into a deep sleep. The fuming, profanity laden entry was far from the tone of a happy bride to be...

God, I can't stand my sister. Of course my mom is with her right now. This should be my day but she stops for coffee at HER stupid bakery first because she can't be bothered to come to my fitting because of work. I just have to get through the next week and I will be done with these people. I also have to put up with Farah because she's making my wedding cake. I hate to give her any credit at all for anything but she is good at THAT. And don't think my folks ever let me forget it. It's Farah this and Farah that. She wins a couple of cake decorating contests and gets a job at one of the most popular bakeries in town and they think she has cured cancer. Fuck! I mean I did get my nursing degree but nothing I seem to do ever gets a rise out of them. Well I am getting the last laugh because I'm about to be Mrs. Carl Crabtree. Ridiculous last name to be stuck with but it comes with a lot of money so I'll live with it. I'll make that sister of mine regret dumping him. She told me she wasn't in love. She thinks she can do better. Who needs love when there's's two karat ring to look at. That's love enough for me and I'm going to flaunt it in her face every chance I get. Oh shit, I'm running way late. I better get this over with. I don't even love the dress. But it was pricy and at least my parents didn't bitch about that. Maybe they feel guilty about treating me like a second fiddle all my life. Or maybe they think my snotty sister won't need a wedding dress because she will never find anyone good enough for her.

My poor delusional sister, Farah thought. If Maryann only knew how much her parents loved and worried about her. And how they felt her unhappiness deeply, considering it one of their greatest failures. *And now she's gone*, she thought as her heavy eyelids closed again.

Farah opened her eyes, and to her surprise, Brandi stood at the foot of her bed. "Hey!" she still had the diary on her lap and swiftly tucked it under the covers.

"Hi," the little girl said back. She had a smile on her face, her hands locked behind her back, and she was swaying side to side on her feet looking proud as a peacock.

And then Farah realized something. "You're wearing one of your new dresses!"

Brandi laughed. The dress was pale yellow with little orange tabby cats running across the round collar and the bottom at the hem line.

"You look lovely, Brandi. Do you like it?" Farah asked.

"I love it."

Farah held her arms out, and Brandi came over to her side of the bed and they embraced. The little girl smelled like maple syrup and butter. "Let me guess what you had for breakfast."

"Maria made us pancakes."

"I knew it. You smell good enough to eat," Farah said, squeezing her as they laughed.

"I hope you don't mind." Farah looked up, and Maria was at the door holding a cup of coffee.

"Mind?"

Maria walked over and handed her the cup. "Opening up the dresses. She was so excited, and I thought you could use a pick-me-up, seeing her in this. I'm so sorry about your sister."

"Thanks," she said, still holding onto Brandi. "This is the best pick-me-up."

"Well, you don't worry about anything around here. We have it under control," Maria said.

"I'll be down in a little while. I'm fine, really. She's been gone for years."

"Don't kid yourself. This is different, and you're allowed to grieve," Maria said, sitting in one of the chairs next to the window.

"Hey, how are you doing, babe?" Robin asked, appearing next in the doorway. He looked like he had already put in a full day's work.

"I'm okay. How are *you* doing?" she asked.

"Not bad enough to have forgotten last night," he said, moving to the other side of the bed and plopping down. "What do we need to do?"

Farah took a sip of coffee. "I don't know. I need to call the facility back. I don't think there is much to do."

"Well, if you need to go, I'm taking you."

Diana was next to stand in the doorway, holding another cup of coffee. "Yes, honey, you should not go alone," she said "Oh, you already have some."

"I'll take it," Robin said, standing to get it.

"Thanks, Diana," Farah said. "I have no idea what I'm doing right now. I need more details."

Diana moved to the chair next to Maria. "Well, you know we're here for you, whatever you need." She looked like she had been crying and Maria patted her hand. "I know you weren't close, but it's still so sad."

"It's been so long. I'm fine, really."

"No, you need closure. Even though you don't think you need it. You should see her."

The thought sickened Farah. "We'll see."

"Let Robin take you. Philip can pitch in more here."

"Take her where?" Rebecca asked at the door next, holding Diego. He squirmed out of her arms and climbed onto the bed.

"Diego!" Maria said, trying to grab him.

"He's fine," Farah said, putting her cup down and hugging the little boy.

"We told you about her sister," Maria said.

"Well, why do you have to leave?" Rebecca plopped down on the foot of the bed.

"Where are you going?" Brandi quietly asked.

Farah sighed, "I'm not going anywhere yet. Please, Becca."

"Sis, we have to figure a few things out," Robin said.

"Well, you can't leave us here with...her," Rebecca pointed over her shoulder.

"Rebecca, *alto!*" Maria said.

"Wow-wee, when Maria talks all Mexicany it must be serious," Barbie said, peeking her head in. "Looks like a party going on in here."

Farah picked up her coffee and took another big sip, finding her room suddenly cramped and stuffy. "Good morning, Barbie. I got news last night that my sister died."

"You have a sister? Or...had?"

"Yes. It's a long story."

"She's been in a deep sleep for a long time," Rebecca said.

Barbie scrunched up her nose. "What does that mean?"

"She was in an accident many years ago," Farah said, rubbing her temples again, her stomach starting to feel queasy with all the motion on the bed. She looked over at Robin, and he wasn't looking good either.

"She's been in a coma ever since," Maria quietly added.

Barbie thought for a moment. "Oh! You mean she was a veggie."

"Oh, *Dios mio!*" Maria said and stood up. "Alright, everybody out." She picked up Diego. "Barbie, are you staying? Because if you are, I can give you some things to do."

"Oh, God, that's our cue. Brandi, let's get our things."

"You don't have to go," Farah said, still holding on to the little girl.

"You just have to pull your weight," Rebecca said, sticking her tongue out at Barbie before hurrying out of the room.

"Won't be as hard as you!" Barbie called after her.

"Out!" Robin said.

When everyone was gone, Farah lay back on Robin's chest, his arms wrapping around her. "How are you really feeling?"

He chuckled. "Not bad, given the circumstances. But let's not worry about me. Well, worry about me if you plan to leave me with all these women."

"We thought it was rough between Becca and Emily, but Becca and Barbie are a whole different level."

They both laughed and then fell back into blissful silence. Farah needed to call the facility where MaryAnn had lived, and then he mortuary where the body would be sent.

"I really should get back to work," Robin said, though not very convincingly.

"Stay here with me. I'll make some calls and get more information. I'm afraid I might need to make the trip."

"I'll go with you. I don't want you going alone."

Farah thought for a minute, listening to Robin's breathing, "Thanks, hon, but if I need to go, I have another idea..."

Chapter 17
Road Trip Revelations

As strange as it was, Farah found herself pulling up in front of Carole's salon the next morning. Truthfully...she didn't need to go anywhere. She could e-sign the mortuary paperwork. She could have MaryAnn's belongings sent to her. But she decided to make this trip for one reason. MaryAnn's story had finally ended, but there was a whole new story starting, and she needed Barbie to start writing the chapters.

Robin offered to go.

Rebecca begged her to go.

Emily thought the timing was lousy. "There is so much to do! My shower and wedding invitations need to get out this week!"

Maria was steadfast. "Emily, we can all stuff envelopes. Farah needs to do this."

"Actually, I had another idea, and this might shock everyone," Farah started, holding her breath, knowing the reaction she was going to get. "Barbie, would you like to come with me?"

Yep, this shocked everyone.

"Sure. I'll go. Not a fan of stuffing envelopes. I'll get the kids back to my mom's today."

"They can stay here," Farah added quickly. "It's just one night away. Is that fine with everyone?"

"We will be just fine." Robin said.

"Well, sure then, I'll go back to Mama's and get mama settled and pack a few things. You can manage things around here, right, Maria?"

"We'll manage."

Later that morning, as Farah walked Barbie out, she handed her a large duffle bag. "I thought you could use this."

"Thought I needed and upgrade in luggage, did ya?"

Farah sighed. "Just take it."

"Alright. You have fun playing house."

Farah turned and let that comment float in the gentle breeze looking forward to the day ahead.

Now Barbie came through the salon door with her new duffle bag hanging heavily over her bare, bony shoulder. In the handful of times Farah had seen this woman, she looked like her clothes came from the closet floor and her hair looked like it hadn't had a wash in a week. Today's outfit and hair were no different. Faded jeans even too faded to even be called fashionable and a sleeveless plaid blouse, tied at the waist, missing a button in the middle.

Farah thought she heard a loud angry voice from inside the salon as Barbie stood at the door. *Not a friend...can't count on you...never listen...*

"Is something wrong? Was that your mom I heard?"

"Yeah. Something's always wrong. She hasn't been herself lately," Barbie said as she threw her bag in the backseat and plopped heavily in the seat next to Farah.

"Is she sick?"

"Can't imagine thirty years of chain smoking and inhaling perm solution could be good for a person. They took x-rays at the clinic. Still waiting."

"Well, if there is anything we can do," Farah said, not sure what she meant by her own words.

"Yeah, sure." Barbie clapped her hands together. "Well, this is going to be fun. I've never been on a 'girls' trip.'"

Farah stiffened. "This is not a girls' trip. We're heading to a mortuary and then to the place my sister lived to get her stuff."

"Well, you're sure dressed all fancy just for that. And you smell good too. You always smell good."

Farah looked down at her long floral dress. She hadn't thought about fancy. She'd thought about cool and comfortable as she put it on this morning, feeling guilty about judging her companion.

"Do you have any other family?" Barbie asked.

"No, just my farm family."

"Where are your folks? I can tell you must have had good folks. A normal mom and a normal dad and family dinners and pancakes on Saturdays and church on Sundays and a house with a picket fence," Barbie said, nodding.

Farah chuckled. "I had great parents."

"Had?"

"They were killed in the car accident that left my sister in this coma. Dead, but not," she said bitterly.

"That sucks."

"It does. It was right before MaryAnn's wedding. They were all at her final dress fitting, and because of my sister, the appointment was pushed back and by the time they were finished and, on the road, a drunk driver hit them."

"That *really* sucks," Barbie said.

"I was supposed to go to that appointment, but I got held up at work. I don't know if it would have made a difference…" Farah said, her voice trailing.

Barbie stared out the window as the countryside rolled by. She always got excited leaving. Somewhere in the back of her mind, where her lost dreams were, she was never coming back. "So, what happened after? You didn't have a guy? You never married before Robin?"

"No. I just threw myself into my work."

"What was work?"

"I owned a bakery."

"Really? Like a donut shop?"

"No, more of a specialty shop. I made cakes for weddings, birthdays, stuff like that. It always shocked me what people would pay for a cupcake. Who can't make a cupcake?" Farah said, shaking her head.

"I've never made a cupcake."

"What about the kids' birthdays?"

"We're not all Betty Crocker, you know."

"I could teach you. For Brandi's birthday."

Barbie sighed. "Sure, sure. So, what happened to the bakery?"

"I sold it after I met Robin."

"Was it love at first sight?" Barbie asked, teasingly.

Farah shook her head and smiled. "Enough. Let's drop this subject."

"Oh, c'mon. Robin is the reason we're both here, right?" Barbie said, staring out the window.

Farah didn't respond, concentrating on the road. They were on the freeway now, leaving rural life behind. Two lanes turned into four. Thirty miles an hour turned into sixty-five, seventy. Cows and pastures turned into strip malls and gas stations, and then housing developments.

They were one hour in with two more to go.

"I want to talk more about your kids," Farah said finally.

"Sure, whatever you want to know me to come. They seem happy there on the farm. That's what I was hoping for." She heard her mother's mean voice again. *Start telling her about our health. Tell her we're sick. Don't waste this chance.*

Farah glanced over. "Why were you hoping for that?"

"You know, I wanted them to get to know family. Real family. It's working out well, I think."

They arrived at the restaurant for lunch at 12:30. While Barbie hurried out of the car to use the bathroom, Farah got them a table outside. It was a beautiful day with a light breeze in the air and Farah breathed deeply, enjoying the warm sun on her face and arms. She took out her phone and texted Robin.

> *{Farah:} Made it. Just stopped for lunch.*
> *{Robin:} Thanks, hon. How was the drive?*
> *{Farah:} Smooth sailing, she is entertaining in her own odd way.*
> *{Robin:} I'll take your word for it. Love you.*

Her traveling companion plopped down in front of her. "Look at us. Dining al fresca!"

Farah smiled, not correcting her.

A server came by and placed two menus down on the table.

"I'll have a glass of Sauvignon Blanc," Farah said quickly.

"I'm good, I don't even know what that is," Barbie said when the young woman looked her way. "Day drinking?" she asked Farah when they were alone.

"I think I'm going to need it."

Barbie whistled. "Would you look at this joint?" She ran her hands over the white tablecloth. "Real napkins, wine glasses, little flowers on the tables. Fancy!" She picked up her menu. "*The Edible Garden*. Huh, let's look."

After the wine and water was delivered, Farah said they needed another minute before taking a wonderful, crisp sip. "I've been here before if you'd like any suggestions."

Barbie looked at the menu, and Farah wondered what she was thinking. She had already gathered from their first couple of meals together that she wasn't an adventurous eater. "I'll have whatever you have," she said quickly as the server approached.

"We will both have a cup of butternut squash soup and avocado toast with tomato jelly. And I prefer a sliced hardboiled egg instead of over easy on top. What about you, Barbie?"

"Your way is fine."

"I think you're going to enjoy this," Farah said, taking another sip of wine.

"Yeah, well, I guess there is more to life than McDonald's."

Farah could feel the relaxing effects of the wine starting to pulse through her. "You know we're not far from the college and Ricky's old apartment."

"Oh yeah? I never spent much time getting to know the area," Barbie said, picking lemon seeds out of her water.

"What did you two do? I mean aside from the obvious. What kept it going after he left for college?"

Barbie sighed heavily. "We were just two misfits who kinda found each other. We became...best friends I guess."

Farah smiled at her, "That is sweet. But...it must have been a little more than that. I mean, because eventually you were intimate."

"If you mean sex, yeah, we had sex," Barbie said as a bright orange, creamy bowl of soup topped off with toasted pistachios and a dollop of sour cream was placed before her. She took a tentative spoonful. "Well, not bad." After another bigger spoonful she said, "It's not like we ever fell madly in love. He couldn't fall madly in love with me."

"Why?"

Barbie put down her spoon. "Ricky was gay!"

Farah put down her own spoon and picked up her wine glass. "Are you sure? Robin never told me that."

"You might need more wine for this," Barbie laughed as two beautiful thick pieces of crusty bread piled high with avocado, bright red tomato jelly, a sliced egg with black sesame seeds and sprouts arrived at the table.

"How did you know he was gay? Did he have a boyfriend?"

"Not in the traditional sense." Barbie sighed. "Ricky was gay, but he didn't *want* to be. He knew it wouldn't fly with the family. He thought that being with me, he could prove something to himself." She took a bite of her toast. "We fumbled through sex a few times. One time too many obviously." Barbie took another bite. "Damn, this is good! Anyway, I wasn't the one he wanted."

"Who did he want? Do you know?"

"Are you ready for this? He wanted Adam."

Farah thought for a minute. "Adam? His cousin?"

"That's the one."

Farah brought her hand to her mouth, losing her appetite, and after eating only half of her toast, pushed it across the table where Barbie eagerly accepted it.

"This is good stuff," Barbie said. "Can't remember the last time I even had guacamole."

"Glad you're enjoying it."

"I can see I shocked you again."

She nodded. "You did. You're good at that. I want to hear more, but right now we need to get going. I have an appointment at the mortuary."

"Great! I've never been to one of those either. Only seen them in the movies," Barbie said then finished the last of her toast.

"Well, I hope it doesn't disappoint," Farah said, draining the last of her wine, thinking, *I'm going to need more of this later.*

Arriving at Lehman and Son's Mortuary, Farah's stomach was in knots, but she wasn't sure whether it was because they were here or from the news at lunch.

"Yep, looks like the places in the movies. Funny, they're always a family affair," Barbie observed. "Sons, brothers, family-owned..."

"I get it," Farah said, getting out of the car. When she pulled open the bulky front door, they entered a large dark room much cooler than she liked and neither she nor Barbie had sweaters. The room looked like it was right out of an old movie, with dark paneled walls, black leather couches against the walls and a big desk in the middle of the room with a black rotary phone on top.

"Feels like a morgue in here!" Barbie blurted out, rubbing her arms.

"Shhh," Farah said, ringing a bell on the desk, rubbing her own arms.

Barbie scooted over to a receiving room with an open door and saw a casket. "I think there's a dead person in there!"

"Get over here!" Farah whispered animatedly as a door in the back swung open and a short, plump man in a tight black suit quickly approached, clutching a manila folder in one hand, and holding his other hand out for Farah. She looked down at his fat fingers and couldn't help noticing a wedding ring that she was sure he couldn't get off.

"Mrs. Robinson, I presume."

"Yes."

"Welcome. I'm Joseph Lehman. We are so sorry for your loss."

"Yes, well, thank you. I'm sure you heard about her condition. This has been inevitable."

"I know, but these things are always so difficult. We're here to ease your sorrow in whatever way we can."

"I'm having her cremated and then the Neptune Society will be taking care of the rest. You oversee this, right?"

"Yes, of course," he sat down behind the desk and opened the folder. "I assume you want to see her first?"

"I don't."

"I do!" Barbie said.

"You're not," Farah replied, not bothering to look at her.

"I want to see what she looked like."

"I'll show you a picture."

"Are you certain?" Joseph asked. "Perhaps it will help with closure."

"I'm good. I just saw her in April. I've had all the closure I need. What and where do I need to sign?"

Joseph Lehman looked up at her. "Fine, then. There are just three signatures needed."

"Who's the dead guy in there?"

"Barbie!"

Joseph cleared his throat. "*She.* It's a woman. And the rest is none of your business."

"Thank you. We will be out of your way," Farah said grabbing Barbie and heading out the door.

"Where to next?" Barbie said when they were back in the car.

"To the facility where she lived. I need to pick up her belongings."

"I hope it's warmer. Guess they must keep it cold in there because of all the dead people. No wonder that little dude was fat. If he was thin, he might freeze to death."

Despite herself, Farah laughed. "You do have a unique way of looking at things."

"So, you're glad you brought me, right?"

She shook her head. "Yes, I'm glad you're here."

Outside *Glen Oaks Rehabilitation*, they saw patients in wheelchairs, sitting outside with nurses or family members. They were mostly elderly, dozing or staring blank in the distance. But some looked younger, with horrible luck bestowed on them.

"That would be the pits," Barbie whispered to Farah as they passed one such man trapped in a lifeless body, sitting with a nurse who was staring at her phone.

At the entrance, the glass doors slid open and warm, pungent air engulfed them. A combination of bleach, urine, food, and floral hit Barbie's nose. "Shit, what is that smell?"

"You get used to it," Farah said, quickly making her way through the hallways to a nurses' station.

"Farah!" A plump nurse in a crisp white dress stood up and came around and pulled her into her ample breasts.

"Hello, Patty."

"We're so sorry, dear."

"Thank you. But it's gone on too long."

"Yes, well, still." Patty took her elbow. "We have put her things in a box. It's on her bed."

"I know the way," Farah said. When they walked in the room, Farah slowly approached the small carboard box sitting in the middle of the neatly made single bed.

"That's it?" Barbie asked.

"That's it," Farah said, staring at the contents. A couple of picture frames, a small album, a hairbrush, and a pink robe. She picked up a picture. "Here she is with my parents and her fiancé. This is from their engagement party."

Barbie took the picture. "She was pretty. She looked like your dad, and you favor your mom."

"Yes, that is what most people said."

"But the fiancé! Not much of a looker. He's got pasty skin...just like me." Barbie looked closely at Carl. There was something about him that sent a strange stir through her. But she couldn't say what it was. Instead, she offered, "She could have done better."

Farah laughed. "No, she couldn't have. He was a nice man. They rushed into a relationship. She wanted to get back at me. Sad."

"Get back at you for what?"

Farah sighed and sat on the bed. "I went out with him first."

"You went out with this guy?"

"He was a good guy! He loved me but I didn't love him. I had to stop it. He came from money, and she went right after him. And he was helpful after the accident."

"Hoping to pick things back up?"

"No!"

Barbie sat. "I learn something new every day with you, don't I?"

"I can say the same thing," Farah said, nudging her arm.

"Not done yet."

"Should I be afraid?"

"Nah," she said, knowing those words weren't true. "Really hard to believe you dated this guy."

Farah laughed. "This was many years before Robin. And we only met because of *his* tragedy."

"Crazy how things work out. Can I ask you something?"

"Maybe," she chuckled, putting the picture back in the box.

"I mean I know you're older and all, but why didn't you two have a kid?"

"I can't have them. I have a condition."

"Huh. I should have had a condition. *And* my mother, and *her* mother."

"Why would you say that?"

"It's just, none of the women in my family were prepared for motherhood. There were never any fathers around. I never knew a grandfather or a father."

Farah touched her arm. "I'm sorry about that."

Barbie pulled away and stood and walked to the door, "Nothing you need to be sorry for. Can we get out of here? The smell is getting to me."

Farah followed her out, wondering why her show of empathy hit such a nerve. *Poor girl really has had a tough life...*

On the nineteenth floor of the Marriot with views of the city's skyline, Barbie squealed like a little girl as she jumped on one of queen sized beds closest to the window. "Get a load of this place. And look at those views!"

"I'm glad you like it."

"This room must have cost a fortune," Barbie said, walking over to the bathroom. "Wow, the bathtub looks like a whirlpool. And there are robes! Big fluffy white robes."

Drained, Farah lay back on a pillow. The wine at lunch, the mortuary, Glen Oaks, the news about Ricky. It had all caught up to her. *And we haven't even had dinner.*

"Can I take a bath?" Barbie asked.

"Sure. Relax and take your time."

"Thanks. I haven't had a bath in a while. I mean I shower, but a bath..."

"I get it. Go for it," Farah laughed, grabbing her phone from her purse, and seeing a text from Robin.

> *{Robin:} Finished for the day. How's it going there?*
> *{Farah:} Good, Just checked into the room before dinner. How are the kids?*
> *{Robin:} All good. Watching tv before dinner.*
> *{Farah } I'll call you later:)*
> *{Robin:} I'll be waiting.*

Barbie came out wearing one of the robes, twirling in front of Farah like a model in a fashion show. "This is the life!"

"It suits you. I was looking at my phone for a restaurant. What do you feel like for eating?"

Barbie sat on her bed. "Don't ask me. I had a coupon once for an Applebee's. The kids liked that."

Farah nodded. "Okay. I'll pick something." She scrolled through her phone before sighing, "Why don't we just eat downstairs. The restaurant is good, and they have a variety."

"Fine with me," she said, and hoped for a cheeseburger.

"Okay, I'll go and freshen up and we can head down." She looked through her bag. She had another dress but decided to just stay in what she was wearing. "Um, I checked and the kids are good, but if you'd like to call go ahead."

"Yeah, I'll call later," she said absently, looking through the duffel bag, pulling out a yellow sundress.

Watching Barbie through the bathroom door, Farah saw her take off the robe and quickly slip the dress over her head. Like all her clothes it was too big. And she was painfully thin. *Was she sick? The family said she was always that way.* She wanted to ask about her clothes, but she didn't want to make her uncomfortable. Not when it had been going so well.

Downstairs, Farah picked a quiet table away from the bar, and TV noise, ordering a glass of red wine for herself and a beer for Barbie.

"It's been quite a day," Barbie said, taking a sip of beer. "Thanks for bringing me."

Farah smiled. "I'm glad I brought you. I've enjoyed myself, even under the circumstances." She took a sip of wine. "I'd like to continue talking about what we were talking about at lunch."

"Oh, Ricky and Adam. Right."

"I mean if you knew he was gay, why did you sleep with him?"

"It was so long ago." Barbie paused, looking like she was trying to remember something. "First of all, we never did anything much before Ricky went to college. You know, kissing and stuff but that's it. But I had already figured out Adam. He hated me. He hated me because he had a thing for Ricky." She chuckled and took another sip. "I can't believe no one else figured it out. Just stupid ol' me."

"You are not stupid," Farah jumped in.

"Well, you know what I mean. I would drive them home from school, and Adam would sulk, giving me the evil eye. And Emily was off in her own world."

This made Farah laugh. "She's always been consistent."

"Anyway, by the time Ricky did leave, I had grown fond of him. We were good friends. I visited him a few times, but still nothing sexual happened. We slept together, hugged, kissed, but that was it. I didn't mind, really." She finished the rest of her beer. "Can I get another one?"

"Sure." Farah waved over the waiter and asked for two more.

"Then one weekend he told me Adam was coming, and for two weeks after that we didn't talk. I called and called, and if he answered at all, they were quick conversations. He kept telling me he was busy at school and he didn't have time for me. But then one day he changed his tune and asked me to come. And when I got there, he wanted to drink. He wasn't much of a drinker, but he wanted to drink. So, we drank...and we did it. That was the first time."

Farah cleared her throat. "Did you, um, enjoy it?"

"Well, the first time hurt like hell, right?"

"Yes, you're right."

"But then, it gradually got better. I mean, not painful."

"Did you two ever use protection?"

"Nope."

"So, you wouldn't have cared if you got pregnant?"

"I never thought anything through. He didn't either. Ricky liked distractions. From school for one. He was never a great student. Of course, I didn't know the extent. And then I found out about him and Adam."

"He told you?" Farah asked, mesmerized.

"No. I found a picture of the two of them in his room. They were kissing. Like, seriously kissing if you know what I mean."

"I got it. Did you say something?"

"No. But I put two and two together. The timing of our 'getting together.' It all made sense. He would never have admitted it. He was already a disappointment at home."

"I'm sure that wasn't true," Farah said.

"Yeah, well try following in Robin's footsteps. He loved the horses and work and crazy hours. Plus, handsome beyond all get-out. He was a real chick magnet, not that he cared or noticed. And then there was Rebecca. The miracle. The *special* baby. They all spoiled her rotten. Ricky was in the middle of all that."

"I'm sure the family didn't see it that way." Farah looked at both of their drinks, "I think we should order dinner before we continue and these drinks are gone."

"Yeah, I'm hungry! All this confessing." She looked at the menu. "Thank the Lord, a cheeseburger!"

After she ordered chicken piccata and a cheeseburger and fries for Barbie, Farah asked, "So then you got pregnant?"

"Yep. But like I said, Ricky never knew. I'd barely found out when he told me he was in trouble at school. He called me, crying hysterically. He wanted me to help think of a story. Like I could do *that*. I had a story of my own growing inside my belly to figure out. But I was secretly thinking it wouldn't be so bad for him to come home. I was thinking once it all calmed down, he might be happy about the kid. The family too. I was thinking I might finally get a real home."

They were both quiet for a minute. Farah could feel the wine, the heat starting in her feet and working its way up, and she was trying not to cry. She picked up her water and drained the glass. Finally, the food arrived. The aroma of lemon and capers hit her nose and she was instantly hungry.

Barbie smiled at her plate. "This smells great. Hey, can I get an extra order of fries?"

They had dived into their meals, and when the second basket of fries arrived, Barbie put it in the middle, and Farah did not hesitate.

"Good chow," Barbie said with a mouthful.

"Really good chow," Farah agreed, nodding her head.

Barbie smiled and looked away, and they finished the rest of their meal in silence. When the waiter had cleared the plates, they both sat back, full and satisfied.

Farah asked, "Are you tired, or can we keep talking?"

"Shoot, I can keep talking. I could even eat dessert."

"Great, you get dessert and I'll get coffee. This has been very enlightening."

Between healthy bites of chocolate cake and vanilla ice cream, Barbie told Farah how she heard about the accident two days after it happened while she was helping her mother in the salon.

"One of mom's regulars broke the news. It came out like she was talking about a sale on milk at the grocery store," Barbie shook her head like she was reliving the day. "It was something like, *'Hey, did you hear, some of them Robinsons were killed. Bad car accident. You just never know.'* I felt like I could throw up. I just knew before my mama even asked which ones." Barbie took a big gulp of water, "And that was it. I knew my dreams would never come true. I hated myself for even having any..."

And after that it hadn't taken long for Barbie to leave Honeysuckle. It wasn't hard convincing her mother she needed a change of scenery. Carole made the call, and within a week Barbie was off to Carson City. She'd planned on an abortion. She'd planned to get a job and a little apartment with little yellow gingham curtains in a kitchen window, learn to cook. Start over. Start fresh.

"Marcy hooked me up with a job at a casino. I was a cashier, handing out winnings to people. That was fun. Sometimes they'd give me a tip! But then one month turned into two and then into three and before I knew it my pants were getting tight around the waist. I went home from work one night and Marcy guessed. She asked when my last period was, and to the best of my recollection I told her. 'Well,' she said, 'looks like you are going to be a mother!'"

"But you never told your own mother?"

"Not right away. When I finally did, I said it was a one nighter. The same way I was conceived. She didn't ask anymore. I never mentioned he was a Robinson until the day she finally met him."

"Why?"

Barbie pushed her empty plate away and wiped her mouth with her napkin. "For one thing, I knew she was never going to be a doting grandmother. Also...I think I felt sorry for her. There would have been a lot of gossip floating around about me trying to trap Ricky. I didn't want her business ruined. It's all she's ever had."

"I don't think her friends would have thought that. I don't think Diana would have. They've been friends for a long time."

"Farah, my mother is her hairdresser. Ask your aunt how many times they've gone to lunch."

Back in their room, Farah was soaking in her own bath. She felt guilty for having such a normal life, with parents who cared for her, nurtured her, educated her. She suddenly admired this quirky woman's ability to get through it all with two children. *And then she brought them to us...*

She called Robin, and he answered on the first ring. "Hey, I was getting worried. Is everything all right?"

"Everything is fine. We had a couple of drinks at dinner, and a lengthy conversation."

"God, what else don't I know about myself?"

She laughed. "Nothing more about you. But...did you know about Ricky and Adam?"

He sighed. "Did she think they were together?"

"She saw a picture that led her to believe that, yes. You don't sound that surprised."

Another sigh. "I saw the same picture."

"Why have you never told me this?"

"I don't know. I found out the day I met you. I was still in shock and it didn't seem necessary to bring it up amid the tragedy. This would have ruined my aunt and uncle."

"Ricky was afraid your parents wouldn't accept it."

"Well, not with his cousin, no. Poor guy."

"Poor girl! He tried to convince himself he wasn't gay, and Barbie ended up pregnant." She sighed. "Anyway, we can talk when I get home. You need your sleep."

"You sound like you could use some sleep too."

"I could. It's been quite a day, my sister being the least of it." She laughed quietly. "I'm starting to like Barbie."

"How many drinks *did* you have?"

"Ha, ha. I thought I pitied her, but now I admire her."

"Well, she did one thing right. The kids are great."

"Have they asked about her? I mentioned her calling home, but she put it off."

"Not one word. In fact, Ben is over with Joe and Maria, and Brandi is sleeping with Rebecca. I didn't want them to wake up alone in the morning. They're completely at ease."

Those words were the perfect ending to an eventful day.

Chapter 18
Me and Bobby McGee

"Oh, no!" Farah groaned, realizing how late it was when she woke up.

"What's the matter?" Barbie asked, coming out of the bathroom, smelling like she had liberally indulged in the little bottles of free products.

"I can't believe the time. I thought we'd be on the road by now."

"What's the rush?"

"Well...six kids for one thing. Leaving Maria with two extra is a lot. Call her and tell her we'll out of here in a half hour."

"Me?"

"Yes, you. They're your kids. I'm taking a quick shower. And be nice." Farah grabbed her bag and went into the bathroom. She could hear Barbie on the other side of the door.

"Hey there, Maria. I have you on speaker phone because Farah doesn't think I can be nice."

"Is everything alright?"

"Going great. We're leaving this lovely hotel in a half hour. Farah thinks she has put an extra burden on you, but I was singing your praises. You got this, right?"

Farah was shaking her head behind the door, sending Robin a text.

"Thanks for the vote of confidence. We're doing fine. Your boy is with the horses, of course, and Brandi is with Emily and Diana. They're working on the dresses for the flower girls. Just in case."

"That's great. I told Farah we weren't being missed, but she insisted."

"She's thoughtful. I hope she's wearing off on you a little," Maria said dryly.

"Okey dokey. Well, we'll see you later. Don't hold dinner, we might..."

Farah came out and grabbed the phone. "Hi, we should be there by four at the latest with no traffic issues."

"No worries, hon. Robin and Joe are heading out for supplies, and they're bringing home pizza! Everyone is excited. Take your time and drive careful."

Armed with fresh coffee and warm croissants as they merged onto the freeway, Farah was eager to pick up where they left off the night before, hoping Barbie was too.

"So let's get back to your pregnancy with Ben. What happened after you decided to keep the baby?""

Barbie polished off her second roll. "Marcy took me to a clinic. I got checked out and got some vitamins. She asked who the father was, and I said the same thing I told mama.

"Luckily, she said I could stay. She liked the idea of a baby around the house. Probably because she never had them. Everyone thinks it's a good idea until they're climbing up your leg all day." Barbie looked over at Farah. "Oops, sorry."

"Half-hearted apology excepted. Please continue," Farah said, shaking her head and smiling.

"She helped me set up a secondhand crib and paid for the baby bedding. I had one of them ultrasounds and found out I was going to pop out a boy. A couple of the girls at work even threw me a baby shower. That was something! I got a stroller and lots of blue clothes and diapers. I was beginning to take to the idea of being a mom." She reached for her coffee.

"Until those labor pains hit. Ugh. He came two weeks early. I was at work. Just got up to take a pee and the water broke all over the floor. The girls went nuts, but I had no idea what was next. They say I was lucky because he came out two hours after I got to the hospital. No drugs. Lucky? I don't think so." She sipped and scrunched up her face.

"Oh my God, when I first saw him, it was freaky. All covered in blood, wailing like a banshee. He was big! Seven pounds. Coming from me, that was pretty good. I was afraid to hold him, thinking he'd slip from my arms. Then they took him away and washed him all up and handed him back all wrapped up. I could really see his hair and face then. He was something. A real Robinson..." Barbie's voice trailed off.

"You know, I'm jealous of you right now," Farah said and laughed.

"Why?"

"Childbirth is a miracle!"

"No, it's a miracle I kept him alive. After I got him home it was bad. Ben was a crier. He didn't like my boobs. Never seemed satisfied. I was at the clinic a lot trying to figure it out. Formula was expensive, and I had to get food stamps."

"I'm sorry," Farah said.

"It got better after a few months. I wanted to go back to work, and one of my coworkers had a mom who offered to watch Ben. I took the night shift so he would sleep. That worked about half of the time, but she didn't mind. She was a grandmotherly type. Gloria was her name."

"Before I knew it, the little guy was a year old. He was walking and into everything. Marcy didn't like that. She was a neat freak. And she had met a guy. He gave me the willies. It was time for me to move on."

"Where did you go?" Farah asked, looking at the road signs, realizing they had already driven an hour.

"Well, Gloria had gotten attached to Ben, so she told me I could stay at her house. That was nice. Her place was bigger than Marcy's and it had a back yard. When the weather was nice, I would hang outside with him. I even bought him one of those little plastic pools."

"It sounds like you were doing a great job."

"Well, babies don't know any better. But, yeah, we got into a routine. And then Gloria got sick. Cancer. She had it before and it came back. Ben was almost two by then. Really active, loud and all over the place. It was getting to be a war zone around the house with all her medical crap and Ben's toys. And she couldn't handle watching him anymore. So, I was screwed. I kept missing shifts. My boss was cool and all, but he could only cut me so much slack."

"So, what did you do?" Farah asked.

"I had a few bucks saved up, so I moved to Reno."

"Reno? What was in Reno?"

"My boss helped me get a job at a larger casino. Paid better. I found a one-bedroom apartment I could afford. It wasn't as nice as that hotel we were just at, but I was kind a proud I finally had a place of my own."

"What did you do with Ben?"

"I found a day care. It wasn't a bad place. I got a recommendation from someone at my new job. He liked day care. They had more to offer him than I did. There were lots of toys and other kids and they took outings to the park and had birthday parties. Things went good for a year. I worked and took care of him and kept out of trouble. And then something happened."

"What?" Farah asked.

"The rodeo came to town."

"Hold that thought," Farah said before pulling off the freeway. "I need gas and a bathroom."

"Good idea. I could use a snack."

"You're a bottomless pit!" Farah said and laughed, getting out of the car. "How are you so skinny?"

After filling the tank, grabbing drinks, a box of red licorice and sending Robin a text, they were back on the road.

Barbie opened her bottle of soda and had a long drink. "So, should I continue?"

"Yes."

"The rodeo came to town."

"A Rodeo?"

"Yep. The rodeo came, and the whole town came alive. All the hotels were booked, and the casino was hopping. There were cowboys everywhere! My boss gave me a ticket for the Friday events, or whatever they're called, but I wasn't sure I was going to go. And then I saw him."

"Who?"

"I'm getting to that. Well, he saw me first."

"Who?"

Barbie laughed and took and stuffed a whole piece of licorice in her mouth and sounded like she was talking with a mouthful of marbles when she said, "The most beautiful man I had ever seen walked by my window, saw me, and stopped."

"Would you swallow that," Farah said, exasperated.

"Sorry," she said, finished chewing and continued, "He...he was wearing a plaid shirt with rhinestone buttons, the tightest jeans you ever saw, boots, and a hat. And guess what? He dipped the hat when he saw me. My stomach did a somersault. Then he walked toward my window. I thought I'd forget how to talk."

Farah laughed, "Then what?"

"Oh, he said, 'hello little lady,' or some smooth talk malarky like that. I said something back and then he introduced himself. You won't believe his name."

"What was it?"

"Bobby McGee."

"Like the song?"

"Just like it. And another B name. I didn't believe him at first. But then he pulled out his ID and proved it. And then he asked what my name was and when I said Barbie, he said the same thing you did, *'like the doll?'* and I fake laughed and then he said I was cuter than any doll he'd ever seen."

Farah laughed. "He sounds like he was smitten."

"I don't think I ever felt like that. All fluttery and all. What Ricky and I had...well I never felt like that. Anyway, he told me he was in the rodeo. He did that horse riding thing, the bucking bronco riding.

"I told him I had a ticket but wasn't sure if I could make it. Then he handed me another pass and said he'd be waiting for me at a special gate. He walked away with a big wink and I scrambled for a sitter. I ended up asking one of the girls who worked at the daycare if she could come and babysit. She said she'd like to, needed the cash, so we were all set."

"When I got there, he led me down to where they keep the horses and where all the other riders hung out. I remember it was hot. Smelly. Horse, beer, and BO." She wrinkled her nose. "He showed me the horse he was going to ride and then led me to a bleacher seat. It's all kind of a blur. It was exciting when they called his name. And boom! Out of the gate and just like that, on the ground and scrambling to get the hell out of the way!"

Barbie shook her head, her lips forming a ghost of a smile. "I thought he blew it, but he was all excited. Said it was one of his better times and said it was because of me. Smooth talker, right? Anyway, he offered me a beer. We talked and stared at each other for a little while, and he asked me out for the next night after the show. And I thought, well here goes, fun while it lasted. I told him I had a kid."

Her smile widened. "But he was cool with it! And I suggested he come over to dinner. Can you believe it? Who did I think I was? But he said sure. And before I left...he kissed me." She sighed. "He kissed me good. I felt it in my belly. I bet like the way Robin kisses you."

"Those first kisses are the best," Farah agreed.

"But by the time I got home I was in a panic. I didn't know how to cook. I was blabbering to the sitter about what I had gotten myself into, still thinking about the kiss. She said spaghetti. Hard to mess that up. So that's what I did.

"I woke up early the next day and cleaned the place. Then I packed up Ben and headed to the store. Got the noodles and a jar of sauce and stuff for salad and rolls and even a bottle of wine. You know the kind where people stick candles in after and the wax melts down. Darn bottle was ten dollars!

"It felt like the longest day ever waiting for him to get there. But finally, seven o'clock arrived and there was a knock on the door. He stood there in a fresh shirt, those same tight pants and his hat pulled down low. He even had flowers. Little yellow daisies." Barbie paused a moment, twisting a strand of hair, thinking back to the happy memory.

"So, he came in and looked around, told me he liked the place. I mean it was no Rebecca Farms, but I tried my best."

"I'm sure it was very nice."

"He peeked in on Ben, who was asleep, and told me how cute he was, and I was thinking, yeah, wait till he wakes up." Barbie sighed again. "Then he took his hat off. I saw his curly blond hair for the first time. I never thought a head of hair could make my stomach do somersaults."

"I can relate," Farah said.

"I opened the wine, and we ate a little and he told me he was leaving the next day. After dinner, I was putting stuff away, trying not to look at him, and he turned me around and kissed me again. He pulled me close, close. I tell you I never felt that way. And the next thing I knew we were on the couch. My dress was coming over my head and he was pulling off his clothes and we..."

Farah jumped in, "I don't need all the details, Barbie. I'm just wondering if you thought about protection, given the circumstances."

"I was just going to tell you. He had a condom, and he used it."

"Well, what happened?"

"The darn thing broke! He said it was old. And I thought, well what are the odds?" She snorted. "Anyway, we said our goodbyes. He promised to call every day, and he did. It wasn't just a one-time thing. He called me as often as he could. And then one day my phone stopped ringing. It took two days before I gave in and called him." Her expression clouded over.

"I remember that day like it just happened. I was at work and on a break, outside taking a walk. I called his number, and someone answered, but it wasn't him. It was a fellow rider. His name was Dale. He said he recognized the name. He had been holding onto Bobby's phone." Barbie took a big breath. "Anyway, Bobby had been kicked in the head, falling off his horse. Didn't get out of the way fast enough. Just like that...I don't remember much after we hung up."

"That must have been so hard. I'm sorry, Barbie."

She waved her off, "It's fine. He gave me a gift before he left."

"What was that?"

"Well, duh. Brandi! She's a cute little thing, isn't she? Looks like her daddy." She sighed once more and sang, *"Me and Bobby McGee..."*

Chapter 19
This Must be Big...

The aroma of fresh, hot pizza could bring a family that rarely ate together to the table with one whiff. But even the Robinsons and the Martinez's, who ate together most nights, couldn't get out to the tables fast enough.

"Now, Rebecca, we should each just have two pieces," Emily said, clearly enjoying her slice of cheesy goodness.

"Two of each! Sure, no problem!" Rebecca said, and everyone laughed.

They ate in blissful silence for a while. Just the occasional, Mmm, this is so good... I'll take another pepperoni... or Throw anything on the plate filled the air.

"How did it go with your sister," Diana asked. "And what happened to Barbie?"

"When we got back, she decided to go home and check on her mother. I don't think she's very well."

"Yeah, Gran coughs a lot," Ben said.

"I'm sorry, that must be hard for you," Farah said.

'It's okay. She doesn't like us around anyway. Says we're loud," he said, stuffing the last of his pizza in his mouth before leaving the table.

"Anyway," Farah started after all the kids started exiting. "It went well, Diana. Just a few papers to sign at the mortuary and a box of MaryAnn's things to pick up. I did learn quite a bit about Barbie's past. She's had a tough time of it. We should be more patient."

"What did you learn?" Diana asked.

Farah looked at Robin.

Rebecca saw the look and said, "This must be big."

"We have kids here, Becca," Farah said before whispering to Diana, "I learned a lot about Brandi's father for one thing I think we should get the kids ready for bed. I'll make popcorn and they can all watch a movie in our house. And then I can fill you in more, Diana."

"I want to get filled in too!" Rebecca said.

"Not going to happen," Robin said.

"Oh, man! I'm not a baby!"

"Alright, let's get going," Maria said and stood up. "Joe, let's get the kids cleaned up."

"Yes, ma'am!"

"You're ignoring me!" Rebecca said.

Farah stood too. "Come on Ben and Brandi. Let's shower before movie time."

"I'll clear up here," Diana said.

"Still ignoring me!" Rebecca said.

"I'll help, Mom," Emily offered, and Josh followed, grabbing boxes and paper plates.

"Hey, look who's snagging the leftovers," Robin said, laughing.

"Hello!!!" Rebecca said loudly. "I know where babies come from!"

"Sis, come with me to check our own expectant mother," Robin said, guiding her away from the table.

"Fine," she conceded. "But I know how that happened too."

An hour later, the kids were settled in front of the TV, each with a bowl of popcorn watching *Toy Story*. Farah, Robin, Maria, and Joe were on the back porch enjoying the warm evening air. In the end, Emily invited Rebecca over to her house to watch an "adult" movie and that appeased her.

"You don't have to tell us anything you don't think is our business," Joe said.

"You're family. It's all your business," Robin said and sighed. "There is something about Ricky and Adam I never told anyone. But Barbie knew," He paused and looked over at his aunt and uncle's house before whispering, "They were gay. I only found out after the accident, and then it didn't seem right to expose them."

"Both?" Joe asked.

"It gets worse. They'd been involved. Robin found a photo of them in a...passionate kiss. Barbie confirmed it was true," Farah said.

"Confirmed what was true?" Diana asked, coming around from the front of the porch. They looked at her like they'd been caught with their hands in the cookie jar. "I knew if you saw me walk out my front door and head towards you, you'd clam up so I went out the side through my kitchen. What was true?"

"This might be too much for you, Aunt Diana."

"Let me guess. My son was gay and in love with Ricky?"

Farah gasped. "You knew?"

Diana let out a big laugh and fell into an empty chair next to Maria. "It feels good to finally say it. For years I saw the way Adam looked at Ricky. He even tried to tell me about it one night, and I dismissed it. Philip wouldn't have understood."

Maria reached and held her hand. "I saw the way Adam looked at Ricky too, but I felt it was one-sided."

"If I had only let him be who he wanted to be." Diana wiped a tear. "Anyway, if that was true, how did that girl end up pregnant with Ben?"

"Ricky and Barbie had been friends for years. Aside from a few kisses, they never did anything. You're right, the boys were together one weekend when Adam visited Ricky at school but afterwards, Ricky freaked out. He couldn't face his sexuality and he used Barbie, in a way, to convince himself he was straight," Farah said.

"So, she got pregnant. And that's why he wanted to come home? He didn't really flunk out," Diana asked.

"No. That part was true. But he just didn't flunk out. Ricky was caught cheating. He traded his car to have a paper written," Robin added.

"Why didn't you tell us that?" Diana asked.

"It didn't seem important afterwards. And I was trying to spare him."

"Barbie found out she was pregnant, but she decided to keep it a secret while Ricky dealt with his school situation," Farah said.

"Oh, my goodness," Diana said. "All these years I've blamed her. Adam hated her because she came between him and Ricky, and then so did I."

"Diana, they couldn't have been together. They were cousins first," Robin said.

She sighed, "Of course they couldn't have been together. What in the world were they thinking?"

Robin chuckled, "They were both really good at not thinking."

Diana nodded, "You're right. I had two like that! Heads in the clouds..."

Maria squeezed her hand harder. "But lovely souls, the both of them."

"Do you think you'll tell Philip?" Robin asked.

"Heaven's no! No good will come of it now. We've come so far. Josh has been a godsend bringing Philip out of a long dark place. And he's really enjoying Ben and Brandi! Nothing better than children around," she sighed and then chuckled, "Well, if you're up to it, who's Brandi's father?"

"Oh good, we're just in time!" Emily said, coming quickly around the porch with Rebecca, greeted by five sets of big eyes. "What? The guys wanted Star Wars and fell asleep. We went looking for you mama and saw the kitchen door open. Here you are!"

"Yeah, and don't leave anything out," Rebecca said as they pulled up chairs.

Robin looked at Farah and shrugged. "Take it away..."

Farah tried to keep the story brief, but Emily and Rebecca were determined to turn it into an epic. By the time they decided to call it a night, Barbie and Bobby McGee's ill-fated encounter had turned into a romance for the ages.

"I always believed in love at first sight," Emily said. "I knew I was going to marry Josh right away. What about you and Daddy, Mama?"

Diana laughed, her cheeks turning a bright shade of rose. "It's been so long, but yes, I knew very early on."

Joe leaned into Maria, *"Amor a primera vista,"* he growled.

She laughed and pushed him away. "Speak for yourself."

"What about you and Farah?" Rebecca asked Robin.

He grabbed his wife's hand. "It was her coffee."

Chapter 20
Plan! What Plan?

The familiar sound of boots quickly coming down the stairs brought a smile to Farah's face as Ben reached the bottom, stopping when he saw her.

"Hey, what's the rush?" she asked.

"Can I go out to the stables?" he asked.

"Um, let's wait till after breakfast. Looks like a couple of horses are heading out. And they are keeping a close watch on the pregnant girl." He looked disappointed, so she added, "Want some hot chocolate? I even have cream."

"Sure," he said and sat down begrudgingly.

"Can I ask you something?" She put a small pot of milk on the stove and sat down next to him. "Have you been to a regular school?" She put a reassuring hand over his. "It's fine if you haven't or don't remember."

"I did kindergarten and some first grade. But then we moved, and I didn't go back to school. Mom said she was going to teach me stuff at home, but she was always busy. And then we came here with Gran."

Home schooling? "Well, I have an idea. Let's spend time each morning practicing reading, writing, and math. We can see what you remember. And then, when Joe Junior goes back to school in August, you can go with him."

"What if I don't remember anything?"

She stood and went to the stove, pulled the pot off the burner, and spooned two heaping teaspoons of chocolate powder into the hot milk. "I bet you'll remember a lot. And if you don't, that's fine too. You'll learn!" She pulled the can of cream out of the refrigerator and swirled a big dollop on the top. "Here, you sip this and I'm going to look for a couple of things."

While he scooped his cream, she went over to the built-in cabinets across the room. There, she looked through books and brought over a stack. "These were Joe's, and now Christina and Marisol reads them. Look through these, and I'll look on my computer and print out some worksheets for math and writing so you can practice."

"Is this what kids do every summer?" he asked shyly.

She smiled. "It's good to keep our brains from turning to mush." She pretended not to watch as he slowly opened a book. He was leery at first, but then Farah saw him mouthing words, and his confidence grew.

Farah poured more coffee and sighed with pride. One horrible person was out of her life, and two more special little people had arrived. Well, three, if you counted Barbie. And she did. She wanted the kids to stay, and she was willing to make Barbie part of the package too. She pulled out her phone and sent Barbie a text.

"Yeah, he's right. He did kindergarten in Reno. Then I went back to Carson City, and he started first grade but it was hard to get him there every day. And when I was late, they got all over me. I mean, it was just the first grade! Good grief," Barbie told Farah over the phone later that morning.

"Well, I was thinking, *we* should get them enrolled here in the fall." Farah emphasized saying *we* on purpose.

"Yeah, well, that's a good idea. I mean I guess if I'm staying. What would *we* need to do?"

"Do you have their birth certificates?" *Please say yes.*

"I bet you don't think I do, but I do."

"Great. Bring them to me, and I'll take care of the rest. Of course, Ben will be evaluated to see what grade he should start. He might be a little...behind."

"He'll be okay. He figures things out quick. Besides, there is something to be said for street smarts. Can't learn everything from a book."

"True. But since he's not on the streets yet, let's just stick with the ABCs and 123s."

Barbie laughed. "That's funny! I'm wearing off on you.

After an afternoon shower, Farah came down to see Barbie sitting between her children on the couch. Ben was reading to her. "Oh...hi. You never mentioned coming over."

"Look at this guy, huh? I told you he would be fine."

"Yes, yes you did," Farah said walking into the kitchen.

"I picked up a six pack. Stuck it in the fridge. Thought it was the least I could do."

"The least," Farah mumbled to herself and walked into kitchen to finish making a pitcher of lemonade. "So, tell me about your mom? How is she doing?"

Barbie stood and walked towards her. "Well, her years and years of smoking have finally caught up to her. She's got that COPD disease. The same thing happened to her mom. I guess I'm lucky I never picked up that nasty habit. But who knows with all the secondhand smoke I've inhaled? My days could be numbered too."

"Are her days numbered?"

Her lips twisted into a grimace. "Maybe a year. She'll be on full time oxygen in a few months."

"I'm so sorry, Barbie. Is this why you moved back?"

She looked out the window, as if searching for her next words. "Um, yeah. Part of it. I mean I did want the kids to meet you. But I had no idea how bad things were with her, the salon, the apartment. And in this heat! Upstairs is like a sauna. Nothing like a fan blowing hot air around to remind you how poor you are."

"You could bring her here," Farah offered. "She could cool off here in the afternoons at least."

"Wow! That's generous of you, considering."

"Don't be ridiculous. Please, if this would make her more comfortable, extend the invitation."

"Thanks, I might do that. It's not like Robin would even recognize her anymore. She is the not the voluptuous woman she once was. She's skinnier than you are now. Don't worry, she won't tempt him."

Farah looked at her and they smiled knowingly at each other. "I'm heading to the stables. We have a girl about ready to give birth."

"Can I come?" Ben asked, quickly standing.

"Let me go out and check with Robin first," she said, grabbing her pitcher and walking out.

Farah was a welcome sight with her pitcher of icy lemonade. Robin and Philip were sponging down the expectant Caramel. A fitting name because of her beautiful color. She was six years old, and this was her first pregnancy, just entering her eleventh month. Everyone was taking extra care with her, trying to keep her comfortable.

"How's she doing?" Farah asked, putting the pitcher down on a work bench.

"She's doing good. Josh doesn't think she's going into labor yet, but we'll all be taking turns staying close by at night. Josh is taking tonight."

Farah pulled Robin from the horse and Philip. "I should have run this by you first. Barbie is back, and I told her she could bring Carole by to escape the heat if she wanted."

"Babe, you don't have to run anything by me. This is your house."

"I know, but she isn't just *anyone*."

"That was a lifetime ago. Two lifetimes." He kissed her cheek. "I better get back to work."

When Farah came out of the stable, Ben was sitting on one of the picnic tables. "Why ae you out here, honey? It's so hot. Where is Brandi and your mom?"

"My sister had to go the bathroom."

"Oh."

"Can I tell you something?" he asked tentatively.

She sat down. "Anything."

"I don't want to go back there."

"Where?"

"I don't ever want to go back to Gran's."

She leaned in closer. "It must be awful in this heat."

He whispered, "It's not just that. It's dark and scary, and all they do is fight."

"Your mom and grandma?"

"Yeah. They think I'm asleep, but I hear everything."

"What do they fight about?"

"Us. Gran says Mom isn't going along with the plan."

"Plan! What plan?"

"I don't know. Something about money. Gran is sick and says stuff like they're running out of time. She also tells my mom not to eat for some reason."

Farah sat up straight. She looked up at the open bathroom window, listening. She heard the toilet flush and the faucet running. She gently grabbed Ben's arm. "Are you sure this is what you heard?"

"Yes. Please, don't make us go back. I love it here."

"You don't have to worry, sweetheart."

"Worry about what?" Barbie said, standing at the door.

A startled Ben shot Farah a look and she squeezed his arm tighter. "It's alright." She looked at Barbie. "Ben's worried about the pregnant horse in this heat."

"Yeah, having Brandi in July was no picnic. I know you fantasized about having a kid and all, but nine months pregnant in the dessert sucked."

"Thanks for always setting me straight, Barbie." She stood, grabbing Ben's hand, turning away from Barbie's gaze, and said, "We'll talk more later," before walking him back into the house. "Are you staying some dinner, or spending the night?" *Please say no*, she was thinking after her conversation with Ben.

"I don't know. The kids should see their granny." She stared at her son thoughtfully. "Right, Ben, time to go see your granny?"

"No! "I want to stay!"

"Well, it's not up to you, young man."

"Let them stay. It's so hot. It won't be good for anyone in the apartment. You said so yourself," Farah pleaded.

Barbie sighed and wiped her brow. "Alright, you win...for now. But I got to go. I got prescriptions to pick up."

"I'll walk you out," Farah said. "Say bye to your mom, kids."

At the car, there was little desire for conversation. Still, Farah, sensing Barbie's suspicion and hoping to defuse it asked, "I'm sure this isn't easy for you...having a sick mom. And this heat can make anyone short tempered."

"Did Ben say something?"

"No!" Farah said, cringing inwardly. She'd denied it too quickly. "Only...that your mom's coughing bothers him. It might be too much for them, watching her decline."

"Huh, maybe." Barbie got in her car eyeing Farah warily as she turned the key and started the loud little motor. Her hair stirred as a rush of air hit her face from the vents. "I'll check in tomorrow," she said as the car grinded into gear.

"Tomorrow." Farah said as she watched the little car drive away in a cloud of dust and smoke.

"Sangria time!" Maria announced, coming into the house carrying a big glass pitcher filled with luscious fresh fruit and white wine."

"Yes, please!" Farah turned and pulled two glasses from the cabinet.

"Where's Barbie?"

"She left, and I'm relieved," Farah said.

"That's safe to say for most of the family, but why you?"

She looked over her shoulders, making sure the kids weren't listening to them. "Ben told me the strangest thing. He said he heard his mom and grandmother fighting about them. Something about a plan that Barbie's not following. It's about money. He begged me not to send them back to the apartment."

"So those two have cooked something up. I guess the apple didn't fall far from the tree," Maria said, shaking her head. "What are you going to do?"

"Have another talk with Ben later and go from there. A couple of rotten apples are no match for us."

After ice cream cones, a run through the cold sprinklers, and cool showers, Farah asked Rebecca to hang out with Brandi while she practiced reading with Ben.

"Sure, she can spend the night in my room!" Rebecca offered, proud to help.

In Ben's room, Farah said, "I have a confession. I told a little lie when I said I want to practice reading. It can be our secret."

He smiled broadly. "I like to read."

"I know! And you're getting better every day. But I wanted to ask more questions about your mom and grandma. And I don't want you to worry about anything. We're going to protect you."

He nodded. "Okay."

"So, you said you heard your grandma tell your mom not to eat. Can you try hard and remember more about that?"

"Um, I heard gran say something like 'I'm the one who is sick but you're the one who is supposed to *look* sick and you're eating over there a lot.' Something like that."

"Huh. And what about money? You said you heard them arguing about money."

He was quiet, trying to remember. "Gran said you guys have money, and it was time my mom got some. I think because of me."

Farah stared at his beautiful little face, still pure, not tarnished by his environment yet. It was all becoming a little clearer, and the hair on the back of her neck stood up. They were going to try to extort money, and these children were their leverage. "Well, that sounds like they wanted you to spend time here, because you're family. And we help take care of you."

"Am I going to get in trouble?"

She hugged him tightly. "You're never going to get in trouble with us."

Much later, Farah looked out her window and saw Robin talking to the owners of Caramel at their car. Her head was still spinning, her body tingling with anger and anticipation. Was this all just a scheme with Barbie and her mother? Did she bring the kids into their lives to get money out of them? Was Barbie supposed to be faking an illness? The baggy clothes were starting to make sense.

After a refreshing shower, she looked at her naked body in the mirror. She knew she had the physique of a much younger woman. She didn't carry extra weight, have a stomach ravaged by stretchmarks, or saggy breasts from years of breastfeeding. She had the body most women envied. Maria and Diana remarked about it often. *The consolation prize for not having any children...unless I want to pay for them.*

Chapter 21
We Must be Creative...

Even before the chickens started welcoming a new day, Farah was sitting at the kitchen table drinking coffee, her laptop open. She quickly closed the letter she was composing when she saw Robin coming down the stairs.

"I thought *you* might need some extra sleep this morning," he said and kissed her on the top of the head.

"I'm sorry. You must have been exhausted last night. You should have told me no."

He leaned down and nibbled her ear. "No husband has ever said no."

She laughed. "I decided to get up and get a head start. Still finalizing the menu for the wedding and shower, and I haven't even figured out what I'm wearing for the big day."

He poured a cup of coffee. "I'm sure you'll look fabulous. The best dressed woman there."

"Don't say that in front of the bride." There was so much she wanted to say but could not. "I guess things are the same with Caramel."

"Yeah, I'm heading out now to give Josh a break," he said walking to the door. "I think I'll benefit from a night in the stables tonight. I could use the rest." He winked and headed out.

An hour later, Farah was out gathering eggs when Maria came out of her house with her constant companion on her hip. "I'm sorry I'm running late."

"You aren't late. I was having trouble sleeping. I thought I'd channel my energy and get a few things done."

"Were you able to talk to Ben again?"

"Yes, and you're not going to believe this."

"It's Barbie. Try to shock me."

"You're right. Those two women are going to try to get money out of us."

"Why?"

"Ben heard things like Carole telling Barbie she is supposed to look sick and have no appetite. And something like we have everything and they have nothing and if we want to see the kids we're going to pay. I think she's supposed to be faking an illness!"

"La Perra's."

"That sounded bad," Farah laughed.

"What are you going to do? Does Robin know?"

"Not yet. I've decided to wait until after Caramel gives birth. But I know what I *want* to do. I'm...researching legal guardianship. It's what's best for the kids, right?"

Maria shook her head. "She's not going to hand them over just like that."

"I know. I haven't thought it all out, and Robin needs to be on board. But I already emailed an old friend of mine who's a lawyer in family court. Carl. I asked him what I needed to do to get the ball rolling."

"Carl? Carl Crabtree? Your ex? Robin is *not* going to be on board with that."

"Leave him to me. I must use the resources I have, and Carl already said he would help."

"I bet he did" Maria said, laughing and shaking her head.

Joe walked out of the house and over to them. "Sorry my wife is a little off her game. I wore her out this morning."

"Joseph!" Maria said, turning bright red.

Farah laughed. "Something's in the air around here."

He lifted Diego from her arms then walked toward the stables. "I'll take him until breakfast."

"Are you sure?"

"Yes." He turned and blew her a kiss then walked inside.

"Alright, what about breakfast?" Maria asked.

"I already have blueberry muffins in the oven. Let's do bacon and eggs."

"Wow! You have been busy."

"You too, apparently," Farah said, nudging her good friend in the arm.

After breakfast, Farah and Maria went back to the vegetable garden and collected more lettuce, summer squash, and zucchini.

"Look at all this ripe squash! What should we do with it?" Maria asked.

"Let's make zucchini bread. We can freeze some for the shower."

"You're on top of everything," Maria said.

Farah chuckled. "Well, I've missed a couple of things. And speaking of that, I'll send Barbie a text."

> *{Farah:} Good morning. How is your mom?*

She hesitated before asking the next question.

> *{Farah:} Coming over today?*

Within seconds there was a response. It was as if Barbie was sitting, staring at her screen...waiting.

> *{Barbie:} Mom's about the same. Not sure about coming over. Not feeling so hot today and I don't mean the heat.*

Farah looked at the reply, trying to read between the lines, not trusting one word that came out of Barbie's mouth or text anymore. A day ago, she'd have told her to come over, rest in the cool of the house, and make her chicken soup. But today was different.

> *{Farah:} Well, feel better. The kids are fine.*

Barbie stared at her phone. "Well, that was odd."

Her mother, sitting across from her at the kitchen table, smoking a cigarette, asked "What's odd?"

"I told Farah that I was sick, and she didn't fall all over herself trying to help. I think Ben said something. Maybe he's heard us."

Carole inhaled sharply, "That's not so bad. It's time to get back to the plan. You're supposed to be sick, like me. You're supposed to be using that boy to get money out of these people and then you can live your life any way you want. You always said I never did anything for you. Well, I *gave* you this great plan."

"It don't seem right anymore. These are good people. They're nice to me."

Carole slammed her hand on the table, "Now don't you go soft on me. You know you don't belong there. Quit making nice with the wife with the funny name. She is just using you to fill her barren belly."

"Farah's not like that. She's not like us."

"Listen, when Farah arrived, she told Diana she couldn't have children. She didn't think she was ever going to marry and then she met Robin. She's nice to you so she can play house with the kids. *Your* kids!" Carole said, smashing her cigarette into a full ashtray. "Maybe I should have let Robin knock me up and I'd money troubles would have been long gone."

"Gross, Mom!" Barbie stood and grabbed the ashtray, making sure the cigarette was out before emptying it into the trash and running it under hot water.

Carole laughed, this time causing a coughing fit. When she caught her breath, she said, "Relax. It's not like he wanted *me*. He was ripe for sex, and I was there. But you got something better than a dick in your vagina from a horny teenager. You got a kid. A kid that's a real Robinson." She laughed again. "And thank God he don't look like Ricky."

"Ricky looked like his mom," Barbie said, sitting down again, staring at her phone, wondering if another text was coming.

"Yeah, well, she was a better-looking woman than he was a man. Now hand me my cigs. I want one more before my first client. You come down with me and help. Get your mind off those kids. The less you see them the better right now."

Carole had only met her grandchildren once before Barbie's return, when Barbie asked for her help when Brandi was born. When she saw Ben for the first time, she had the look of recognition but didn't put it together as she laid eyes on her three year old grandson. "Look at the beautiful head of hair on that one! And those eyes! Man, the daddy must have been good looking. Too good looking for you. Are you sure this kid wasn't switched at birth in the hospital?"

"Mom, he's Ricky's son. And thanks for the vote of confidence."

"Ricky who?"

"Ricky Robinson."

Carole's eyes popped. "Well, I'll be damned. Only you'd get knocked up twice by guys who died."

Touching, Barbie had thought. These weren't the first words most grandmothers would say when meeting their grandchildren for the first time. "Mother, you are so cruel!"

"Why didn't you tell me about Ricky's kid?"

"I found out right before he died. You would have told me to have an abortion. I originally planned that, but I just never got around to it."

"Yeah, well, it's a good thing you didn't stick around. The talk in that town would have been too much. Not good for business, if you know what I mean."

"Yeah, Mom, nothing I do has ever been good for business."

But Carole's tune had changed by the time Barbie arrived back in Honeysuckle. "I've been thinking about it, and I think it's high time they took responsibility for their flesh and blood. I'm not going to live forever."

"By the looks of things, you aren't going to live a month," Barbie said her first night back. "What have you got up your sleeve?"

It didn't take long to figure it out. The shop, the business, and the apartment were a mess. And there was no money.

"How have you been surviving?" Barbie asked, turning the pages of the old ledger that Carole still used. "Why isn't this stuff in the computer?"

"Computer? I never had a computer."

"And I suppose you never heard of online banking?"

"Online what?"

"Are there any savings?" Barbie asked.

"Nope. I never made that much and put it right back into the shop and paid the rent, just the way my mom did."

"Mom, I know you like your customers and all, but you could have charged a little more throughout the years. And maybe if you had updated this place, you could have attracted new customers."

"Well, listen to you, miss know-it-all. It hasn't been easy since other shops have opened…and…I don't have an updated license. I let it go some years ago."

Why am I not surprised? Barbie thought.

The building was owned by the Brickson family, who owned several buildings along Main Street. They were committed to keeping the town looking quaint and had updated the salon's storefront. And luckily for Carole, they were rich enough not to be greedy and kept the rent low. But Walter Brickson stopped by the salon soon after he heard Barbie was back. He told her that they were buying an ice cream franchise and renovating the apartment upstairs as soon as the space was available.

"That means when you kick the bucket," Barbie told her mother after his visit.

"That's why *we* must be creative, young lady. Those Robinsons got lots of money. Diana has told me Farah's got a few bucks from her dead family. She sure walks around town with her nose in the air. Of course she's too good to come in my salon. Trust me, those kids of yours are our ticket out of this."

"And how am I supposed to go about this?"

"Well, I ain't got all the answers yet, but the first thing you need to do is introduce the boy to them. There is no way they aren't going to want him at that farm. Little Brandi is the bonus. A boy and a girl. The perfect addition. We get them good and attached...and then spring it on them. We're sick. Mainly me. And I've run the business into the ground. We need money for medical expenses. You'd like to take me on a vacation before I croak. If you don't figure out a way to get some fast money you're going to have to leave with the kids and head back to Reno for a better paying job. Unless..."

Barbie laughed, "Geez. You could have written a soap opera, mother!"

Carole laughed too, "This could work!

At the time, Barbie thought it was a clever idea. As her children grew older, she was finding it harder and harder to care for them. Why not turn them over to a good family who could give them more than they could? Why not have money for a change? The minute she had met Farah, she'd hated her. Fancy clothes, fancy perfume, fancy house, fancy food...

But things have changed.

Chapter 22
A Timely Birth

On the last Sunday in June, which fittingly fell on Day Fathers's Day, Robin rushed into the house and announced the foal had been born. He was as giddy as any new father, taking Farah into his arms and twirling her around. "I've seen it dozens of times, but it never gets old." The kids gathered around, begging to go out and see. He picked up Brandi and kissed her cheek. "Let's give the mommy a little time alone with her new baby, and we can all go visit later."

Farah handed him a fresh cup of coffee. "Is it a boy or a girl?"

"It's a boy!"

"Wow, something else to celebrate today!" Farrah announced.

"While you work on the celebration, I'm going to get back out there," Robin said, putting Brandi down. He beamed at Farah again and there was a certain twinkle in his eyes. It truly was as if he was a new father. "I'll be back later. Oh, and the owners are coming over and bringing donuts. Don't worry about breakfast."

"Yeah!" The kids all squealed in unison and ran outside.

Farah and Maria decided to order ribs from town and have Emily and Rebecca bring them home after work. Then they would work on baked beans, coleslaw, and cheese biscuits. Farah had just pulled ingredients from the pantry when her phone beeped.

{Barbie:} Heard the big news! I'll come and get my kids off your hands. There must be a lot going on.

She hesitated, but there was no getting out of it.

{Farah:} Sure, come whenever you want. We're celebrating later so stay.

A week ago, Farah might have pitied her, but what a difference a week made when she arrived wearing another loose-fitting faded floral sundress. Still, she smiled and even gave her a hug as she came into the kitchen. "Hey, Barbie, good to see you. Feeling better?"

"Yeah. Where are the kids?"

"All outside. The owners brought them donuts and blue lollipops and asked them to think of a couple of names for the new arrival. They're having fun and getting big sugar highs. How did you hear about it?"

"I was picking up a few things from the grocery store and overheard someone talking about it."

"Wow, I guess this really is a big deal," Farah said.

"Yeah, well, not as good as an affair as far as gossip goes, but we'll take what we can get in this town."

Farah laughed. She hated to admit it, but she had become fond of Barbie and her quick wit and take on things.

Barbie walked to the door. "Good grief, who are all these people?"

"Oh, neighbors and the horse's owners and some of their neighbors. They're probably already thinking about selling the new little guy. In the end, it's all a business. Hopefully, he can stay with his mama here."

It's just business, Barbie thought. *The horse will go to the highest bidder. And so will the children...*

Later, Farah was upstairs in Brandi's room, putting on a new quilt they had picked out together. It was pale pink with little peonies all over. There was a matching rug and decorative pillows. She was just walking downstairs when she saw the postman's truck drive in.

"What is he doing here on a Sunday?" She opened the door, ready to intercede, but saw Robin, saying goodbye to Cal from across the road and saying hello to the mail carrier as he handed him a package. After handshakes and shoulder smacks Robin turned and looked at what he was holding. Then he looked up and saw her at the top of the porch.

He slowly walked up, "Carl? Your Ex? Now what have you gotten us into?"

"I'll fill you in later. Right now, it's a celebration!"

Downstairs, Barbie was sitting on the couch, her children standing in front of her. "These two have been filling me in on the new pony. When can I get a peek?" she asked Farah as she came downstairs.

"Um, Robin can take you out later. Along with Father's Day, we're celebrating the new foal. So...please stay for dinner," Farah said with a smile and grit teeth.

Barbie snorted. "Father's Day? We never celebrated that one in the Fletcher household. I was thinking of taking the kids home. Their granny has been missing them."

"No, Mom, we don't want to go back there. We want to stay here. We're having ribs tonight. Can we stay? Please?" Ben pleaded.

Brandi, wearing a bright a bright orange seersucker top and shorts with matching ribbons in her hair, ran over to Farah, clutching her leg. "We don't want to leave."

Barbie sat, arms folded, crossed legged, one shaking vigorously up and down. "Alright, we can stay for dinner. I see my little peanut is all dressed for a party in another new outfit. But after that, we're going home." And before she could stop herself, she said, "Me and my mom were thinking of taking the kids to Carson City to see Marcy over the 4th."

"NO! I don't want to go there!" Ben wailed.

Barbie stood and wagged a finger at him. "Now, you watch your tone young man. Your gran is not getting any healthier here. There might be better options for treatments there or in Reno. Um...Marcy is looking into a couple of options for us."

Oh my God. "Barbie, is it necessary to take the kids? What will they do there? And driving in that cramped car of yours?"

"Never mind about my car." She paused. "Unless I can borrow yours?"

Farah's mouth opened but no words came out. Brandi was still clutching her leg. Ben had moved over to her side too and she put her arm around his shoulder. "You're not on my insurance policy. But nice try."

"Such a goody two shoes, always following the rules. Anyway, I'm waiting to see how Mom feels in a couple of days."

Farah stared at her. They were in the middle of a game, and she had to play it right. She squeezed both children tightly. "Go on out and play now. I see Uncle Philip out with watermelon." Ben and Brandi hurried out. She waited a beat to give them time to get farther away. "You can see they don't want to go. Do you have to upset them like this?"

"Me? I'm their mom. A few new outfits don't change that. You should not be undermining me. I can do whatever the hell I want."

"Yes, you can. And I'm sure a long ride in a hot stuffy car to a place where there is nothing for them to do, is the right decision," Farah said before heading outside.

"Mother," Barbie hissed, looking out the window at the family gathering at the tables. "Why did I agree to this..."

Farah doesn't look like she's at a celebratory dinner, Barbie thought, watching her pick at her food with Ben and Brandi on either side. It sure didn't take long for her to turn my kids into little Robinson's, sulking and all...

No one else seemed to notice. Robin was at the other end of the table engaged in the lively conversation about the events of the day with Joe, Philip, and Josh. Maria and Diana sat across from Emily and Rebecca talking about all things wedding.

"I can't believe how fast time is flying," Emily said. "July is a few days away, the shower is in August, and then the big day just three weeks after!"

"Forget that. Who's throwing you the bachelorette party?" Barbie asked, picking up her third rib.

"What's that?" Rebecca asked.

"You never heard of a bachelorette party?"

"It's a silly tradition where men, the bachelors, and women, the bachelorettes, get together separately for a party before the wedding. Often involving too much alcohol and God knows what else," Farah said with an obvious edge in her voice.

"The 'what else' is the best part!" Barbie said. "I've seen plenty of them when I worked in the casinos. Groups of drunk women and men parading around with big fancy drinks in their hand. It's the last fling before the ring!"

"We're not into that kind of thing, right, Josh?" Emily said.

He turned his attention her way, "What?"

"You aren't having a bachelor party, right?"

"Well, um, not exactly." He looked at Robin, "We might get away on the day of the shower for the night."

"And do what?" Emily asked, her voice raising several octaves.

"Yes, what?" Farah asked.

"We thought we'd head to the rodeo in Carson City. It just happens to be the same weekend. All of us. Joe, Philip, Josh's brother and dad, the other guys in the wedding, and the boys," he said, gesturing to Joe Jr. and Ben. "I'm just making sure things are covered around here."

"Oh, that's a good rodeo. Lots of hot chicks roaming around looking for cute cowboys. Joshy here will be quite popular," Barbie said, licking her sticky fingers.

"When were you going to tell me, Josh?" Emily asked.

He shrugged his shoulders, "Now, I guess, babe. Sorry."

"It's no big deal, honey. It's a rodeo. He'll be with the old man here," Philip said.

"A bunch of old men," Joe said. "And a couple of young ones."

"I don't like the idea," Emily said, sounding more like a child than a woman.

"It's fine, honey," Maria said, reaching across the table and patting her hand. "I trust Joe Junior and Ben here to keep a close eye on things." She winked at her son.

"It's a great idea," Farah agreed. "Our High Tea will be no place for a bunch of cowboys."

"God. High Tea. I'd rather be with the boys," Barbie said.

"No girls allowed," Ben said, quieting the whole table. His anger toward his mother was palatable.

"You never know, you might enjoy a nice, refined tea party," Farah said.

"Well, that's a while away. I can't commit just yet." Barbie pushed her plate away. "Alright. kids, let's get a move on."

"What? The kids are leaving tonight?" Robin asked, standing up.

Farah stood too. "Yeah. Barbie is taking them tonight. And possibly away for a few days."

"We don't want to go," Ben said defiantly.

"Well, too bad, little cowboy. Let's go."

With that, you could have heard a pin drop. Emily stood and hurried into her house. Josh shrugged his shoulders and went after her. Diana and Maria stood and started clearing plates. Joe and Philip mumbled about getting back to check on Caramel and invited the kids in one last time for the night.

"You two don't budge!" Barbie said.

"Oh, let them go. I thought you wanted to see him. Go ahead and I'll pack some of their clothes," Farah said.

Ben and Brandi didn't wait for another word before running after everyone else.

"You sure know how to ruin a party," Rebecca said before walking toward the stables herself.

"I was thinking the same thing," Robin said, moving next to Farah.

"For the last time, I'm allowed to take my kids whenever and wherever I want!" Barbie stared at them, arms crossed, holding her ground. She had to keep the upper hand, but it was getting tough. She knew they were good people who only wanted the best for her kids, but she had her mother to worry about. It was her mother's mean, sick voice that was drowning everything else out. *"They're good and attached now. Bring the kids home and let them worry for a while. This will work well in our favor."*

Farah touched Robin's arm. "Of course you are. You can do whatever you want."

"Yeah, well, like I said, it depends on how my mom feels in a day or two."

"Then let them stay here until you know," Robin said.

Barbie was looking into his beautiful eyes, his hair, just starting to get gray streaks. His perfect wife at his side. She could hear the children in the stable, chickens clucking, dogs barking in the distance. She didn't want to leave any more than she wanted to take them. But they hadn't asked her to stay. "I promised mama." She turned and walked to the stables.

Farah wrapped her arms around his waist and watched Barbie walk to the stables. "I hate the idea of them leaving too. That's what the package in the mail was about. I have an idea."

"And I guess I'll be meeting the ex," he chuckled, kissing her cheek before heading to the stables.

"Nice new touch to the rooms," Barbie said, standing in the doorway, watching Farah lovingly put clothes in the duffle bag.

"Thank you."

"And I really do appreciate the new clothes. Brandi looks just like an orange creamsicle tonight. I haven't thanked you properly for that."

"No worries. I've also packed books and daily work pages the kids have been doing in the mornings."

"Good Lord! Ever heard of summer?"

"Yeah, well, since Ben hasn't had a regular school schedule, this has been incredibly good for him. They start school the last week of August and he's being evaluated to see what grade he'll be in. It's all arranged. Remember you asked me to do that? Well, I did. And they enjoy spending time everyday learning. So, I hope you encourage this on your little road trip. And I also hope you remember your daughter's upcoming birthday We would like to have a combined birthday with Christina. I hope you won't let her down." Farah walked up to her, shoved the duffle bag against her chest and scooted past, not waiting for another word.

Pulling up behind the salon to the stairs that led up to the apartment, Barbie thought, *now what*? There were no plans to take the kids away. There were no plans besides making Farah and Robin sweat.

"Alright, let's go," she said to the kids. She got out of the car and held the seat back for them, but they didn't budge. "C'mon Ben." He still didn't move. "I said—"

"I told Farah you and Gran are mean and all you do is fight."

"What did you say we fight about?"

"Me and money."

So he did say something. "Well, kids aren't cheap. Takes money to put food on the table and clothes on your back. Now get out of the car."

Ben reluctantly undid his seatbelt and helped Brandi with hers. They stepped out of the car, hand in hand, staring at the ground. He remembered the piece of paper in his pocket, and touched it, bringing him instant peace. Robin had written down his phone number and told him to call if he needed anything. *"Anything at all,"* Robin had said. *"Wherever you are."*

"So you really want to pursue this? Legal custody? You're not even sure he heard what he says he heard. He's just a kid," Joe said as Farah and Robin shared their plans.

"Robin might agree with you, but it makes sense. Carole is sick and by the looks of the way Barbie dresses, she is *trying* to look sick," Farah said, pouring coffee into mugs.

"So, what are the first steps?" Maria asked.

"Well, my old friend, Carl," Farah paused and glanced at Robin who had an amused look on his face. "...will represent us, but he can't represent Barbie or the kids. He can assist can help find her an attorney. Then, Child Protective Services will need to come to the house and make sure it's suitable. I think that will be the easy part." Farah smiled, touching Robin's hand.

"You can see my wife has gotten *all* of the steps covered."

"If she was planning on trying to extort money out of you, why would she agree to this?" Joe asked, shaking his head before adding, "I just used the word *extort* for the first time in my life."

Robin laughed, "To think, Joe, we just were just two country gentlemen taking care of horses a mere two months ago."

Farah slapped his arm, "We don't have all that figured out yet."

"What figured out?"

They all turned toward the staircase and saw Rebecca at the bottom.

"I thought you left for the shop with Emily," Robin said.

Rebeca walked over to the table. "Nope. She needed more time to get ready. She slept in the stable with Josh last night. She told me she was helping with Caramel and her baby, but I'm not stupid. I think they were doing things that should be kept for the wedding night."

"Let's keep that a secret," Robin said, laughing.

"So, what were you talking about?"

They looked at each other before Joe said, "If she knows what goes on after the wedding, I think she can handle this."

"If we tell you, you must keep this to yourself. You cannot let it slip out. Especially to Barbie," Farah said.

"I promise, promise, promise!"

"Alright, we want to ask Barbie if the kids can live here permanently. We would make all the decisions involving their care. Food, clothes, medical, school. Things like that," Robin said.

"Isn't that what is going on now?" Rebecca asked.

"It is, but she can still come and go with them as she pleases. It...um...makes us nervous. We like them here. And we think they like being here. These are papers from a lawyer, guiding us on how to do it legally. Don't you think they would be happy here?" Farah asked.

"Yes! They love it here. They hate that apartment and their stinky old grandmother. They say all she does is smoke and complain."

Emily burst through the back door with Diana and Philip trailing behind. "Ooh, fresh coffee!"

"Help yourself," Farah said.

"Everything alright with you and Josh this morning?" Maria asked.

"Everything is fine. Why would you ask?"

"It's just that you seemed upset last night about the boys leaving for a night."

"Oh that. I overreacted. My dad will be there. And his. And Robin and Joe. All these old guys. I don't know why I got so upset. He assured me there's nothing to worry about." She took two big sips of her coffee. "Ready, Becca?"

"I'm ready. Been ready. And don't ask me what we have been talking about cause it's a secret," she said as she rose.

"What is she talking about?" Emily asked.

"If you don't know by the time you get to work, I'll be shocked," Robin said, shaking his head as the girls headed out.

"Can we ask?" Philip said, pouring coffee.

"Uncle Philip, Aunt Diana, we have some news to share."

"What is it, honey?" Diana asked.

"We want to try to get full legal guardianship over Ben and Brandi," Robin said.

"Wow! That's big. What brought this on?" Philip asked.

"Well, we think it would be good for the kids. Much needed stability," Farah said.

"I think it's wonderful. They do need stability," Diana said. "But how are you going to get rid of Barbie?"

"She can be as big a part of their lives as she wants. But they will live here."

"Do you think she is going to agree to this? I mean, has she said eluded she doesn't want them?" Diana asked.

Farah wanted to be cautious, knowing Diana and Carole were friends. "No, not in so many words. It's Ben, that's told me there is a lot of tension in the apartment. Especially with Carole's health. We are looking into options."

"What if she wants to stay here too? Have you thought about that?" Philip asked.

"Emily's leaving. You'll have an extra room, right." Robin laughed, standing. "Just kidding."

Joe stood with him, "I can't believe Emily called us old."

"I know, like we couldn't show the lads a good time."

"But you're not, right?" Maria said.

"Hey, what happens at a rodeo stays at a rodeo," Joe said, kissing his wife on the cheek before both men hurried out the door.

Chapter 24
Unexpected Fireworks

Independence Day in Honeysuckle was as picture postcard perfect as anyone could imagine. The storefronts on Main Street were decked out in red, white, and blue bunting, flags, streamers, and balloons. There was a parade with decorated cars, the marching bands from the middle school and high school, Uncle Sam on stilts and many horses. Two regulars from Rebecca Farms adorned in patriotic colors, including red and blue ribbons woven into their manes.

After the parade, there was a celebration in the town square. Hot dogs, cotton candy, pink popcorn, chocolate covered frozen bananas, bright red candy apples, and other carnival treats were enjoyed. As well as games, including the popular dunk booth.

Farah had been in awe the first year she arrived, watching the parade, munching on popcorn, and taking in the small-town charm. This year she was apathetic about going. There had not been one word from Barbie, but then Robin gave her the news for which she'd been hoping.

"Hey, Ben just called me."

"He did? Where are they?"

"They're here. Never left. He wants us to get them."

"Sure. Let's do that."

'Well, I don't think Barbie knew he called. He said she was in the salon."

"Should I call her? I'll call her. I'll invite her to join us. I'll play dumb." Farah took her phone out of her purse.

Barbie was downstairs with Carole as she put the finishing touches and half a can of sticky hairspray on Betty Strickland's fancy updo when her phone rang. Excusing herself to the mayor's wife, she picked up the phone.

"Well, well, well," she said aloud as she read the screen. *What took you so long?* She turned toward the window, away from her mother before she answered. "Hello there! Happy Fourth!"

"Same to you," Farah said, her voice sounding a little too cheerful. "Just wondering how things are going. Um....are you in town?"

"As it turns out, we're here. Mother never felt up to a road trip."

"Well, sorry to hear that. Listen, we're heading to the parade. Were you planning to go with the kids?"

"Oh, that. I guess there's no escaping it since it passes right by the front door."

"We can come and get Ben and Brandi," Farah said eagerly.

How did I guess? Barbie sighed. "Yeah, that's not a bad idea."

"Great. We'll be there in about an hour. Please join us...if you can."

Pulling into the back of the apartment to park, Robin, Farah, and Rebecca got out of the truck. They hadn't reached even the back steps when the door flew open and Ben, in his new normal, jeans, plaid shirt, boots, and a hat raced down the stairs followed by Brandi in her little red dress, hair in pigtails with a red ribbon bouncing with each step.

They ran into the open arms of Robin and Farah. "So good to see you guys," Robin said.

"We missed you," Farah said.

"We missed you too," the children both said simultaneously.

"What about me?"

They all looked up.

Barbie slowly walked down wearing blue shorts, a red sleeveless tee shirt and her hair pulled back in a ponytail with the same red ribbon as her daughters. A strong and inviting breeze blew through the parking lot. Hot dogs were on a grill somewhere, sugary cotton candy was being spun, and popcorn was being popped. Then the faint sound of a marching band started.

"Well, sounds like it's show time! We should get our seats," Barbie said, walking away.

After the last firework had exploded in the sky, they walked back to the apartment and Ben asked, "Can we go home with Robin and Farah?"

Barbie looked down at him, holding his sister's hand with a firm grip. "Not tonight."

"C'mon. It's not fun here with you and Gran. And it's so hot!"

"That's just too—"

Then, out of nowhere, the heavens seemed to open in the form of projectile vomiting from Brandi. The contents of the afternoon came up all over the little girl and the ground beneath her. Robin, Rebecca, Barbie, and Ben backed away as quickly as they could.

Farah knelt as little girl burst into tears. "It's okay, honey."

And Barbie said, "Yeah, go ahead and take them."

"Can I come in and get her cleaned up a little?" Farah asked.

Barbie grunted. "I guess so."

Entering the dimly lit apartment, Farah caught her breath. It was like nothing she had ever seen. Deep rooted cigarette odor, peeling wallpaper, a worn dirty carpet, stained lampshades on two old lamps and a whirling fan over the small kitchen table that shook and made ticking sounds as it spun. That was where Carole was sitting, smoking a cigarette. She wasn't faking death. It was closing in on her. This was no place for Ben and Brandi.

"Well, well, well. Look what we have here. Farah Robinson in the flesh after all these years. The beautiful out of towner that turned ole Robin from confirmed bachelor to married man and here you are. To what do we owe the pleasure?"

"Hello, Mrs. Fletcher. Brandi had an accident downstairs. I came to change her." She had a tough time not staring at the woman her husband had lost his virginity to.

"Yeah, I can smell her from here." She waved her hand in front of her nose. "Even my smoke isn't hiding the stench."

"Room's right here," Barbie said, pointing to a door. "Bathroom right next to it. Can't miss it."

Farah led Brandi into the bathroom and carefully pulled her soiled dress over her head. "Feeling better, baby?" Brandi nodded yes, and Farah ran a washcloth under cool water and gently wiped her face and hands. "Now let's find something to put on and we'll be on our way."

Farah could hear Barbie and her mother arguing in loud whispers, Carole was upset the kids were leaving. She quickly dressed Brandi in pajamas and grabbed the pile of clothes that were lying on the bed and stuffed them into the duffle bag. They looked like both children's clothes, but she didn't bother to sort, planning on throwing them all in the washing machine.

Back in the family room, Farah asked for a plastic bag for the dress. "I'll take it home and wash it."

"Knock yourself out," Barbie said, handing her a bag at arm's length.

"Okay then. I'll call you tomorrow, and let you know how she's doing," Farah said.

"She'll be fine, won't you, peanut?" Brandi nodded again, hiding behind Farah.

"Come and give Granny a kiss," Carole said, putting her cigarette out in a full ashtray.

But Brandi didn't budge.

"Get over here!" Carole barked.

Farah grabbed Brandi's hand and walked her over. "Kiss your grandma goodnight, honey."

Up close Carole looked worse. Her skin was gray, her hair also gray and wiry. The skin on her thin arms hung loose, her fingernails permanently stained yellow. Brandi reluctantly leaned in and kissed Carole's wrinkled cheek. Farah wanted to gag and was thankful Brandi didn't.

Farah turned to leave, but then remembered, "And oh, the birthday party is next weekend for Brandi and Christina. I'm going to teach you how to make cupcakes, remember?"

Carole laughed, unlodging phlegm from her lungs. "This I got to see."

"And of course, you're invited, Carole."

"That's kind of you. I've never been out that way. I've cut all the Robinson's hair through the years, but this is my first invite."

Chapter 25
Cake and Confessions

Farah was feeling nostalgic, piping pink and purple buttercream onto cupcakes for Brandi and Christina's birthday party. *Just like riding a bike.* Pink and purple were the colors of the day, including balloons tied all around the porch, a princess jump house, and a Sno-Cone machine.

"It's not every day we have a giant castle in front of the farm," Robin said coming in the kitchen. "I've let neighbors know what's going on."

"That's a great idea."

"Is all of this necessary?" he asked.

"Yes! I'm sure Brandi has never had a birthday party. And Five is a big year. It's for Christina too. It's for all the kids," Farah said.

"Well, be careful because you've set the bar high for the rest of the kids when their birthdays roll around." Robin gave her a quick kiss before heading out. "A mere country gentleman," he laughed as he walked through the door.

Farah laughed too, knowing she was going overboard, considering the many times she complained behind her own customers' back at their elaborate orders for children. But these children deserved a little spoiling after Farah saw how they were living on the 4th.

By two o'clock, the party was in full swing with children in party hats running around everywhere. Tiaras for the girls and crowns for the boys. Josh and Philip had a gentle Morgan named Kelsey out, giving children rides in the arena. Robin and Joe were at the barbecue grills taking hot dog and hamburger orders while neighbors and friends gathered around sipping on beer or iced tea. Maria, Diana, and Emily were at the pink and purple decorated picnic tables helping with fruit, macaroni salad, and chips, while Farah watched the kids in the jump house and Rebecca handed out cherry snow cones.

Barbie and Carole arrived fashionably late, carrying two carefully wrapped packages topped with bright pink bows. Barbie looked like she had taken more time with herself, wearing a pair of white capri pants and a pink tee shirt. Farah even noticed shiny gloss on her lips. *The sick routine must be over. Now what?*

"Sorry I haven't been around to help. My mother is not doing well," Barbie said to Farah when she joined her on the porch with a beer.

"No worries. I have plenty of help here. You look nice today."

"Thanks! I was picking up supplies for Mom and she told me to get a few things for myself. I guess that's her way of saying thanks. Not natural for her. Maybe she knows something I don't know..."

"You mean about her health?"

"Yeah," Barbie said, taking a sip of beer. "Maybe she wants me to enjoy what little there is before she kicks."

Farah wanted to pick her brain about the apartment and Barbie's plans after Carole died. But this wasn't the time to tell her she had already contacted the owner of the property, and that she had made him an offer he was mulling over.

It took some convincing when she brought the idea up to Robin after seeing the apartment. "When does that brain of yours stop?" he'd asked, lying in bed with her, his finger circling her bellybutton. "I didn't know I was marrying such a conniver."

She chuckled. "It's the perfect solution. We offer to renovate the apartment. On a strict budget, of course. If she works, she can stay and pay the same rent her mother has been paying."

His finger traveled down running back and forth along her panty line. "We're *still* essentially buying her off. And she's never mentioned money, babe. Maybe Ben has stretched a little." He let his fingers travel further, hoping to get her mind elsewhere before adding, "And maybe you are hearing what you want to hear."

She stopped his hand and playfully said, "Now who's conniving to get what he wants. I don't think Ben made this up. And if he did, well, after seeing the apartment, I can't blame him. This way Barbie has a chance to work and live in a nice space and get to know herself. And she's not here."

"That's worth every penny," he winked, pulling her on top of him.

Though no one was in a hurry to leave, enjoying Robin's and Farah's hospitality and a break from their ordinary routines, the guests started clearing out by 7:00. After Brandi and Christina opened more presents than they had ever seen, ate cupcakes, and passed out goodie bags to all their guests, both girls fell asleep on the couch still wearing their tiaras before Robin and Joe carried them to their beds.

Barbie had been drinking beer all afternoon, and Farah insisted she stay the night with her mother. "Wow, you, my mom, and Robin in the same house!" Barbie said, helping Farah clean up the kitchen when the last of the guests had left.

"Ha, Ha. She'll be with Diana. They have a downstairs bedroom," Farah said, pouring a glass of white wine and heading outside, collapsing on a chair on the back porch.

Maria joined Farah after she put Diego to bed and the two women sat in blissful silence. The sun was setting, and the little white lights on the gazebo and around the porch of the house started to shimmer.

"Thanks for all of your help today," Farah said to Maria, squeezing her arm.

"Oh, my goodness! Thank *you*. You're so good to my children. Christina has never had a party like this."

"I guess I went little overboard." Farah laughed.

"Well, we all benefitted. You've got to stop spoiling us." Maria got up. "Want another glass of wine?"

"Sure," Farah said.

"I got it!" Barbie called from inside. "Sit down, Maria." Barbie came out with the bottle of wine and glass for Maria in one hand and another beer in the other. She filled both of their glasses before plopping down hard on chair. "Whoa, what a day!"

"Tired, are we? Must be exhausting being you," Maria said.

"Hey, I did my time with the jump house. Dealing with all those sweaty kids and Rebecca took its toll."

Maria saw Joe come out of one of the stables heading home and she stood up. "You are an odd woman, Barbie." She kissed Farah on the cheek. "I'll see you in the morning."

"Yeah, better get home so your Mexicali horse whisperer can whisper a few things in your ears," Barbie said, taking a long sip of beer.

Maria scoffed and laughed, slapping her knee. "*Eres horrible.*"

When they were alone, Barbie said, "My mom enjoyed today."

"That's great. I'm sure your kids enjoyed seeing her...outside the apartment."

Barbie took another swig of beer. "So listen, I need to come clean about something."

Farah swallowed hard. "What is it?"

Barbie sighed, "I wish I were a better mom. I don't seem to have any...instinct for it."

"You've done okay."

"Maybe. At times. I think the one good thing I've done is bring them to you." She sighed again, heavily. "I came back because my mom asked me to. I had not decided anything about the kids yet. Soon after, I saw what a disaster I walked back into. She's sick, broke, the salon is a wreck and, well, you've seen the apartment. After I was there a couple of weeks, we...well mainly her..." She took another sip. "This is hard."

Farah was on the edge of her seat, not moving, hardly breathing. "What is hard?"

"We thought we might get some money out of you. In exchange for time with the kids. She told me to pretend I was sick. She don't have to pretend, as you can see."

"So what? You want to charge us a fee to spend time with them?"

"Sounds bad when you put it like that, don't it?"

"Sounds pretty bad," Farah agreed. "And when was this going to start? And how?"

Barbie scoffed. "The Fletcher women might have a few street smarts but that's about it." Barbie picked at the label of her bottle. "I look at Ben, and I see Robin. I mean I should see Ricky, but I see Robin, and this place, and somewhere I'll never belong. Then I look at Brandi and I see Bobby, the one guy I could have been happy with. And poof! He was gone."

Farah should have been livid, but she felt compassion. "You've had your share of crappy breaks."

"Yeah, but still, you've grown on me. And I know my kids are better off here. But I don't want your money anymore. My mom don't know that yet. Maybe a night here will rub off on her too."

Farah stood, leaned down, and gave her a hug, feeling the tears rolling down her cheeks.

"Whoa, whoa," Barbie said, laughing and pushing her off and standing up, unsteady on her feet. "I think I've said too much. I need to go to bed."

Farah guided her up the stairs, and at the top of the landing said, "I'm sorry you felt you couldn't have been honest about Ben from the beginning. He would have been loved and welcomed...and I'm sure you would have too."

Barbie swayed back and forth. "That might be true, but then I would have never met Bobby McGee, and there would never have been a Brandi."

Chapter 26

The Morning After...

"**W**ow! I can't believe she told you all that," Robin said, pulling on his boots the next morning."

"I guess I fell asleep before you came in. Where were you?"

"Oh, you know, checking on the horses I guess."

"You mean hiding from Carole."

He laughed. "I said hello."

"Anyway, Barbie was pretty drunk. I wonder what she'll remember. We should tell her about *our* plan as soon as she's up to it."

"Doesn't that change things now that she's not going after our money?"

"Well, It's still a positive solution for her. She *does* need income and that apartment *desperately* needs an overhaul. I can't imagine the children spending one more minute there."

"Let's try not to insult them. A person's home is their castle...or something like that."

"You wouldn't put one of your horses in that castle."

He chuckled and walked to the door. When he opened it, Brandi stood there and he picked her up. "What's going on, sweetie? Do you feel okay?"

"I feel okay, but my mom is snoring really loud and it smells in there. Can I come in?" she asked quietly.

"Of course you can," Farah called from the bed, holding her arms out as Robin handed her off. "You get under the covers with me for a while."

"Ugh," Farah said as she made her way over to the coffee pot, pouring a big cup, the house looking like the aftermath of a big party, inside and out.

A few minutes later, Maria came in and put Diego on the couch, then walked toward Farah, who was holding out a cup of coffee for her. "Thanks. What's for breakfast?"

"Let's do frittatas. I'll go gather eggs in a few minutes." She looked back toward the stairs. "You're not going to believe this, but Barbie spilled the beans last night. She *was* planning to get money out of us."

"What did she say?" Maria asked, wide eyed.

"Well, it wasn't a well-designed plan, but they were going to ask for money in return for time with the kids. Poor Brandi came in our bed trying to get away from her snoring...and odor. She had too much to drink so her memory might not be that clear."

They drank their coffee in silence. "Well, I guess I'll..." Farah started before they heard loud footsteps upstairs, a door open, a door slamming and then the obvious sound of retching. "It's going to be a long day."

When they gathered around the picnic tables for a late breakfast, the only two people not present were the two overnight guests.

"Where's Barbie?" Diana asked.

"She's sleeping next to the toilet," Rebecca said, putting a piece of frittata on her plate.

"What does that mean?"

"Well..." Rebecca started.

Farah broke in. "I got this." She looked over at Ben, engrossed in a conversation with Joe Jr. "She's sick. She had a little too much beer yesterday," she said quietly. "Where's Carole?"

Just as she asked that, Carole came out of Philip and Diana's house and walked gingerly down the front steps over to the table. She looked around and whistled. "Is it a holiday or something?"

"No, just Sunday morning," Philip said.

"Yeah, I heard you people spend a lot of time together. Where's my daughter?"

"Asleep in the bathroom," Rebecca blurted.

"What?"

"It seems she had a little too much to drink yesterday," Diana said gently.

Carole snorted. "Chip off the ol' block."

"She's probably going to be sleeping it off for a while," Farah said.

"Well, shit. I didn't want to be here all day," Carole said.

"I can take you into town. I'm heading there in a little while," Emily said to everyone's relief. "Josh and I are meeting with the pastor today."

"That's kind of you. I'll take you up on it." She looked down at her grandchildren. "I can take the kids off your hands if you want."

"No!" Ben called from the other end.

"Don't sass me, young man," Carole croaked, bringing the table to an eerie silence.

Robin stood up. "Let them stay here, Carole." He looked around, the eerie silence lingered, but all eyes were upon him. He felt oddly exposed as she stared up at him, feeling all of eighteen again. "Just let them stay until their mother surfaces," he said hurrying towards the stables.

Carole coughed. A deep, wet cough, killing everyone's appetite. Forks hit plates, and plates were pushed forward. Joe was next to excuse himself from the table, followed by Philip, and soon the children started departing one by one.

"I'm just going to get ready, Carole. We can leave in a half hour if you want," Emily said rising from the table, grabbing a stack of plates.

"Yeah, fine. I guess I can see I won't be missed," Carole said.

I'm sorry, Carole. I'll apologize for Robin too. It's just that we have all gotten attached to the children," Farah said.

"Forget about it. I ain't thin skinned. I told Barbie you'd take a liking to those kids. I knew they would pay off at some point."

Barbie sat by the window in her room and listened to the conversation float up. Unfortunately, the aromas from breakfast were also floating up, making her nausea worse.

My big mouth mother. Her head was pounding as she tried to piece together her conversation with Farah last night. *Did I confess to everything? How did she react?* She climbed back into the fluffy bed and pulled up the bedding. *Might be the last time I'm ever in it,* she thought as she drifted back to sleep.

When she opened her eyes again, it was nearing 2:00 PM. Her headache and nausea were gone, replaced with hunger pains. As she walked downstairs, she could hear children talking. They were all seated at the kitchen table working on a puzzle.

"Hey, Mom," Ben said when he saw her, then quickly went back to his section.

"Hey. Where's Farah?"

"Outside," he answered, head down.

Barbie walked out back to find Farah sitting on the same chair as last night, reading a book. "Hey," she said as she sat down next to her.

"Hey back," Farah closed her book. "How are you feeling?"

"Better. Sorry."

"We've all been there once...maybe even twice."

"Yeah. I guess. If I'm remembering things correctly, we were talking right here at the end of the night?"

"We were. Do you remember what about?"

Barbie stared straight ahead. "Not word for word. Want to fill me in?"

"Sure. A little later. Robin wants to be part of the conversation."

Barbie looked at Farah. "Why do I feel like I'm in trouble?"

Farah laughed. "You're not in trouble. We just have an idea we'd like to talk about. It's about the kids. We think it's a little better than your plan."

*My plan...*Barbie mouthed, looking straight ahead. She could hear her kids talking and laughing, happy and content. *Turned out to be a pretty good plan.*

Chapter 27
A Lot to Think About

Robin and Farah sat across from Barbie and her mother in a booth at Sam's. Farah and Barbie sat on the inside, with Robin and Carole sitting on the outside, both looking like they were ready for a quick escape. It was another warm morning that would be turning into a stifling hot afternoon, and the three overhead fans were whirling away on high, circulating the last of the cool morning air.

Bev came to take their orders, and they all just asked for coffee. "We have that pie you like, Barbie," she offered.

"No, just coffee today. Too hot to eat," she answered.

"Okay, gang. Let me know if you change your mind."

"Well..." Robin cleared his throat. "Let's just get to it. The reason we asked you here is..." He looked at Farah for strength, seeming to have lost all of his, staring across the table at the woman he once found so desirable. Though now she was a shell of her former self.

"We're waiting..." Carole said.

There was a pause as Bev put four mugs of coffee and a bunch of creamers on the table. "Let me know if I can get you anything else."

"First of all, we want you to know how blessed we feel to have Ben and Brandi in our lives. They have become part of the family," Farah said.

"Well, I'm happy about that too," Barbie said, watching a steady stream of sugar pour into her cup like a waterfall, feeling her mother's jittery leg against her thigh.

"Just get to it," Carole said.

This time Farah cleared her throat. "We want the kids full time...with us."

Carole slammed her hand down on the table, rattling everyone's cup. "I knew it! I knew that was what this was about."

"Mother!" Barbie said. "Let me handle this. What do you mean full time?"

"Well, we would like legal guardianship of them."

"WHAT!" Barbie and Carole cried at once.

"You want to get rid of me?" Barbie added. "Is this because if what I told you the other night?"

"What did you tell them?" Carole asked her daughter.

"Hear us out," Robin said. "We're not trying to cut you out of their lives. But...you have...issues that we don't have."

"We want to be able to make the decisions involving their health, schooling, welfare...everything," Farah paused. "I mean, we have been doing a lot of this already. This agreement will...protect us."

"From what?" Barbie asked.

"From you leaving and taking them away," Farah said softly.

"Money isn't everything," Carole broke in.

"Oh really? You weren't going to try to extort money out of us to see them?" Farah asked.

Barbie and Carole looked down at their coffees.

Carole looked at her daughter and spoke with gritted teeth. "You and your big mouth."

"It was who Ben brought it to my attention. He overheard you fighting, and it was always about money. And then, yes, you confirmed it the other night after the birthday party, Barbie."

Carole sighed heavily, "Well, Barbie. I mean I'm happy for the kids and all but we're still screwed."

"Actually, we have come up with a solution," Farah said, leaning forward. "First of all, I've talked to Walter Brickson, and Robin and I have offered to pay for a renovation of your apartment. Barbie, you can live there with no rent increase for the next two years...if you work. He mentioned an ice cream franchise replacing the salon after..."

"After I'm dead," Carole said and snorted.

"But you can work anywhere. That's part of the agreement. It will be good for you. It will be good for your kids to see you working. And you can be as big a part of their lives as you want. But..."

"But they won't live with me anymore?"

"They would not," Farah said.

"Will they still call me Mama?"

"Of course they will! We're not trying to take your place."

"The hell you're not!" Carole said.

"Mother! Pipe down. I need to think. How is this all supposed to happen?"

"You are considering this?" Her mother scoffed.

"We have a lawyer who will help us with the process," Farah intervened quickly.

"A lawyer? We need a lawyer?"

"Yes, to do it legally," Robin said.

"Do we need to go to court?"

"Yes, we will be going to court. And there is more to it," Farah said.

"Wow. I've never even met a lawyer before. That's something. How did you find him?"

"That's not important right now," Robin said, rubbing his temples.

Farah touched his arm measuredly. "I told you about him. He's...an old friend. Carl Crabtree."

Barbie's eyes widened. "Carl? Your ex who got engaged to your dead sister?"

"The one and only," Robin said.

Barbie laughed. "Boy. Sitting here we got two women who have been with Robin and soon I might be in the room with two men that have been with Farah. What are the odds?"

"I need a cigarette," Carole said angrily, sliding out of the booth before adding, "This is already wrapped up with the big bow as far as I can tell."

"And I need the restroom," Robin said sliding out of the booth.

As they hurried away, Farah said, "Barbie, you'll be getting your own lawyer. Carl can't represent you, but he will help find you one. Unless you know someone."

The two women looked at each other and laughed before Barbie said, "I can't afford a lawyer, you know that."

Farah grabbed her hand. "Robin and I will take care of it."

"I don't need my own lawyer. I trust you."

Farah shrugged. "It's the way the laws work. And it's for your own protection." She paused before asking, "What do you think?"

"I don't know. I really thought I wanted a break from them. I really thought I'd hate you all. But I don't. I like you, and I like seeing how the kids are changing. I don't think I want to miss it."

"Barbie, I didn't think I'd like you either. But I do. It might be easier if I didn't."

"Well, I got a lot to think about."

"Carl sent me the paperwork. It's quite a process and will take months. You can start looking it over, and I'll arrange a conversation with Carl. Whatever you need," Farah said as Robin came back.

"Well, where are we?"

"Barbie is going to start looking over the paperwork, right?"

"Right."

"Fine. Let's get going," he said, getting his wallet out of his pocket.

"I could eat a piece of pie now. If that's okay," Barbie said, waving Bev over.

"Some of us have work," he said.

"Just a little while longer," Farah said, touching his arm.

"I'll take some pie now with a scoop of ice cream," Barbie called to Bev.

"Alright, hon. Any other takers?" she asked.

"Maybe Mama," Barbie looked out the door.

"Oh, we just had a ciggy together and she told me to tell you she was heading home. Something about having enough of her walk down memory lane for one day," Bev said, shrugging her shoulders. "So...no other takers?"

"Unless you've got whiskey, no," Robin said.

Chapter 28
No, Tomato-y!

Barbie watched the assembly line in the kitchen from the couch. Farah, Diana, and Marie were filling small mason jars with the bright red preserves.

"What are those for?" she asked, holding several sheets of legal-sized paper, with another large stack next to her on the couch.

"It's tomato jelly for wedding favors," Farah smiled, holding up a jar. "We've ordered stickers with Emily and Josh's names and the wedding date to go around them."

"Lordy. Only you." The children were running in and out and up and down the stairs, in constant motion. *Isn't this bothering anyone else but me,* she wondered. "Maybe I should take this stuff home and look over it. It's so loud around here. I can't concentrate."

"I don't want the paperwork leaving the house," Farah said. "Remember, you have a meeting with your lawyer, with Eden Green tomorrow morning, and then we follow up with both Carl and Eden together in the afternoon. He can go over anything we don't understand."

"You can go over to my place," Maria offered.

"Huh, maybe." The truth was Barbie wasn't going to understand it. Words, words, and more words. Words like *relinquishing, sole custody, parental rights.* Words she had only heard on Court TV, not in real life.

Furiously puffing on a cigarette when Barbie had returned to the apartment after the meeting at Sam's, Carole had screamed, "I should have known you'd mess up having a Robinson heir. You had the ticket out of here! Two tickets! And now all we get is a coat of fresh paint and *you* have to get a job. This whole thing backfired because you fell for a Farah. The whole family did, starting with Robin." Carole smashed her cigarette into the full astray and stood, mumbling as she walked toward her bedroom. "What the hell kind of name is that anyway..."

"There was no *real* plan mother. But we sure could have plead insanity when they took us to court for extortion." Barbie chuckled at this, but the response from her mother was the loud slam of her bedroom door.

Barbie sighed, looking at the professionally prepared papers on her lap. There weren't as many as she would have thought, but even fewer pages didn't make them easier to understand. *Maybe this was all a trick. Maybe Farah was the evil mastermind and this whole place was under her spell. It was unnaturally happy around here all the time. Not that I got anything to compare happiness too,* Barbie thought, looking at Farah, who caught her eye as she returned from the pantry.

"Everything alright, Barbie?"

"Peachy."

"No, tomato-y," Farah said, laughing.

Barbie groaned. "That was bad, even for you."

"Listen to this," Emily said as she flew in the back door.

"Don't say anything!" Rebecca said running in behind her.

"What is going on girls?" Farah asked.

"Rebecca got asked out on a date!" Emily said.

"A date?" Farah asked.

"Yes, every afternoon at three o'clock she walks over to the PW and gets us sodas. She used to complain about it, but lately she can't wait to go. And today I found out why. Gabe."

"Oh, Gabe. He seems like a good guy," Maria said.

"I'm not sure I know who that is. Is he respectable?" Farah asked and winked at a blushing Rebecca.

"He's nothing to worry about. He's like her," Barbie said absently, sliding the papers back inside the manilla envelope.

"What? You mean kind, smart, and funny?" Maria asked.

"I know what she means," Rebecca said, turning toward Barbie. "She means retarded."

They all glared at Barbie.

"What? I'm just saying he's cool. He bags my groceries nice. Steady employment is a good thing."

"You should try it," Maria said.

"Ha, ha."

"Anyway, what about this date?" Farah asked.

"He wants to take me to the movies this Saturday afternoon. He says he can come and pick me up from the store, and his dad will drive us to the theatre. He's going to get a ticket but not sit with us. And then he will drive me home. But I'm not kissing him on the first date," Rebecca said, looking closely at the jars of jelly, trying to hide her embarrassment.

"That sounds lovely," Diana said, stacking cooled jars into a box. "I know his parents. Good family. They're all invited to the wedding."

"Well, we have to check with Robin," Farah pointed out, "but I'm sure there'll be no problem."

Rebecca sighed and rolled her eyes, "He's going to ask a million questions. He'll want to go."

Farah laughed. "I'm sure that won't be the case. He'll be excited for you. His little girl on her first date."

"He's my brother!"

"You know what I mean. He's a big brother with fatherly tendencies."

"Tomato jelly. Didn't we have that at that place we stopped for lunch on the way to see MaryAnn? Her box, anyway," Barbie asked, putting her papers aside and joining the group in the kitchen.

"We did, smartass. Here, taste it," Farah said, pushing a jar toward her with a bowl of crackers. "Let me know if it's as good."

She dipped a cracker in the jar and popped it in her mouth. The tart taste exploded on her tongue. "Yeah, not bad." She licked her fingers. "Well, I gotta head out soon and pick up something for Mama for dinner."

"Do you have any questions about the paperwork?" Farah asked. "Should we make a list of questions for Carl? He thinks you and Eden will be a good fit."

Everyone was staring at her. "Does the entire farm know what's going on? I mean I expected Maria here to be in on it since you two are joined at the hip, but Diana and these two blabbermouths?"

"Hey!" Emily and Rebecca said in unison.

Farah hesitated. "Well, sorry. We do share everything. Like I said, we have already come to think of them...and *you* as family."

"Yeah, well, this is a lot of family to get used to. And I don't even know what we're going to tell the kids. If I decide to do this, I mean."

"We'll talk to the kids together," Farah said. "Let's get through the meetings with Eden and Carl first."

"Alright then. I'll say goodbye and be on my way."

"Hey, let me get you some leftover fried chicken for you and your mom," Diana said. "This way you don't have to stop."

"Yes, and I have a few things in the freezer. And take a jar of jelly and I'll make you a fresh salad," Farah said, not waiting for an answer but going straight to the fridge.

"This should get you by for a couple of days," Farah said as she walked Barbie out to her car.

"Are you all really this nice or is this part of you buying me off? First with a new apartment and now with food. That's what my mom thinks anyway." Barbie chuckled, embarrassed, staring at the ground.

Farah put her hands on Barbie's shoulders. "We really are this nice. You should have tried to get to know us before you cooked up that half-baked plan with your mother."

"Well, the fully baked plan has me a little freaked out."

Farah pulled her into a hug. "I know. That's why we are starting with the meetings, so you fully understand. We want you to be happy," Farah said, releasing her embrace. "Be here by 10:30 tomorrow and remember, it's a Zoom call, so...think about what you are wearing. Eden and Carl will be able to see you. First impressions matter."

"What do I need to make a good impression for? I'm the one signing them over to you. You're the one that needs to make a good impression. Oh, wait. You already did."

Chapter 29
Zoom to the Rescue

Farah was pacing the floor in the dining room where they would conduct the Zoom meetings when Barbie drove up. She was pleased to see Barbie wore the outfit she'd worn on the Fourth, with her hair pulled back into a neat ponytail. She greeted her at the door and said, "You look great. Thanks for taking this seriously."

"Actually, I was waiting for you to call and tell me what to wear." Barbie chuckled, walking past her into the dining room.

"Ha, ha. Did you write down questions for your lawyer?"

"I was hoping you could sit in with me. I know you're full of questions."

"I can't. That would be a conflict of interest."

"Oh God, all these big terms." Barbie sighed.

"Just take lots of notes, and don't be afraid to ask questions. You'll be great."

"Where will you be?"

Farah looked at her watch. "I'm going upstairs," she said before giving her a quick hug.

"Hello, Ms. Fletcher. My name is Eden Green, and I've been asked to help you with—"

"Yeah, yes, I know why you are here. You can call me Barbie."

"Alright…Barbie…"

Barbie stared at the woman on the other side of the screen. She was in her twenties, her own dark hair pulled back like Barbie's, wearing a white blouse and dark jacket. "My goodness you are young! Am I your first client?"

"I assure you, I've passed the bar and am prepared to represent you."

"Okay, tell me, tell me. Are you in your full business suit or are you wearing a pair of shorts or something and slippers? I always wonder about news people when you can only see half of them."

"I'm in my full suit...but because I walk on my lunch break, I have tennis shoes on. Now, can we please get to your case?"

"Sure, sure, whatever you say."

For the next thirty minutes, Farah paced at the top of the stairs, fingers crossed, and listened while Eden and Barbie talked. It went as smoothly as she could have hoped. They discussed the proposed terms for the guardianship; including where the children would live, Robin and Farah taking over the children's financial responsibilities, health decisions, education decisions and daily schedules.

"In return, the Robinsons have generously agreed to remodel your apartment and keep the rent the same for two years," Eden said.

"Yeah, that's great and all, but Eden, let me tell you, the room I'm sitting in now is just about as big as my entire place."

Farah covered her mouth and chuckled.

Eden cleared her throat. "And you'll have to have meaningful employment."

"Now wait a sec! I didn't know it had to be meaningful." Barbie chuckled.

Farah chuckled at this too.

"And you have to agree on a visitation schedule."

"Yeah, that seems like a bit much. And I don't like the fact that they can't stay with me more often," Barbie said.

Farah sighed.

"Well, it looks like they don't want the kids there because of your mother's smoking...and other reasons."

"Right. Yeah, they don't think my mom is a good influence. They're right. But it's going to be weird. At least in the beginning."

"And it's good that we're talking about this. And I'm reading that the schedule is strictest during the school year, and more flexible in the summer months," Eden offered.

"Yes, I read that too. And speaking of school, I would like to be involved in the education stuff. Well, not math, but other stuff. I want to see the report cards too and go to the open houses."

She replied, "Alright, we will make sure your wishes about that are included. Anything else?"

"Uh, well, yeah, I definitely want to be in the loop with health stuff. I mean, just cause they're paying for everything doesn't mean I don't want to know about it. I can sit with them when they need shots sometimes and the tooth fairy *can* come to my house occasionally, ya know."

"We will let all parties know about that, including the tooth fairy," Eden said with a slight giggle, trying to keep her emotions out of this, as she feverishly typed on her keyboard.

By now Farah was sitting at the top on the stairs, grateful for Eden's patience.

"Do you have any more questions?" Eden finally asked and Farah held her breath.

"Oh, well, Eden, I guess not. Just add that stuff for now. Farah said she wasn't going to listen. She said something about a conflict, but I just bet she was so worried I'd mess this up that she couldn't help herself. She probably took my notes for me."

"Barbie," Farah hissed.

"I didn't hear a thing," Eden said and ended the session.

"How'd I do?" Barbie asked after Farah bounded down the stairs and stopped at the dining room entrance.

"You did great. And you asked all the right questions. We really do want you to be a part of the family. You have done a wonderful job with Ben and Brandi under some tough circumstances. We want to make things easier for you."

"And you finally get to be the mom you've always wanted to be."

"I do love being a 'mom-figure' in their lives, yes. But I'll be happy to send the tooth fairy your way."

Barbie whistled as Farah came down the stairs, "Boy howdie, this a quite change from this morning. And you smell good. Is this smella-vision?" She had just come back after leaving for a few hours.

Farah wore a sleeveless white linen blouse, accentuating her bronzed summer arms, her curly hair pulled back in a soft ponytail, accentuating gold hoop earrings. "Go and splash some cool water on your face," she urged as Robin came in from the stables. "Carl is calling in thirty."

"He doesn't care what I look or smell like. It's you he can't wait to see. Doesn't the little woman look great, Robin?" Barbie asked.

"Knock it off. Now let's get questions together while we have the time," Farah said.

"I'm going to shower," Robin announced, heading upstairs.

"Oh, you got nothing to worry about. I've seen his picture. You win, cowboy," Barbie laughed.

Robin came into the dining room just before 4:00, freshly showered, wearing a white button-down shirt. He pulled the glass doors closed, leaving children with big curious eyes wondering what was going on.

"This should be interesting. Your ex and your husband face to face," Barbie said, clapping her hands together.

"Let's just stick to the subject," Farah said.

Three minutes later they were all looking at Carl and Eden, live and (sort of) in person.

"Farah! So good to see you again. You haven't changed a bit!" He beamed.

"Very good to see you too, Carl. We appreciate your helping with this. This is my husband, Robin." She put her hand on his shoulder.

Robin held up his hand and waved. "Hi, Carl."

Farah turned the other way. "And this is Barbie."

"Hello, Barbie! I've heard a lot about you," Carl said.

"And I've heard a lot about you too! All good, Carl," Barbie said, looking closely at him. That same strange feeling ran through her, just like the first time she saw his picture. *Had they met somewhere?*

Carl cleared his throat. "So, Farah got in touch with me a few weeks back and asked for some information...about what it would take for her and Robin to assume legal guardianship of your two children."

"That is why we're here, right?" she said.

"Right. And I told them you would need your own lawyer. You had a talk with Eden this morning and she's joining us this afternoon."

"Yeah, what did she say about me?"

"I can hear and see you, you know," Eden said.

"She said you are...funny and...interesting. Right. Eden?"

"Those were my words."

"In other words, she thinks I'm crazy."

"Barbie!" Farah and Robin said in unison.

Carl laughed nervously. "Barbie, I assure you that is not the case. Farah has filled me in on your...circumstances, and we all want to work together."

"What has she told you?" Barbie asked.

"That things haven't always been easy for you. This seems like a workable solution for you to get back on your feet, while being a big part of the children's lives.

"Could this thing be temporary?"

Farah and Robin spoke at once. "No!"

"Until they're eighteen," Carl said.

"It would be too confusing for them otherwise," Farah said, touching Barbie's arm. "We want them to know where home base will be and... that's here of course."

"And they're being very generous financially," Carl said.

"If I get a job. Yeah, Eden and I went over that part, right Eden?"

"That's right," she said.

"Barbie, considering what you and your mother had up your sleeve..." Robin started.

"Oh, the handsome husband speaks. Here's where we play good cop/bad cop, Carl." Barbie looked over at Robin. "He really is a looker, isn't he, Carl? It must be weird for you two, sitting here, staring at each other."

"Barbie, please," Farah pleaded.

This time Eden did giggle.

"Alright, let's get on with it. Yeah, I'll do it. Probably." She rubbed her temples. "I just don't want them to think I don't want them."

"We will talk to them together in simple terms they can understand," Farah said. "We won't even talk about the legal stuff until they're older. And of course, you are welcome here."

Robin quickly added, "On the agreed schedule."

"See? He's bad cop, Carl," Barbie said, slapping the table.

"Well, a visitation schedule is common," Carl said, wiping his forehead with a tissue.

"I know. I went over all of this with Eden too. And I added some stuff."

"What stuff?" Robin asked.

"Very simple stuff. And the schedule doesn't have to be that strict," Farah said, grabbing her husband's leg. "But Robin is right. It would be better for Ben and Brandi to keep their lives and schedules as consistent as possible."

"Apparently I'm disruptive, Carl."

"I'm sure they don't see it that way. You might appreciate a schedule so you can plan your hours at work around it."

"Yes, that's exactly right," Farah said.

Barbie sighed and looked around the room. The dining room she'd fantasized about for years. The room where she had thought she'd never fit in. And now here she was. It wasn't quite what she'd imagined, but she was here. And with a couple of signatures, she would ensure her children's place at this table for years to come. She thought of Ricky and Bobby. They would both want this.

"When we tell the kids, can we do it in here?" she asked.

Farah and Robin looked at each other. "Sure," they both said.

"And I mean, just us and the kids. I don't need the other twenty people in here."

"We will include Rebecca," Robin said.

She shrugged her shoulders. "Alrighty then. What's next, Carl? Or should I only be talking to *my* lawyer?"

Carl cleared his throat. "Next, we'll get the paperwork filed in probate court in your county and get a court date to go before a judge. But even before this, Child Protective Services will visit the farm and make sure it's a suitable home."

Robin groaned and stood up. "What kind of time frame are we looking at, Carl?"

"Oh, this could take months. Child Services is spread thin."

"But then we get to go to court? I've never been in a courtroom," Barbie said.

"Yes, we will need to go before a judge," Carl said.

"Where do you think that will be?" Robin asked.

"I'm guessing the closest is Carson City."

"We really appreciate this, Carl," Farah said.

"It's fine, really. I'm happy to help, Farah."

I bet you are, Barbie thought, glancing up at Robin, wondering if he was thinking the same thing.

Farah gently nudged Barbie. "We get our outside chores done early in the summer. Everyone helps. And I mean everyone."

"What? What do I have to do?" Barbie asked, looking up, horrified, gasping as she checked her phone. "It's early," she complained.

"Well, I think I'll put you in charge of the vegetable garden on this fine morning. There is lettuce, cucumbers, and ripe tomatoes to be picked, and then the plants need a good watering."

She left her guest looking bewildered and, she thought, a little horrified.

"Is this your scheme to get her out of here for good? Hard labor?" Robin teased when she came back into the bedroom.

"She's going to have to get used to work. I figure a couple of mornings in the hot sun might make a job indoors more palatable. So yes, not here."

Robin laughed, "I can't believe this is going so smoothly. I'll have to give it to Barbie, she handled the conversation well with the kids last night..."

"What's going on?" Rebecca asked from the door of the dining room as Farah spooned out vegetable pasta alfredo, salad, and garlic rolls. "This room is for special holidays or celebrations." She looked around. "But it can't be a celebration without everyone."

Farah sat and took a sip of red wine. "Come in and sit. We have some news. And it's good news. Barbie wanted it just to be us when we discussed it...and she wanted to be in here."

It was quiet again, all eyes on Barbie as she rolled pasta on her fork, never lifting it from the plate. "Here's the thing, kids. You like it here, right?"

Ben and Brandi nodded.

"Well, I think this might be a good place for you to live. Like, every day."

"Really?" Ben said with a big smile on his face. "You mean it? We can stay here and not go back to Gran's?"

"Don't sound so upset," Barbie said.

"There is a little more to it. Your mom has agreed with Robin and me, that we have...more control over things like your schools and doctors and dentists, and any activities you're interested in. Stuff like that. And, yes, you will live here." Farah said tentatively.

"But I'm still your mom," Barbie interjected firmly. "And I'm still going to be around. Just different...around."

"How different?" Ben wondered.

"Well, I'm going to take care of Gran. And Farah is going to help me with the apartment. Make it nicer. And then I'll live there and work somewhere in town. And you can come and have sleepovers from time to time. "

The children ate in silence, not daring to lift their eyes from their plates. "What will we call you if we live here?" Ben finally asked his mother.

"Mom!"

"And we are your aunts and uncle," Robin said, looking at Farah and Rebecca.

"Aunt Becky! I like the sound of that," Rebecca said.

"So, what do you think? Do you like this idea?" Farah asked.

They looked at each other and smiled, Brandi breaking out in the giggles.

"We like it," Ben said. And then he looked at Barbie and said, "Thanks, Mom."

Farah thought she was going to cry.

Robin also looked away and quickly picked up his glass of water.

"I guess this is kind of like a celebration," Rebecca said with a wide smile.

So, while Joe Jr. and Ben picked up the eggs from the chickens, and Farah was busy wrapping white lights around Maria's porch, she could hear Barbie in the garden with a big basket.

"God damned bugs! Who the hell needs all this green stuff? Ouch! What bit me?"

"How ya doing over there?" Farah called from the porch.

"Fine, I guess. What are you going to do with all this stuff?"

"I use everything. I can send more home to your mom too."

"Yeah, well, if she cared at all about her health we wouldn't be here now," Barbie said as she carried her basket up to the porch.

A minute later, Emily came flying out of her house and down the steps with a sheet pan of cooked bacon. "My God, if I have to cook any more of this, I'm going to start smelling like it."

"Well, I'm sure that won't bother Joshy one bit. He'll want to eat you up if you know what I mean," Barbie said.

"That's gross," Emily said as the two women stood face to face on the porch.

Barbie laughed. "If you need a little talk about the birds and the bees before the big night, let me know."

Emily playfully slapped her arm. "I know all about the birds and the bees."

"I'm not talking your ma's version. Wink, wink."

Maria went to the door and swung it open. "Alright, that's enough of that talk for now, you two." She glanced over her shoulders. "We have impressionable ears in here."

"I know what you're talking about!" Rebecca called from the kitchen. "Don't worry, there are no birds or bees coming on my first date."

Chapter 31
Something in the Air...

The birds and the bees were in the air in the days leading up to the shower. Fragrant lavender and salvia lined the fronts of the houses, including the lucky chickens' house. Pink climbing roses and star jasmine were blooming on the gazebo, and when afternoon breezes kicked in, their floral perfume traveled all through the farm.

The three flower girls' dresses were finished, and their white Mary Janes and laced socks had arrived. Emily would have preferred it if they were *all* dressed in Jane Austen Regency-style gowns, but Farah, Maria, and Diana held their ground and ordered their own.

Emily would have also preferred every man on the farm clad like *Mr. Darcy*, but that wasn't going to happen either. Instead, she conceded that only her father had to wear the same matching dark gray suit as Josh and his groomsmen. Robin and Joe agreed on dark slacks and white shirts with straight collars. Joe Jr. and Ben hoped to hide in the stables the entire day, but their hopes were dashed when their own slacks arrived and they were sent over to Diana's to have them hemmed.

Farah's offer to help Barbie find dresses for the wedding and the shower was met with halfhearted enthusiasm. What she *was* enthusiastic about was the thought of living alone in a new apartment, and she asked Farah if they could get the ball rolling.

"I've been looking at some things, and I want to get your opinion," Barbie said one afternoon, "I've always liked yellow. It's popular again, by the looks of things online."

Farah sat down with her to look at her ideas. "I like yellow too and it works well with the blue couch you're considering," she reassured.

"Remember I'm taking Mom to see Marcy tomorrow. That's for real this time. Then I can start the cleanup."

"So, she's gotten used to the future plans?"

"Well, I think she liked *her* plan better. She wanted a quick fix. But she wasn't thinking long term. She was only thinking of herself and some immediate payback. She's just like her mom. Dumb and selfish. I don't want Ben and Brandi to end up like us."

Farah was surprised and moved by this statement. "I think you've broken the cycle."

"I had a little help."

After dinner, as they enjoyed ice cream, Rebecca said, "I can't wait for the wedding so Gabe can see me in my dress."

"Have you two gotten to first base yet?" Barbie asked.

"What's first base?" she asked.

"Holding hands and a kiss on the cheek," Farah said, smiling across the table at Robin.

Rebecca giggled and brought her hand to her cheek. "He has kissed me."

"Lordy, at this rate she is never getting to home plate," Barbie said, spooning more ice cream in her bowl.

"So how long are you going to be gone?" Robin asked Barbie, changing the subject.

"Just two days. I'm taking Mom, spending the night, and heading back the next morning. She's staying a few more days before taking the bus home. It'll be nice to see Marcy. Although when her and mom used to get together all they talked about was their 'dates' at the bars. I'm sure my existence is the result of my mama getting to home plate with one of those dates."

Robin looked up, "Make it stop."

"What's home plate?" Rebecca asked.

"It's when you score in a baseball game. You have to get on first base, then second, then third, and then you have to cross the home plate and not get tagged out. Then it's a score!" Ben said. "Duh."

"Exactly," Robin said, glaring at Barbie.

"Relax, the girl's got to know this stuff if she's going to be dating."

"Baseball has nothing to do with kissing," Rebecca said.

"It's a different kind. Think if that kiss on the cheek as getting to first base." Barbie chuckled.

"Barbie," Farah cautioned, though holding back laugher.

"No, I want to know these things," Rebecca said.

"Barbie," Robin cautioned next.

Barbie laughed. "I got this. Let's say first base is a kiss on the cheek. Then second base will be a kiss on the mouth and third is a kiss and a hug. And then home plate will be..."

"Wedding night stuff!" Rebecca said.

"Right. Wedding night stuff," Barbie said.

"Baseball games take a long time to play," Robin said, scooping the last of the mint chip into his bowl. "Nine innings. Sometimes more."

"Yeah, well this kind of baseball seems better," Rebecca said.

Chapter 33
A Fellow named Crabtree?

The air conditioning provided little relief from the heat, compounded by the open windows swirling toxic fumes from Carole's cigarettes on the ride to Carsen City.

"Jeez, Mom, ever heard of secondhand smoke? Trying to put me in an early grave too?"

"Oh, all right. Pipe down," Carole said, throwing the lit cigarette out.

"Holy crap! Now you want to start a grass fire?"

"Well, looky here who's become a...whachamacallit... an environmentalist."

Barbie looked over at her mother and they laughed. "I guess I have changed a little."

Carole was quiet before saying, "It's for the better."

Barbie couldn't remember the last pleasant thing her mother had said to her. She wanted to say something, but she couldn't get her mouth to move, so she savored the moment quietly. She didn't even protest when Carole lit another cigarette within minutes, and she breathed in the smoke as if she were puffing on her own.

They arrived at Marcy's a little after 5:00. Marcy was the same age as Barbie's mom but the years had been much kinder. She had moved into a retirement community, and she proudly showed the property off from her third-floor balcony after they unpacked the car.

"Look over there. You can see the pool, and right behind it is the gym. Over there, there's a café and a lounge and on Saturday nights they have live music. If you're up to it, we can go, Carole."

The inside of her apartment was spacious with two bedrooms and baths, a modern, open kitchen, and a living room. Marcy liked blue, starting with a light shade on the walls, a darker version in wall-to-wall carpet, and royal blue couches. "And I finally got central air!"

"And leather sofas! I'd say you did all right for yourself," Carole said after they all sat down with a beer.

"They're *pleather*. But you can't tell, right? Joining the casino workers union turned out all right. Those monthly dues have given me a good pension," Marcy said. "You should have stayed here, Barbie. You liked the work."

"She found another way to fund her retirement," Carole said sarcastically.

"And what's that?" Marcy asked.

"It's a long story," Barbie said.

"Well, I got the time," Marcy said. "I'm going to make us a nice dinner and you can fill me all in. Come into the kitchen with me."

"It all started when mom thought it was high time the Robinson's knew about Ben. I told you all about them and the whole family tragedy that led to me coming here. Robin and his wife Farah are in charge now," Barbie said, sitting down in a chair at a small round table.

"Farah? You don't hear that name often. Is she as pretty as the one on the poster?"

"She is."

"She was. We *all* age." Carole chimed in from the balcony.

Barbie shrugged. "Well, in the beginning, we, mainly mom, thought Ben was the way to get money out of them. We, mainly mom, thought when they heard about him being blood and all, they'd want him with them. And they'd pay to spend time with him, and Brandi of course."

"Like extortion?"

"In a nutshell."

Marcy laughed, "You know that's illegal, right?"

"It wasn't going to be a lot of money!" Carole called.

"Yeah, well they were onto our plan and came up with a better one."

"And what's that?"

"I'll get to all that later," Barbie whispered.

Soon they were all sitting down to Marcy's chicken in mushroom sauce. "It's just sauteed breasts with a can of mushroom soup on top, but, hey, I've never had any complaints." She also cooked the dickens out of a can of green beans, made mashed potatoes out of a box and biscuits from a can.

"This is darn good," Carole said. "Barbie's been bringing home all this fancy stuff from her 'new family.' God forbid they ever cook their vegetables."

"They're better for you raw. More vitamins," Barbie said, buttering a biscuit.

"See what I mean?" Carole said. "She's turning into one of them."

"Mama let's drop it and enjoy the meal. It's delicious, Marcy. And even *their* biscuits come out of a can."

After dinner, a walk around the complex that included dipping their feet in the pool, Carole was ready to call it a night. Marcy and Barbie sat out on the balcony with another beer.

"So, what happened when they found out what you and Carole were up to?" Marcy asked.

"I'm going to give them guardianship of the kids," she said quickly...like ripping off a brandade.

Marcy gasped, "Are you sure about this?"

"It's not as bad as it sounds. I'm going to see them as much as I want, but they will live on the farm with their financial needs taken care of. And mine too! They're remodeling the apartment and I'll get to stay there for cheap rent. And I'm going back to work. I did like to work."

"You must really like these people."

"I do. At first it was suffocating. They do everything together. I mean everything. Ben and Brandi took to it right away. After a couple of weeks, it was like they had always been there. Of course, it helped that Farah started dressing them up like they were always hers." Barbie chuckled then sipped her beer.

"But are you sure you want to sign them over? That's so final."

"Yeah...it's freaky. And your reaction doesn't help. But I can go to all the school stuff and spend time a lot of time at the house. I can even have sleepovers at the apartment. It's all in the papers."

"Papers?"

"Yep. They are doing this all legally. And *I* even have my own lawyer. They helped me with that too."

"Wait a minute. That sounds suspicious. How can you trust a lawyer they found for you?"

"Nah...they aren't like...us. They are good. But this is funny. Farah dated this guy, and when she dumped him, he ended up engaged to her sister. But *then* the sister got killed right before the wedding. Well, not exactly killed. She was a veggie for years. Like a coma. Anyway, Farah kept in touch, got ahold of him and here we are. His name is Carl Crabtree. What a name, right? I have a different one. We can't share. I don't get half of it, but this is how it works."

Marcy thought for a minute. "That's funny. I think me and your mom knew a fella named Crabtree. Never forget a name like Crabtree."

"From where?"

"Oh, he used to frequent one of our favorite watering holes. He didn't live here but came for business. Or so he said. He was from the Sacramento area. Married, but liked a fun time if you know what I mean. Come to think of it, he was a lawyer too. In fact..." She stood and walked inside, returning with an old showbox. "I haven't looked at these in years," she said removing the lid. On the top was a little blue photo album with *Grandma's Brag Book* on the cover. She handed it to Barbie. "Remember this?"

"Oh yeah. You were always taking pictures of Ben with that little camera of yours. You were good with him." She slowly looked through the album. "Can I have this?"

"Sure." She continued looking through the box, placing pictures on her lap. Marcy and Carole in their glory days. Both pretty, ruby red lips, cigarettes between fingers with long painted nails. "I don't know why I was always taking pictures of these dudes. We had *relations*, not relationships." Then she stopped at one and held it up. "This is him with your mom!" She turned the photo over. "Yep, Ray Crabtree, May 1988." She handed the picture to Barbie.

Barbie sat up straight and sucked in her breath. Her mother, thirty years younger. Beautiful red, wavy hair resting on her shoulders, a fitted black dress hugging her hourglass figure, sitting on a bar stool, bare legs crossed. "What the hell!" She walked into the apartment, holding the picture under a lamp, her heart and pulse racing.

Marcy followed her in. "What is it, honey? You look like you've just seen a ghost."

"Not quite a ghost." Barbie turned the card over. "May 1988," she whispered, counting with her fingers, June, July, August, September, October, November, December, January, February. Did my mom sleep with this guy?"

"I'm fairly sure she did. Why?"

"Holy Shit! I think I might have just found my daddy."

"What makes you think that?"

"Well, the date in this picture says May of 1988, and I was born the next Valentine's Day 1989. Mom always said I was born out of lust and not love." Barbie scrunched her face. "She thought that was so funny."

"Well, maybe there was someone else...around that time."

"Yeah, maybe," Barbie said absently, still engrossed in the picture.

"And even if he is your father, what would you do about it? He'd be an old man by now. Possibly dead. How would you go about getting any info?"

"It's going to be easier than you think, Marcy."

Chapter 34
Big Brother

Barbie hardly slept, staring at the picture for hours. She had fantasized about a father when she was a little girl, wondering if he was looking for her. What little girl wouldn't fantasize about getting a heart-shaped box with chocolates from her daddy on her birthday...

She was still staring at it when her mother joined her at the table for breakfast. "Morning, Mama. How'd you sleep?"

"Like a baby. That air conditioning makes all the difference. I didn't even hear you come in or get up."

"I slept on the couch. Marcy and I spent the night looking through old pictures. This one caught my attention." She pushed it across the table.

"Huh." She turned it over. "Good ol' Marcy. She loved her camera. Didn't know she knew all the names."

"You wouldn't know his name?"

"Well, now that I see it, I guess so. Yeah, he was Ray. He liked redheads."

"And you two...had a thing?"

"If by thing you mean sex, yeah. So what?"

"Look at the dates, Ma! I think this guy could be my father!"

Carole looked again. "Well, I'll be damned."

"Was there more than one at that time?"

"I don't think so. It's not like I slept with every guy I met. And no one in Honeysuckle. Well, except the one. I just liked to have a little fun when I visited. Right, Marcy?"

"Yeah, we mostly kissed, played footsies and gave the occasional massage for free drinks." Marcy set a platter of scrambled eggs, leftover biscuits, and bacon in the middle of the table. "But once in a while they made offers, we couldn't refuse."

"I get it. Did you ever see him again?" Barbie asked, grabbing a slice of crispy bacon, and biting off half.

"Hell, no! I came home, found out I was pregnant, and didn't see Marcy again for three years."

Marcy sat down with a cup of coffee. "I saw him again a couple of times. He asked about you, Carole."

"Really? That's nice. He was one of the better ones."

"Gross," Barbie said, stuffing the other half of the bacon in her mouth.

"Well, so what if he was your sperm doner. He was a rich lawyer with a family of his own. He mentioned two boys, I think. Or maybe that was someone else. You're not thinking about looking for him, are you?"

Barbie took the picture back and grabbed another piece of bacon. Then she picked up her phone, swiped the screen and handed it to her mother.

"What the hell?"

"Notice the resemblance? This is Carl, the lawyer. The one helping with the kids. I don't have far to look, do I?"

Barbie opened the windows, all four of them, when she got home. The fan just circulated warm air, but Barbie didn't care. She was sweating from head to toe, but it was liberating ridding the apartment of junk and bad karma. She quickly filled three large trash bags with her children's old clothes, broken toys, dated newspapers, magazines, and junk mail.

It felt good to give the apartment a thorough cleaning, even though it was going to get gutted. It reminded Barbie of when she'd had her own place in Reno. She hoped to find similar curtains for the kitchen. She remembered Bobby complimenting her on the place. *Yep, yellow gingham curtains...*

Three hours and a long cool shower later, Barbie sat at the table, looking at Grandma's Brag Book. There were three empty pages in the back. In two of them she put pictures of Brandi as a baby, and on the last page she put the picture of Ray and her mother. She couldn't wait to see the look on Farah's face.

"Barbie's back and asking to come over," Farah said as Robin came inside.

"It was peaceful while it lasted."

"I can't say no." She laughed and typed on her phone. "I'll invite her to dinner."

"Every time she comes over, I fear what's going to come out of her mouth."

"I think we're all out of surprises." But when her response text came back there was a sudden pit in her stomach, and she knew she had spoken too soon.

{Barbie:} I have some big news!

By the time she arrived, the entire family was around the kitchen island building tacos. She tried to get Ben and Brandi's attention but the big bowl of chips and Maria's homemade salsa were making it impossible.

"I see I wasn't missed," she half joked.

"They're just hungry kids," Farah said, holding up a small mason jar filled with salsa. "Look. Aren't these cute?"

"Let me guess, more stuff for the wedding? Do you people have to feed everybody?"

"Ha, ha. These are favors for the shower."

"Was your mom okay with you leaving her there?" Diana asked.

"Oh yeah. Marcy has a real nice apartment with fancy pleather couches and air conditioning. I left them looking through a box of old pictures reminiscing about all their conquests."

"Conquests?" Emily asked.

"Oh, you know, guys have notches on bedposts and Marcy had a box of old Polaroids."

"Of what?"

"Men."

"Doing what?" Rebecca moved closer.

"Once again, not appropriate dinner conversation," Robin said, pulling her away.

Barbie laughed, grabbing a taco shell, "Aren't you glad you asked, Emily?"

"Speaking of pictures, I was hoping to get my hair done for the shower. It's in a week. Will your mom coming back?" Diana asked.

"A week? Boy time flies. I forgot all about the shower."

"How could you forget?" Joe said, grabbing a beer from the refrigerator. "I've almost forgotten we board horses here."

"Hey," Emily said, laughing with everybody. "Mama, you can come with me and Becca to my girl. She's doing our hair that morning."

"Yes, we're all looking forward to the shower because we're going to the rodeo! Right boys?" Robin said to Ben and Joe Jr.

"Right!" they said in unison.

"Don't remind me," Emily said, working on her second taco, more lettuce than meat.

"It's not going to be all pleasure. We're taking two horses up for sale," Philip said. "We won't have time to look at the pretty girls."

"Dad!"

"Well, the boys shouldn't have all the fun. Did you hire a stripper, Farah?" Barbie asked.

Farah snapped her fingers and gave a shake of her head. "Oh, too bad. Honeysuckle is fresh out."

After dinner, Joe, Philip, and Diana took the kids outside to eat Popsicles and cool off in the sprinklers while Farah and Maria cleaned up the kitchen and Robin worked on his laptop at the table.

Barbie went over to her purse and pulled out the little blue book and sat down with it at the table by Robin, who eyed her suspiciously. "What's that?" he asked, reluctantly.

"It's Ben's baby book. I thought you'd get a kick out of it."

Farah came over and sat next to her. "Let's see!" She smiled as she slowly turned the pages. "He was an adorable baby. Come see, Maria."

Maria stood over her shoulder. "He really was. Robin, he's always looked like you."

Farah kept turning. "Oh look, here's Brandi. What a little butterball she was."

"Yeah, she was chubby," Barbie said. "My boobs could barely handle her appetite."

Robin groaned, closed his laptop and was about to stand when Farah turned to the last page, having the same reaction as Barbie the first time she saw the picture.

"Look familiar?"

"I knew this man!" Farah gasped.

"Knew? He looks like Carl, with hair?" Maria said.

"It's not Carl...it's his father."

"Let me see," Robin said, taking the book from her. "This is Carl's dad...with your mother?"

"Yes. But that's not the best part." Barbie grabbed the book back and took the picture out. "Look at the date on the back. May 1988. I was born nine months later."

"Are you saying your mom and Ray had a relationship?" Farah asked.

"Well, they rolled around in the sheets once or twice. He used to come into town for a fun time every few months according to Marcy, and he met my mother when she was visiting. Anyway, it looks like I found out who my daddy is. And that means Carl is my brother! And mom thought there were two boys. That means *two* brothers!"

Robin sat back down. "It never ends with you."

"This isn't my fault! What is wrong with wanting to know my father is?"

"This can't be true. Did Carole confirm this?" He asked.

"As best she could recollect. The date on the back of the picture says it all. This is even before you, Robin. I guess you knew she wasn't a virgin."

"That's enough out of you," Robin stood defiantly again.

"Alright, let's all calm down," Farah said. "I'm sorry to tell you, Barbie, but Ray died a few years ago of cancer. And Carl's mother followed shortly after."

"And how would you know that?" Robin asked her.

"Carl and I have exchanged emails over the years."

"Well, that sounds like Fletcher luck," announced Barbie. "At least I know I have a couple of siblings. That's something. It's like a reality show. Orphan Annie meets the brother's she never knew she had."

"Except you're not an orphan. This must be handled delicately. Dr. Phil is going to have to wait," Farah said.

"He might not know his father was unfaithful," Maria said.

"Ray Crabtree had a reputation around town, and his wife looked the other way because she liked her social status," Farah said quietly. "Carl and his older brother Dale knew he cheated. But, Barbie, you are not to say a word about this before I speak to Carl."

She pouted, "All right. But when?"

"Not right this minute. We've got a shower in a few days and a wedding after that. You've gone this long without knowing. What's a while longer?"

"Yeah, well, you all have taught me the importance of family. And I think ol' Carl is going to like having a sister," she said, hurrying out of the house like a child.

"This really is incredible," Maria said shaking her head. "I don't remember Carole ever looking this good. She was attractive."

"She was, and Ray Crabtree was a cad. I'm sure he's her father," Farah replied. "Or was."

Robin sighed and walked toward the back door. "Something tells me Carl isn't going anywhere after the court date."

Chapter 38
Here Comes the Bridal Shower

Rebecca Farms hummed with activity the morning of Emily's bridal shower. While Robin, Philip, and the boys tended to the horses, Joe and Josh were hitching the trailers to the trucks. Diana was trying to keep her daughter focused on helping with the morning meal, but all her excitement about the afternoon, coupled with her apprehension of Josh leaving for the night, made that tough.

Farah was busy, icing the small three tier white cake with berry filling and orange buttercream. *Riding a bike...*

"You have outdone yourself," Maria said, whisking eggs.

"Maybe I have! And there's still the wedding cake," she said with a laugh.

After breakfast, they all gathered around the trucks to say goodbye. Joe Jr. and Ben were excited and anxious and couldn't stand still or bother with hugs and kisses. Philip was just as giddy as the young boys, but he pacified Diana with a warm embrace before climbing into the truck.

Joe hugged Maria and Diego with his little girls wrapped around his legs. "It's just for one night," he laughed, peeling them off.

Emily clung to Josh, "Promise me you'll call when you get there. Promise me you won't drink too much. Promise me you won't look at any girls."

He promised everything before kissing her like she was the only girl in the world.

"I think that's second base!" Rebecca said.

Robin and Farah looked at each other, smiling, shaking their heads at all this love and good fortune. "Don't tell me you're going to miss me," he said.

"Heck, no! We have too much to do. But don't you be looking at too many pretty girls either," she wagged a playful finger at him.

He grabbed it and kissed it. "I only have eyes for one pretty girl, he said as he climbed into the front truck, Joe driving the second. Eager men and horses ready to go. "I'll call later," he said before kissing her mouth. "Have a wonderful shower."

"And you have a wonderful rodeo."

It was a scene out of the movies as the trucks gently pulled away with all the women furiously waving their arms.

"Alright, alright, we have work to do," Farah said, clapping her hands together, heading back into the house. "Four hours until High Tea...and it's just you and me!" She laughed.

"What's my assignment?" Maria asked, putting Diego in front of the TV with his blocks.

"You can work on the cucumber sandwiches," Farah said, smiling at her printed-out menu that she had framed for the table. "I'm going to tackle the flowers."

"Gotcha," Maria said, beginning to trim the crust off the white bread. "I know you have done so much already but this is a lot even for you. It's too bad you don't have more help."

"I'm having fun! I'd rather be here with you than at the salon with the girls. I feel sorry for the hairdressers," Farah laughed, arranging yellow and white Gerber daisies in mason jars. "And Diana is going to see Carole. I *really* don't want to be there with all that energy. I can just see Barbie announcing the news of a brother to everyone who walks through the door," Farah rolled her eyes.

"Have you mentioned her to Carl yet?"

"I did," she said raking her phone out of her apron pocket and handing it to Maria. "Read this."

> *{Farah:} I want to send you a picture that recently*
>   *came into my possession.*
> *{Carl:} How did you get a picture of my dad? And who*
>   *is this woman?*

{Farah:} She lived in Carson City.

{Farah:} Wait, that's not correct. She visited Carson City, where they met, but she lives in Honeysuckle.

{Carl:} Lives? I remember he traveled to Reno for business, or so he said. Didn't know he made it to Carson City or Honeysuckle. How did you get this? Who is she?"

{Farah:} Are you sitting down? This is Barbie's mother.

{Carl:} WHAT???

{Farah:} There is something else. This picture was taken in May of 1988. Barbie was born the following February. She's convinced herself you are her brother...

"Oh wow, what did he say after this?" Maria wondered.

"He called me. We both agreed that we can put this aside for now, considering we might not go to court for months and they won't meet until then. I've told Barbie I'm not even talking about this until after the wedding. We have some breathing room."

Emily gasped, "It's all so beautiful!"

"And you two are beautiful," Farah said, eyeing the blushing bride to be and Rebecca as they admired the beautifully prepared food. "I love your hair!"

"Yes, I thought I'd try this out before the wedding." Emily turned, showing off the back of her hair, upswept and intricately pinned and curled.

Rebecca's hair was woven in a beautiful braid with a yellow ribbon. "Look, the yellow matches my dress dress."

"It's perfect. And speaking of dresses. We had all better get ready!"

The theme of the day was yellow, with all the ladies of Rebecca Farms in dresses of assorted styles and shades. Farah couldn't resist and ordered the little girls white cotton dresses with lemons embroidered throughout.

A white linen tablecloth covered the farm table, and Gerber daisies lined the center. The kitchen island played host to all the expertly plated food. And just after 1:00, the ladies of Honeysuckle started to arrive. Bridesmaids, family friends, future in-laws, and longtime neighbors all there to celebrate Emily. A role she was relishing as the afternoon started.

Barbie and Carole arrived, both looking better than Farah had ever seen. And she was pleasantly surprised to see Barbie wearing a yellow and white checkered skirt and short sleeved white blouse, and Carole, sporting red hair again, wore white capri pants and a yellow tunic.

"I see you went back to your red hair," Farah commented to Carole as she brought her a glass of champagne."

"Yes, Marcy helped me with it. You know we were in beauty school together. But she went another route."

"I had heard that. It's nice to have a friendship last that long."

"I'm sure a woman like you has friends all over the place."

Farah thought for a moment. Nothing could be further from the truth. She'd really had no friends before she came here. She had employees and regular customers and acquaintances, but no real friends. Looking around at the house filled with warmth and love and friendships reinforced how lucky she was. "All my friends and family are here." She touched Carole's arm. "And I'm glad you're on that list too."

After everyone had their fill of food and drink, Emily started opening her gifts with the three little girls eagerly at her feet, taking turns handing packages to her. She squealed with delight after each opening. Sheets and towels, homemade aprons, homemade recipe books, kitchen cookware, and small appliances.

With the help from both of their parents for the down-payment, the soon to be newlyweds were purchasing a home in one of the new developments nearby. It was supposed to be kept under wraps until closing, but after two glasses of champagne and a fancy new mixer in her hand she burst out, "Oh, a red one! This will go perfectly in my new kitchen. If it all works out, we can spend our first night as husband and wife there."

After all the excitement died down from the news, there were two gifts left. In one beautifully wrapped box from her bridesmaids was a long silk robe and nightgown in pale lilac. The ladies of Honeysuckle laughed nervously, nudging, and giving each other knowing looks, and murmurings of "perfect for the wedding night."

The final package was from Barbie. It was a small giftbag.

This is not a kitchen appliance, Farah thought.

"Now, this is for the wedding night!" Barbie said. "Open 'er up!"

After pulling the top layer of tissue out, Emily stalled, looking in the bag, her eyes squinting, her head tilting to one side. Then she gently pulled out a small piece of black fabric.

Farah was afraid of this.

"What's that?" Rebecca asked.

No one spoke.

"It's a thong!" Barbie laughed. "*That* is what you need for the wedding night. And there's a few more in there for the honeymoon."

Emily quickly put it back, "Thank you so much. I love...everything."

"It's been such a wonderful day. Better than I even imagined," Emily said after the last guest had left.

"Yeah, and just think. The boys are just getting started in Carson City. Better take a little selfie in the thong," Barbie said.

"Our party doesn't have to end!" She sent a warning glare at Barbie. "We have a full bottle of opened champagne and it's just going to go flat."

Sasha and Anna had stayed because their husbands were with the Rodeo party, happily accepted another glass.

"Hey, what about me?" Rebecca asked.

"Did you have one already? I wasn't keeping track," Farah said.

"None. I promise. I was watching Diego, remember?"

"She's right," Maria said. "You did an excellent job, *mija*."

"Thanks. So, I can get a glass of champagne and my ten dollars?"

"Ten dollars! You're getting ripped off," Barbie said, taking a glass for herself and bringing one to her mother.

"Alright, Becca, I'm giving you twenty dollars and one half glass," Farah said.

Diana brought a glass over to Emily, who was sitting in the middle of all her gifts. "You really got some wonderful things."

"I did, didn't I? I can't wait to show Josh."

"He's only going to care about my gift," Barbie sang out.

"Get your mind out of the gutter!" Maria sang back, picking up the last of the discarded wrapping paper on the floor.

"Actually, let's take a look at them," Diana said, taking a sip of her champagne. "What are they called again?"

"Mother!"

"Oh, relax, Emily. I'm not a prude."

"Thongs!" Barbie said, grabbing the bag and handing it to Diana. "Lots of women wear them all the time. Not just before hanky-panky."

Diana dumped the bag over on her lap. Along with the black one there were red, purple, and white varieties. She picked the red one up. "I don't get it. I mean I *get* it. But this doesn't look comfortable."

Farah came and sat down, "I'm with you, Diana. Never been a fan."

"Don't tell me you wear granny panties to bed," Barbie said.

Farah shook her head as they all laughed. "I think we need some music and maybe a little dancing."

While the women of Rebecca Farms danced, ate High Tea leftovers, and finished the champagne, the men of Rebecca Farms were checked into a hotel suite two hours away, eating pizza and drinking beer, enjoying the break from the daily routine and the women who were multiplying.

"And they never stop talking," Joe Jr. said, laughing as he stuffed pizza in his mouth.

"Son, that is your mother you are talking about. Shame on you," Joe said, kidding with his son. "But he's right, Josh. Welcome to the family."

"I've got sisters. I'm used to it."

"Just don't bring them to the farm," Joe Jr. said.

They were all laughing as Matt and Steve came into the room, freshly showered. "So, are we heading out after we eat? Maybe have a couple of strong drinks and a ride on a mechanical bull?" Matt asked, rubbing his hands together.

Josh looked at his future father-in-law. "I don't know. Maybe we should just hang here."

"Oh, go on and have a good time. My lips are sealed," Philip said.

"Really?"

"Really. In fact, why don't you join them, and I'll stay with the boys," he said looking at Robin and Joe.

"Really?" They said together with big smiles building.

"Yeah, go and show these boys an enjoyable time," Philip said, grabbing another slice of pizza.

"Well, I guess it'll be all right," Josh said. "I'll call Emily while it's quiet. I'm sure their party is over by now, and I don't want to call her from anywhere noisy giving her any ideas."

"We should call too, Joe, and get this out of the way," Robin said and winked at the two young boys, who were smiling broadly at the budding scheme.

But when the three men went to three different corners of the suite and dialed their significant others, loud music and laughter rang in their ears. The party had taken a turn from the refined and lady-like tone of High Tea. The men could barely get a word in, or any interest in what they were saying as Farah, Maria, and Emily went on about the wonderful time they were having.

It was best to get off their phones as soon as possible, the three men concluded as they prepared to head out.

"I can't believe Emily didn't grill me about the rest of our night," Josh said, laughing as they walked to the elevator.

"I didn't know tea could have that effect on a person," Joe said, shaking his head. "My wife sounds a little tipsy."

Robin laughed. "No doubt Barbie is there trying to fill Emily's head with crazy ideas about us and tonight. I bet Farah changed gears a little and is keeping their party going."

"Well whatever she's doing, remind me to give her a big hug when we get back," Josh laughed.

"Get in line, buddy," Robin said, putting his arm around this much loved, soon to be family member.

Chapter 36
Carl has some Clout!

"Just one big happy family," Barbie announced on the morning of the first day of school, coming down the stairs as Farah and Maria made lunches.

"Wanna help" Maria asked.

"Taking notes. So what has Carl said? He knows about me, right?"

"He does. But there is more to take into consideration. And right now *that* consideration is it's the first day of school. *You* should be thinking about this."

"They get up a little earlier than usual and let someone else take over for a few hours. Done. Now what has he said about me?"

"You're impossible. He hasn't said much. You know he does have a full-time job and a family. Do you really want to steamroll in and change their lives like you did ours?"

"Worked for you, didn't it?

Farah sighed, "He said he's looking forward to meeting you when we get the court date."

"That could still be months!"

"So, in the meantime, let's keep busy. Go upstairs and get the kids up."

"I never thought the first day of school was something to get excited about, she mumbled as she went back up the stairs."

Soon, five anxious children were scrambling around the kitchen. Marisol, Christina, and Brandi, showing off new outfits and backpacks, could barely sit for breakfast. Joe Jr and Ben were looking and feeling out of sorts in shorts and playground-friendly tennis shoes.

"What's wrong with my boots?" Ben asked.

"Hard to run around and play tag in boots," Farah offered.

"Tag?" Joe Jr. laughed. "We don't play tag anymore."

"Well, whatever you do these days, boots won't work. Eat your toast."

Entering the school, Barbie could have been one of the students dressed in shorts and a tee shirt, her head bobbing up and down in pigtails. She walked ahead of Farah and Robin, holding her children's hands, the three of them looking around in wonder.

Make that the four of them as even Carole made the excursion. "This place is awesome! I don't remember it ever looking this nice. Do you, Mama?"

"I don't remember ever being here!" Carole said, and both women laughed.

Robin put his arm around Farah's shoulders and squeezed as if he knew she would have liked for them to be the ones holding Ben and Brandi's hands. "Don't worry, this will get old with her," he whispered in her ear.

"I guess, but I'm not going to be completely at ease until we've made it official."

Afterwards, Farah, Barbie and Carole went to the apartment. "Boy, who would have thought? Dropped kids off at school and now looking at floor samples. I sound like a suburbanite! Oh, and I want to be there to greet the bus today too," Barbie said.

Give me strength, Farah thought, climbing the stairs. And just before she got to the top, her phone pinged in her back pocket.

She glanced at the incoming text. "Oh, my God!" She covered her mouth.

"What?" Barbie asked.

"Child Services is coming to the farm."

"When?"

"The day after tomorrow!"

"Well, shit! Ol' Carl must have a little pull."

Farah's phone pinged again, and she gasped. "And he thinks he's secured a court date."

"When?"

"TWO DAYS BEFORE THE WEDDING?" Emily, Maria, Diana, and Rebecca exclaimed in the kitchen later that afternoon. Their loud and shocked voices sending the children, the dogs, the cat, and the chickens scrambling.

"That's not possible!" Emily screeched. "That is not possible!"

"What's not possible?" Robin asked, coming into the house with Joe. "Or do I really need to know?"

"We got ourselves a court date! Carl knew a judge!" Barbie said.

"Two days before the wedding!" Emily yelled again. "This is impossible."

Joe turned slowly, hand on the door.

"Don't even think about it," were the words coming from his wife.

"Can we push it out?" Robin asked.

"I don't think it works like that. I'm going to talk to Carl after dinner," Farah said, taking a deep breath. "We'll have to make this happen. The kids will need to be there too. They'll have to miss a day of school."

"What's one day of school? They'll survive," Barbie said.

Emily walked over to Barbie. "This is the worst timing thanks to you."

"Hey, this court stuff was Farah's idea," she said, shrugging her shoulders.

"Honey, everything is going to be fine," Diana said.

"Your mom is right," Maria said.

Sitting on the island, Farah's phone pinged. They all leaned over and looked at it. Carl. She took a deep breath after reading the text.

"CPS is coming at three o'clock on Wednesday afternoon." She looked around, taking a deep breath. "The kids will be home by then. We need to get this place in top shape."

"This place is aways in top shape," Maria said, coming over and putting her arm around Farah's waist.

"Yeah, I think you'll pass inspection," Barbie said. "But let me know what I can do to help."

Chapter 81
A Good, Soft Feel to It

Wearing white capri pants and a gold, silk tank top, Farah stood at the back door, looking down at the porch steps and colorful new additions of flowerpots which lined both sides. The porch furniture and colorful rugs had been cleaned and rearranged.

Inside, as she moved over and picked up a red gingham pillow from the couch, Maria came through the door. "I don't think you can fluff that any fluffier," she said.

Farah held the pillow to her chest. "I won't be able to relax until this is over."

Maria breathed deeply. "The place smells as good as it looks. And so do you."

"Thanks. I thought I'd make cookies."

"Yes, if all else fails, let's bribe them."

Both women laughed.

"I was thinking about the first time I came here. Do you remember?"

"You bet. I was very pregnant with Christina," Maria said with a gentle smile. "Robin drove up and this tall, beautiful drink of water emerged from the truck and gracefully ascended the steps."

"Graceful? I was a nervous wreck."

"Well, you'd never have known it."

"As we were driving in, I told Robin I didn't want you to think I'm taking over, and eventually resenting me." Farah breathed in. "Oh, the cookies!" She threw the pillow down and rushed to the oven. With her hand in the oven mitt, she pulled the cookie sheet out of the oven. "You never felt that way, did you?"

Maria poured them a cup of coffee. "Sit down for a minute." When Farah had joined her, she said, "I was a nervous wreck the first time I came here too. *At that* time I was pregnant with Marisol. But Rachel and Robert, Diana, and Philip welcomed us with open arms. Joe and I had left Utah and our troubled families right after we got married and were going it alone. Right from the beginning here we felt like we gained a new, happy family and they treated us like equals. It was such a happy place until the accident. And then it seemed for years, there was no more laughter. Until Robin met you."

"You make me sound like some sort of miracle worker," Farah laughed.

"I might have thought so at first. But after a while I realized something."

"What was that?"

"I realized...you might have needed us just as much as we needed you."

Farah grabbed her hand. "I did need you...and all of this."

"And now, there are two more little ones who need you. Actually, make that three."

"And speaking of three...I hear her car."

"Please, please, please be presentable," she said, as she hurried to the door.

Barbie hopped out of her car wearing frayed denim shorts and a white tee shirt, her hair piled haphazardly on top of her head. "Well, look at you. Didn't know this event was formal."

"I told you to dress properly."

"What the hell for? I'm not the one making the good impression."

"You look like you just rolled out of bed!"

"Relax, I look fine. I've been busy at the apartment. You know, making the place livable for the kids. The bunkbeds arrived today."

"Just get in the house and splash water on your face or something. Maybe comb the hair."

But just as Barbie reached the door, another car drove up...

Barbie smirked. "Looks like showtime!"

The young woman looked nothing like any social worker Farah had ever seen on television. She was young, mid-twenties, dressed in a tan skirt and jacket, white button-down blouse, and white tennis shoes. Her hair was blond, cut short and probably naturally curly. The kind of curly that could get unruly in a hurry if one didn't know what to do with it. She was holding a clipboard in one hand and a pen in the other.

"Hello," Farah said, walking down the steps. "You must be Christy." She held out her hand.

"Christy Tanner, at your service," she said, sticking her pen behind her ear and taking Farah's hand. "I hope it's okay I'm early. Wasn't sure of the traffic."

Farah stared at her. *This is the woman determining my fate today...* "No, the timing is good. Where do you live?"

"Sacramento."

"Oh, goodness. Are you driving back?" Farah asked, still holding her hand.

"No. I drove here with my girlfriend. We're staying over." She tried to pull away. "Shall we get started?"

"Sure. Of course," Farah laughed nervously and dropped her hand. "Let's go in the house."

At the top of the steps, Barbie was waiting. "Man, you look young! I was expecting an old woman, gray hair, pot belly, jaded." She squinted at the social worker. "You don't look jaded yet."

"Thanks...I think."

"Yes, so this is Barbie. She's the mother of the children."

"Nice to meet you, Barbie," Christy said.

"Well, welcome to our home," Farah said, opening the door.

Inside, Christy looked around. Farah followed her gaze. The beautiful kitchen straight ahead, the doors leading outside. The dining room to her right with a large vase of fresh flowers on the table, the gleaming staircase. "Very, very pretty," she said.

"Right?" Barbie said. "I don't know what your file says there, but I've been coming to this place for years, and Farah here has worked wonders."

"Barbie," Farah cautioned.

"Where is everyone? Where are the kids?" Christy asked.

"Out back. They get out of school early on Wednesdays. They ride the bus. It's very safe. Same driver for many years." She stopped, knowing she was rambling. "Do you want to meet Ben and Brandi?"

"Well, of course I want to meet them. That's definitely in the file." She tapped her clipboard again, chuckled, and then cleared her throat. "But can I see upstairs first?"

After she looked at the children's bedrooms, Farah and Barbie walked Christy through the kitchen and then outside. A pitcher of lemonade, cookies, and another vase of flowers waited on a patio table. The children were at the picnic tables under the blooming gazebo, the older ones doing homework, the younger ones were coloring. Uncle Philip sat with them reading his paper.

Christy could hear horses and laughter coming from the stables. She could see chickens roaming, dogs lazing in the sun. Maria was on her porch reading to Diego, and Diana sat with Carole on her porch sipping iced tea.

"I know just what you are thinking. Too good to be true, right, Christy?" Barbie said.

"It's pretty amazing," she said, lifting a page from her clipboard. "Where's...Robin?"

"I'll go and get him," Farah said, walking down the steps toward the stables.

"You think all this is pretty, wait till you meet *him*," Barbie said.

"Well, we can talk for a second," Christy said. "Can we sit?"

"Sure, have a cookie. I can guarantee they're homemade and delicious."

Christy sat. "Maybe later. Which two kids are yours?"

"Isn't it obvious?"

Christy looked at the table again. "I guess so. Sorry about that." She looked at another page on her clipboard. "I gotta say. This case is unusual. Usually, the mother terminating her rights is kicking and screaming. You are really on board with this?"

"Terminating? That's quite a word. I mean I'm still going to be around."

"Yes, of course. But the kids will be here, under the Robinsons' guardianship until they're eighteen. That's many years."

"Are you trying to freak me out? Cause you're freaking me out. Am I not supposed to do this?" Barbie asked.

"No, I'm just relaying the facts. And determining if this is the best solution for the children."

Barbie looked at her. "Do you have good parents? Like, you know, encouraging, shit like that."

Christy looked down at her papers. "Um, I guess so."

"Well, see that woman on the porch over there? The one lighting a smoke. That's my mother. I can't remember a time as a little girl when I didn't feel like...I was just in the way. I was raised with a grandmother too and felt the same way about her. Hard women. They made me hard."

"I'm...sorry," Christy said, clicking her pen open and closed.

"I used to come here as a teenager, and it was always a happy place. I could tell they were all about family. I fantasized about being part of it, even managed to get knocked up by the gay brother. You'd think that was a sign, right? Is that in your file?"

"It's not."

"Well, anyway, I stayed away for years. And then when I came back, with two kids in tow, me and Mom cooked up an idea. It involved money...and the kids."

"That probably isn't relevant," Christy said, looking uncomfortable.

"I get it. The point is, Farah and Robin are good people. The whole family are good people. They've changed me...my thinking. I want my kids around that good thinking." Barbie paused before adding, "This place softens you, Christy. It really does. I want my kids around it."

"Well, that is very thoughtful, Barbie. And yes, this place does have a good...soft feel to it."

Just then, the second stable opened and out came Robin and Farah, walking hand in hand toward them.

"Well here comes the perfect couple. See what I mean about pretty?" Barbie said.

Christy stayed much longer than she'd intended. After she met Robin, they joined the kids under the gazebo for cookies and lemonade. Maria, Joe, Diana, and Carole made their way over, and just after 6:00 Emily and Rebecca came home.

"This is Christy, from Child Services," Farah said. "Remember we talked about this the other night, Rebecca?"

"Of course. She's deciding if this is a good place for Ben and Brandi to live." She grabbed a cookie and looked at Christy. "Please say yes!"

"This is a beautiful place. And these are delicious cookies. But I really should get going. My girlfriend will be wondering." Christy finally stood up. "If it's alright, can I have Ben and Brandi walk me out?"

"Of course, come on kids," Robin said, lifting Brandi up from the table and walking her around. "We'll be on the porch waiting for you."

Robin, Farah, and Barbie stood on the porch, watching Christy talk to the kids. It looked like a lighthearted conversation, and all were smiling.

"I think this went well," Farah murmured.

"I think you're right," Robin answered, kissing her on the side of the head.

"Yeah, I talked you two up. I might have mentioned the scheme. I told her what a crappy mother I had. It all worked in your favor."

As Ben and Brandi turned and ran back to the porch, Christy waved to them. "Thanks for the...well, nice afternoon. I think this will go smoothly for you all in court."

"Yep, you are welcome," Barbie shouted, waving back before looking at Robin and Farah. "I need a beer."

Chapter 38
A Little Law & Disorder

Farah and Robin piled two tired children, their ornery mother, and one excited sister into the van.

Well, truthfully, they were all tired and ornery, especially Farah, who'd not had much sleep as both big days approached. She was up extra early making sure everyone was dressed for the occasion. Robin, used to jeans and boots at this early hour, was feeling nervous and out of sorts in his new wedding slacks, blue button-down shirt, and sports jacket that Farah had found in the back of the closet.

Farah, Rebecca, and Brandi wore their dresses from the shower, and Ben reluctantly put on his school clothes.

Barbie wore black. A black sleeveless dress, tightly cinched at the waist, black pumps, her hair pulled tightly back in a bun, and black glasses.

"Black? And what's with the glasses?" Farah asked, rolling her eyes as she came down the stairs.

"I watch a lot of *Law and Order*. Everyone wears black, and I figured the glasses make me look smarter."

"Good grief," Farah muttered, pouring more coffee.

Maria and Diana were there for the sendoff, their lists in their hands. "We have it all under control. Don't worry about a thing," they both assured Farah.

"This is a special day!" I feel we should have some sort of celebration later, but with everything..." Maria said then grimaced.

"Thanks, Maria. Robin and I will bring something home. We should be back by five at the latest. Carl said we should only be in court for an hour or so. Depending..."

"I'm not going to cause trouble. Jeez. Let's just go," Barbie scoffed.

Two hours, two bathroom stops, one donut shop, and one upset stomach stop later, they arrived at the Carson City Municipal Court.

"Sorry, Brandi is a barfer. Not great in the back seat," Barbie had said as Farah held a plastic bag for her outside of the car on the side of the road.

"You might have mentioned this."

They were all overwhelmed standing at the bottom of the steps of the beautiful, modern building. As they slowly ascended, Farah held the children's hands, Robin held Rebecca's, and Barbie rushed ahead, spotting Carl at the top with Eden Green.

"Well, well, well. We finally meet face to face. Hello, brother."

Looking nervous, his furrowed brow sweating, Carl took out a handkerchief and dapped himself, "Nice to meet you, Barbie." He held out his hand to her.

"I knew the minute I saw your picture we had a...connection. I felt it in my bones."

"Barbie, easy. Hi, Carl," Farah said coming up behind. "It's so great you're helping with this."

"Yes, it is," Robin said, holding his own hand out to Carl.

"I know the timing is crazy. A couple of things fell off the judge's calendar. We lucked out."

"It pays to know people," Farah said.

"Where's the rest of the family? Thought they would be here," Barbie asked Carl.

"Yes. Our youngest fell asleep in the car. They'll come in when she wakes up."

"I can't wait to meet them. Just think kids, more cousins!"

Inside, it was hard to say who got the biggest thrill out of going through the metal detectors, Barbie, Ben, Brandi, or Rebecca.

"Thank God the kids have their good socks on," Barbie said after they all had to remove their shoes.

"No, thank me," Farah responded, ushering the group toward Carl who was waiting at the escalator to take them to the second floor.

They sat nervously in the front rows of the cool courtroom. Along with Eden, Barbie and her children sat at one long table that would be to the Judge's left, and Robin, Farah, Rebecca, and Carl sat at the other table, to the Judge's right.

Barbie looked around. *This is nothing like I've ever seen on television.* There were two other women sitting at desks with computers. And there was a big, beefy guy in a cop's uniform standing near the door. *Wonder if he's packing?*

"This should go pretty quick," Carl whispered to Robin and Farah. "We're all in agreement here. There are no opposing parties. When..." he began, but the door behind the bench flew open and Judge Abbot appeared.

He was tall, broad, and quite intimidating in his black robe, but he had a big welcoming smile when he called out, "Hey, Carl, I heard this was you! How long has it been?"

"Hi, Judge. It has been years. I left corporate law a long time ago."

"Yeah, me too. This is more rewarding. And the hours are better." He chuckled, opening the folder in front of him as he sat. "Sorry about your dad. We had some good times together."

Barbie leaned over. "Maybe he knows my mom too," she whispered loudly to Carl.

"Oh, um, she's not supposed to talk unless spoken to. The same rules apply here in little old Carson City. Please remind your client, Miss Green," the judge said then went back to reading the file.

"Just like Law and Order!" she called out.

Eden grabbed her hand and glared at her.

The judge glanced up. "Are you Barbara Fletcher?"

She stood up quickly. "Yes, your honor, I am. Friends call me Barbie."

"Well, I'm going to go with Miss Fletcher. Or is it Mrs."

She laughed. "Nope. Never."

"Alright, you can sit. And Mr. and Mrs. Robinson?"

Farah and Robin both looked at each other, not sure what to do.

"Yes, Judge, let me introduce you to Farah and Robin Robinson," Carl said, standing.

They stood and said hello.

"And who is the young lady with you today?"

"I'm Rebecca!" she said and quickly stood. "I'm the aunt."

"Wonderful," he said, giving her a warm smile.

"Robin is my brother. But he is kinda like my dad. Our parents died in an accident. My other brother died too. His name was Ricky. And…"

Robin grabbed her hand. "Honey, you can sit."

"No, she can continue," Judge Abbott said.

"His name was Ricky, and he knew Barbie from school, and right before the accident, they did…wedding night things. I know all about wedding night things and even though I have a boyfriend now…"

Robin grabbed her arm again, but the judge put up his hand and chuckled. "Miss Robinson, you can continue, but let's keep to why we're here today."

"Okay. After the accident Robin became my dad. And then he met Farah, and she became my mom. And then she showed up with Ben and Brandi." Rebecca pointed to Barbie. "Because of the wedding night things *she* did with Ricky, she had a baby. He's Ben. And *then* she did wedding night things again, and she got Brandi."

"I object!" Barbie stood and called out.

Carl stood, but again the judge waved him off. "What are you objecting to, Miss Fletcher?"

"I…um… She's making me look bad. I'm not bad."

"Okay, sustained. Miss Robinson, why are we here today?"

"We're here because even though I'm their aunt, I'm kinda like their sister. And we have all had a lot of fun since they came to the farm. Right?" She looked down at Ben and Brandi, who nodded in agreement. "Robin and Farah want them to live there all the time. And I do too," she finished and plopped into her seat.

The judge was thoroughly amused. "What a wonderful witness!" he said, looking down at the file. "So, Ben and Brandi why don't you stand?"

They looked at Eden, who nodded and gently pushed them up.

"It looks like your mom and the Robinsons have come to an agreement so you live at the farm full time. Would you like that?"

They looked at each other, and then back to the judge and nodded, yes.

"Tell me why you want to be there, Ben."

"Well," he started slowly, "it's a cool place and there's lots of room for us. And we just got to start school. Farah is a good cook, and we have chickens and horses. And we have even more family there with Joe and Maria, Joe Jr. and Christina and Marisol and Diego. And then there's Emily. There are lots of girls around."

Judge Abbot chuckled. "Yes, I've read the report from the Department of Social Services, and it does seem like a wonderful place and a wholesome environment. The Department, after meeting with the children and each of you has endorsed the petition." He looked at the little girl and leaned forward with a smile.

"Now, Brandi, what do you have to say about the farm?"

She looked down at her dress and quietly began. "Farah got this dress for me. She's gotten me lots of new things. And we have family dinners every night. And I like the animals."

Judge Abbot looked over at Robin and Farah, who were holding back tears. He cleared his throat before he began. "And in this agreement, your mom will still be in your life. In fact, it looks like they're encouraging you, Miss Fletcher, to be as big a part as you wish and are being very generous to you in other ways too."

Barbie stood again, looking at her children and then at Farah and Robin. "I remember going to Rebecca Farms as a young girl. I used to fantasize about it being my home. If you saw it, you'd agree. These are good people. I want my kids there. Then my fantasy can become their reality."

Judge Abbot cleared his throat again, holding his hand over his mouth, gently shaking his head before he began. "I have seen a lot of tears in this courtroom over the years. Most out of misery for children who had fallen through the cracks. I didn't think anything could change my crusty old demeanor, but I was wrong. Carl, Ms. Green, it looks like this is an easy one," he said.

Carl stood. "Yes, we have had several meetings to make sure everyone is...happy."

"Mr. and Mrs. Robinson, are you happy?

They quickly stood. "Yes, yes, we are very happy," they said together.

"Miss Rebecca?"

She stood. "Yes!"

"Ben and Brandi?"

They both nodded yes with big smiles on their faces.

"And Miss Fletcher?"

She paused. "You know, your honor, for the first time in a long time I can honestly say *yes*, I'm happy."

"That's great," he said, closing the file. "My clerk will take you in a room and get everything signed, notarized, and filed. It was good to see you again, Carl." He stood to leave.

"Wait, don't you need to do that gavel thing?" Barbie asked.

"I don't. But I can." And he did. "Case closed!"

Judge Abbott walked out, and parties in the first row hugged and laughed with relief. And when they turned around, they saw a petite woman with two little girls enter the courtroom.

"Oh, hi, Dorothy. You just missed all the fun," Carl said as he walked over to greet them.

"This day just keeps getting better," Barbie said. "Kids, I think it's time to meet your cousins!"

After court, Carl and his family joined then they had celebrated with hamburgers, French fries, and milkshakes at a diner much like Sam's. Carl's daughters Violet and Poppy, Rebecca, and Brandi and Ben became instant friends and were in a booth, feeling very independent all by themselves. And right behind them, Farah, Robin, Carl, Dorothy, and Barbie sat.

When their milkshakes arrived, Farah picked hers up. "This day calls for a toast! Thanks again, Carl. You made this process so easy."

"Yes, Carl, we're so grateful," Robin added.

Carl blushed, clearly not comfortable with being the center of attention. "Well, this was easy with this family."

"Yes, I hear horror stories. Most children are pawns," Dorothy added. Patting Carl's hand. "You all have only wanted what's best for the children."

"We all lucked out. Good thing Farah has always stayed connected with you, 'ay Carl," Barbie said.

He blushed again, "It hasn't been much."

"It really hasn't," Farah reassured.

Robin jumped in. "Don't worry, Carl. She's just trying to start something."

"No, really! If she hadn't been in contact, I wouldn't have found my brother!"

"We're not...completely sure." Carl squirmed, looking at his wife.

"How do we find out for sure?" Barbie asked.

"Barbie, can we digest one major change at a time," Farah said.

"And maybe this lunch, "Robin dryly added.

"The timing of the picture makes this pretty obvious to me. And this is nice for the girls," Dorothy pointed to the booth over her shoulders. "His brother's children are much older and we rarely see them."

"Too bad you don't live closer. At least we all have the weekend together," Barbie said.

Robin sighed, taking another big bite of his burger.

"Carl and his family are coming to the wedding?" Robin asked as they got into bed the night before the court date.

"Well, on the Zoom call with Carl this afternoon, Emily and Rebecca came in. One thing led to another, and Emily invited him. His wife was there, and she thought it would be fun. A little get-a-way. Everyone loves a wedding!"

And where are they staying? Are we going to be out in the stables?"

Farah laughed. "No. They're staying downtown at the hotel."

"Thank God. I mean he seems nice enough, but I don't think I want to share our house with your ex," Robin said, playfully pulling her close.

She laughed again. "I barely consider him an ex. He was more of a friend. And a good friend to have, right?"

"Yeah, well, I guess if you had to keep in touch with an ex, he'd be the one."

And as they pulled into the driveway, they could see in the distance on the porch, the family standing, holding balloons, cheering as they approached. Even with everything going on, they'd made this happen.

"Wow! My mom's even holding a balloon," Barbie said. "Maybe all that nicotine has finally gone to her brain."

Inside the house, everyone was talking at once. Between asking questions about their day in court, to Maria and Diana filling Farah in on all their prep work today, to Barbie going on and on about Carl to her mother.

Finally, Farah said, "Okay, everyone, take a breath! I've got a cake to make."

Robin went to the refrigerator and grabbed beers for Joe, Philip, Josh, and himself. "Let's go to stables and fill the horses in." He winked at Farah before walking out.

Farah wrapped a white apron around her waist and went to the pantry. "Maria, after Carl and his family check into the hotel they're coming here and bringing dinner." She came out with a large jar of flour. "Then he had a good idea for tomorrow. He's invited the kids over to go swimming at their hotel. It will be great for them and us."

"Yeah, I'll drive us all over," Barbie said.

"In what?" Farah and Maria said in unison.

"Well, maybe just this once I can borrow your car, Farah."

Farah looked at Maria. "What do you think?"

"You can trust me, Maria. It's better for me to get out of your hair too."

"Well, when you put it that way," she said, bringing eggs over to Farah.

Emily, who had been munching on carrot sticks, asked, "What is Carl bringing over for dinner?"

"Pizza," Farah said.

"Pizza? I can't eat pizza two days before my wedding."

Chapter 39
And Finally

Mr. and Mrs. Philip Robinson
Request the Honor of your Presence...

Rebecca Farms had been transformed into the bride-to-be's vision thanks to Farah, the rest of the family and the catering company hired to assist for the day. The long picnic tables were replaced with eighty white chairs, neatly lined rows of six on either side of the aisle lined with pink rose petals. The bridal party and Emily would come out of the main house, her father waiting at the bottom of the stairs to escort her the rest of the way, to where Josh would be waiting under a white arbor covered in eucalyptus.

After the ceremony, round tables covered in white tablecloths would be ushered in for guests to sit and eat. And then, after the meal, the tables would be removed to make way for the dancing.

The menu was set. Though an English countryside was the theme of the décor, and the fragrant flowers Farah had been lovingly tending to all summer were playing their part, the menu was modern, tasty, and hearty. For the cocktail hour, while three wait staff would walk around with trays holding champagne flutes, Farah, Maria would bring out big bowls of chips and Maria's salsa and two cheese boards to the picnic tables, now lined up in front of the chicken house, who, despite some loud protests, were watching the festivities safely tucked away inside their fancily adorned home.

After the picture taking and the bride and groom saying hello to their family and friends, platters of grilled chicken with tomatoes, fresh mozzarella and a basil vinaigrette, a creamy pasta and pea salad, fresh fruit, and rosemary sourdough rolls would fill the tables.

"What are we going to eat?" the kids had asked when they heard the menu. There might even have been a few *"yucks"* under a few breaths, so a big platter of hot dogs was added to appease the kids, and the kids at heart.

Soft music would play throughout the meal, the DJ set up in front of Philip and Diana's house, and the cake would be displayed on the porch of the main house. Another of Farah's creations, three-tiered but square this time—and because it was Josh's favorite—chocolate cake with mocha buttercream filling was hiding under smoot white fondant and several shades of pink buttercream roses.

"Those flowers look so lifelike..." Farah can hear her mother's voice again as she fusses over her creation one more time. She could also hear the hairdryers humming from Emily's upstairs bedroom where the bridal party had gathered, signaling the hair and makeup team had started. Later they would help with the eager flower girls, who would already be in their dresses if allowed. Right now, they were over with Maria. She was making an early lunch for the children and encouraging naps before the photographer arrived at 3:00, but Farah doubted that would happen.

Robin came out of one of the stables and headed to the other, his two young protégés behind him. While the girls were chomping at the bit to get ready, the men of Rebecca Farms were keeping a low profile this morning.

Barbie had left for town with her mother. Carole. She looked to be on death's door when Farah first met her on the Fourth of July, but had made quite a turnaround. Since coming to the farm, she'd cut down on her smoking, gained weight from the healthy meals, and her mood had changed for the better. This morning they were heading back to the shop so she could do the hair of three of her regular customers invited to the wedding. One of these was Sadie Brickson, who would be attending the wedding with her son

Walter. He was in for a revelation, as it appeared Carole wasn't going anywhere, and his franchise might have to wait.

Barbie also had invited Carl to see her newly renovated apartment this morning. It was quickly nearing completion. New furniture was on the way, and her yellow gingham curtains were already in the kitchen window. He seemed as happy to have her in his life as she was to have him. There was a definite connection they both felt.

Farah, just putting her cup in the dishwasher, saw one of the hair/makeup team head over to Maria's house. She smiled, knowing how decadent this all felt to her closest friend. "We're pampering ourselves today," Farah had said. "You deserve it."

That was her cue to take her own shower because she was next on the list. As she walked up the stairs, she was awash in emotions. She had been a successful business owner the day she'd met Robin. It was professionally and financially fulfilling. but it was nothing compared to the fulfillment she felt here.

At the top of the stairs, Emily's gown and the bridesmaids' dresses were hanging on the backs of bedroom doors. The landing looked like a bridal boutique. Her own dress hung on the back of the bathroom door. It was a simple, yet elegant sleeveless A-line crepe dress in blush. High heeled silver ankle strap shoes sat next to the bed. She was excited to get all dressed up. It had been years since she needed to.

It was a perfect 75 degrees when the wedding march started, and all eyes turned to the porch.

Marisol, Christina, and Brandi were first, the three girls holding hands and giggling as they walked down the stairs. Their long curls topped with wreaths of laurel and baby's breath, bounced with each step.

Next was Cassie, followed by Anna, followed by Sasha. The three women looking even more lovely than the first time they put their dresses on.

Finally, it was Rebecca's turn. She wasn't used to heels and was proudly sporting two inches. Also, she wasn't used to all eyes being upon her and was loving it, waving to everyone. She was loving it so much, Robin feared she was going to miss a step and decided to go and escort her down by the elbow.

And then Emily appeared in the doorway, and it seemed like over eighty people took a deep breath at the same time. She was the most beautiful bride ever. Not that this crowd was impartial or anything.

Her upswept hair, her glorious gown, her blush pink peony bouquet. She was perfect. So perfect, her father started to cry. So perfect, she was finding it hard to move, looking over at her adoring groom to be. Finally, Robin scooted back around, walked up, and took her hand, guiding her down to her emotional father's arm.

And after that, it all went like clockwork. The ceremony, the cocktail hour, the tasty buffet. The champagne that flowed, the wine on the tables, the keg of beer that seemed to appear out of nowhere. Emily wasn't sure if Jane Austen would have approved, but the thirsty men and women were happy.

When the tables were cleared, Mr. and Mrs. Joshua Marshall prepared for their first dance. He held her close as they swayed back and forth, stealing kisses. Romance was in the air, and after the father/daughter and mother/son dance everyone took to the dance floor.

Philip and Diana were cheek to cheek, their daughter happy, a new son, and visions of grandbabies filling their heads. He leaned in and whispered, "You're the most beautiful one here."

Joe, his slacks long gone and his familiar jeans on, held Maria tight. His eyes nearly popped out of his head when he saw her in her dress for the first time. Hers was like Farah's, a simple A-line that hit just past the knees. It was sleeveless with a rounded collar and a deep v in the back. He leaned in and whispered, *"La mas hermosa."*

"And I bet you didn't know you liked dancing so much," Farah said to Robin, her arms wrapped around his neck.

"I don't," he said, both arms wrapped around her waist. "But I like this. You really pulled off a miracle here today. Everyday."

"I had a lot of help. And I had the perfect place to start. This beautiful farm."

Robin pulled her closer if that was possible. "Speaking of beautiful, you're the most beautiful woman here."

Later, they retreated to their porches, giving way to the younger generation and music they had never heard before. Philip and Diana sat on theirs with Josh's parents, laughing and talking and forming a bond to last for years to come.

Robin and Farah sat with Maria and Joe, a sleeping Diego on his chest, Barbie, Carole, Carl, and Dorothy. They already talked like old friends and family, watching their children on the dance floor.

The boys had long ditched their wedding clothes, but the girls would gladly sleep in theirs, and they were all showing off their best moves.

"It's been such an enjoyable day," Carl said. "We can't thank you enough for including us."

"The timing was perfect. And look what you did for us," Farah said.

"I mean *I* really started the whole ball rolling," Barbie said.

"Yes, you did," Farah agreed. "And we're so blessed because of it."

"Yeah, they didn't like me much when I first arrived. It's a long story," she said to Carl.

"One we don't need to get into tonight," Robin said.

"Right. Let's just say, me and Mom were a little misguided."

"Leave me out of this," Carole said, laughing.

Soon they were all laughing, the animosity and bad feelings long gone. They had turned into a family. Not so traditional, but a happy family just the same. And now Carl and Dorothy and their two girls would be part of the family. And speaking of family...

"It's been a while since I've seen Rebecca," Robin said, glancing around the crowded dance floor.

"Look, she's in the middle dancing with Gabe," Joe said.

Suddenly, like a parting sea, the dance floor opened, and they were front and center. The group on the porch leaned forward in their seats because they saw what was coming.

Gabe leaned in. Rebecca leaned in. And...

"Second base!" screamed Barbie.

The End

About the Author

I have been writing for over thirty years. People who can't find me in Barnes and Noble don't get this…but other writers will.

I have also been working part or full-time since high school in many industries ranging from retail, and office work to manufacturing. None of them were rewarding, they just paid the bills. Other writers will get this too.

I was able to take several years off to be a stay-at-home mom. I raised three children and am now an over the moon happy grandmother.

I am an indie author and proud of it. The best is yet to come…

Heather Fahy Serrano

Made in the USA
Monee, IL
13 November 2023